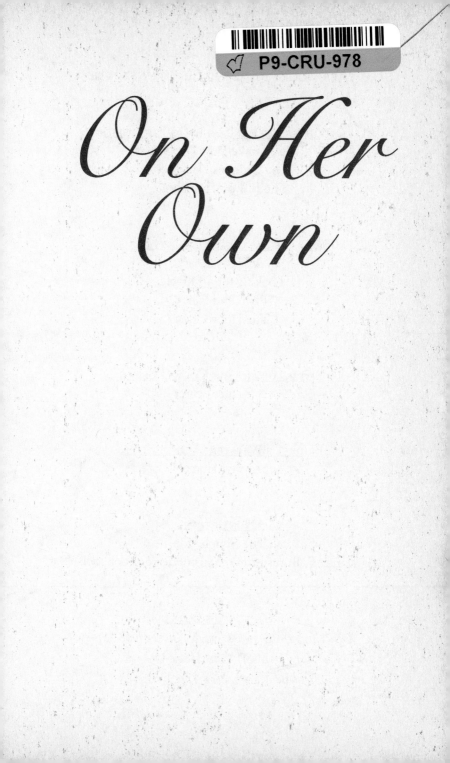

On Her Own

On Her Own

WANDA & BRUNSTETTER

BRIDES OF WEBSTER COUNTY

BARBOUR
PUBLISHING

ISBN 978-1-59789-610-8

All scripture quotations are taken from the King James Version of the Bible.

All Pennsylvania Dutch words are taken from the *Revised Pennsylvania German Dictionary* found in Lancaster County, Pennsylvania.

For more information about Wanda E. Brunstetter, please access the author's Web site at the following Internet address: www.wandabrunstetter.com.

Cover design by Müllerhaus Publishing Group

Published by Barbour Publishing, Inc., P.O. Box 719, Uhrichsville, OH 44683, www.barbourbooks.com.

Our mission is to publish and distribute inspirational products offering exceptional value and biblical encouragement to the masses.

ecpa Member of the
Evangelical Christian
Publishers Association

Printed in the United States of America.

DEDICATION/ACKNOWLEDGMENTS

To my friends Holly Stoolfire, Sandy Fisher,
and Marge Schaper, who were on their own for a time
and learned to rely on God for their strength and support.

Two are better than one;
because they have a good reward for their labour.
For if they fall, the one will lift up his fellow:
but woe to him that is alone when he falleth;
for he hath not another to help him up.

ECCLESIASTES 4:9–10

Chapter 1

Cradling the precious infant she had given birth to a short time ago, Barbara Zook lay exhausted, her head resting on the damp pillow.

"We have four sons now, David," she murmured into the stillness of her room. "I wish you were here to see our *boppli*. I'm planning to name him after you." Unbidden tears sprang to Barbara's eyes as she struggled against the memory of what had happened almost eight months ago. If she lived to be one hundred, she would never forget the unsuspecting moment when her world fell apart.

Barbara squeezed her eyes shut as her mind drove her unwillingly back to that Saturday afternoon when she'd been happy and secure in her marriage—when she'd been full of hope for the future.

Barbara sat in the wicker rocking chair on the front porch, watching her three young boys play in the yard and waiting for her husband's return. It was their tenth wedding anniversary, and David had taken their horse and buggy to Seymour to pick up her gift. He'd said it was something Barbara both wanted and needed.

She patted her stomach and drew in a deep breath as the rocking chair creaked beneath her weight. "When David gets home, I'll give him my gift—the news that I'm pregnant again," she whispered. Barbara had known for a couple of weeks that she was carrying David's child, but she had wanted it to be a surprise. She was sure her husband would be happy about having another baby, and she was hopeful that this time it would be a girl.

She planned to share her good news the moment David arrived. He had been gone several hours, and she couldn't imagine what could be keeping him.

Barbara's stomach rumbled as she noticed that the sun had begun to drop behind the thick pine trees on the other side of the field. It was almost time to start supper. She had just decided to head for the kitchen when the sheriff's car rumbled up the driveway.

She stood and leaned against the porch railing while Sheriff Anderson and his deputy got out of the vehicle and strode toward her.

Barbara shuddered. Something was wrong. She could feel it in every fiber of her being. "M-may I help you, Sheriff?" she asked as the two men stepped onto the porch. Her voice cracked, and she swallowed a couple of times.

"Mrs. Zook," the sheriff said, moving closer to her, "I'm sorry to be telling you this, but there's been an accident."

"An accident?"

He nodded. "It happened about a mile out of Seymour."

Barbara's heart thudded in her chest. "Is it. . .David?"

"I'm afraid so. We were called to the scene by one of your English neighbors who'd been heading down Highway C and witnessed the accident. He identified your husband's body."

My husband's body? The words echoed in Barbara's mind. *It's not true. It can't be. David's alive. Today is our anniversary. He'll be home soon with the surprise he promised me. David's always been so dependable. He won't let me down.*

"I'm sorry," Deputy Harris said, "but a logging truck pulled out of a side road and hit your husband's buggy. The stove that was tied on the back flew forward and hit David in the head, killing him instantly."

The porch swayed in an eerie sort of way, and Barbara gripped the railing until her fingers turned numb. *David's dead. He bought me a stove. David can't be dead. Today's our anniversary.*

The wail of an infant's cries pushed Barbara's thoughts to the back of her mind, and her eyes snapped open. Her nose burned with unshed tears as she focused on the joy of having a new baby in her arms. Little David needed her. So did Zachary, Joseph, and Aaron.

"I'll do whatever I need to in order to provide for my boys," she murmured.

A knock sounded at the bedroom door, and Barbara called, "Come in."

The door creaked open, and David's mother, Mavis, stuck her head through the opening. "How are you doing? Are you ready for some company?"

Barbara glanced down at her son, who was now enjoying the first taste of his mother's milk. She nodded at her dark-haired mother-in-law. "You're welcome to come say hello to your new grandson, David."

Mavis entered the room and closed the door. "Alice told me it was a boy and you'd named him David." She moved closer to the bed and sniffed deeply, her brown eyes filling with tears. "My son would be real pleased to know he had a child named after him."

Barbara swallowed around the fiery lump in her throat. "David never knew I was pregnant. He died before I could share our surprise." She stared down at her infant son. "It breaks my heart to know this tiny fellow will never know his *daed*."

Mavis reached out to touch the baby's downy, dark head. "If I could do something to help, I surely would."

"You already have, Mavis. You and Jeremiah have helped us aplenty, same as my folks."

Mavis nodded. "Your *mamm* has been real good about watching your *kinner* so you could keep working in the harness shop, and your daed's been willing to help there despite the arthritis in his hands."

"That's true." Barbara thought about how determined her

husband had been to open his own business here in Webster County, Missouri. Because of it, they had made enough money to put food on the table and pay the bills. The truth was Barbara actually enjoyed working in the shop. To her, the smell of leather was a sweet perfume. These days she found the aroma even more comforting because it reminded her of David.

"This is a day of beginnings for David Zook Jr., and it's a day of endings for our friend Dan Hilty."

Mavis's statement jolted Barbara to the core. "Has something happened to Dan?"

Her mother-in-law nodded soberly. "You didn't know?"

Barbara shook her head.

"I thought Alice might have told you."

"Mom didn't say anything. What happened to Dan?"

Mavis took a seat on the chair next to the bed. "He died of a heart attack early this morning."

"*Ach!* How terrible. My heart goes out to Margaret and the rest of the Hilty family." Barbara felt the pain of Dan's widow as if it were her own. It seemed as if she were living David's death all over again. Giving birth to her husband's namesake was bittersweet, and hearing of someone else's loss was a reminder of her own suffering.

"Death comes to all," Mavis said in a hushed tone. "It was Dan's time to go."

Barbara had heard the bishop and others in their Amish community say the same thing when someone passed away. Some said that if the person hadn't died one way, he or she would have died another. "When your time's up, it's up," someone had told Barbara on the day of David's funeral. She wasn't sure she could accept that concept. Accidents happened, true enough, but they were brought on because someone was careless or in the wrong place at the wrong time. If David hadn't gone to town the morning of their anniversary, she felt sure he would be alive today.

Barbara saw no point, however, in telling David's mother how she felt about these things. She'd probably end up arguing with her. "When is the funeral?" she asked instead.

"In a few days. As soon as Dan's brother, Paul, gets here." Mavis patted Barbara's shoulder. "You'll not be expected to go since you've just given birth and need rest."

Barbara nodded. Rest. Yes, that's what she needed. She closed her eyes as the desire for sleep overtook her. "Tell my boys they can see their little *bruder* soon. After Davey and I have ourselves a little nap."

When Barbara heard a familiar *creak*, she knew Mavis had risen from the chair. The last thing she remembered was hearing the bedroom door click shut.

Alice Raber sat at the table where her three grandsons were drawing on tablets. "Your mamm just gave birth to a boppli," she said. "You have a new little bruder."

"What'd Mama name him?" Aaron, who was almost nine, asked as he looked up from his drawing.

"David."

"That was Papa's name," said Joseph, who would soon be turning six.

Alice nodded. "That's right. Your mamm wanted to name the baby after your daed."

"Nobody will ever take Papa's place," Aaron mumbled.

She touched his shoulder. "Of course not. Your mamm just thought it would be nice to give your little bruder your daed's name so you could remember him."

Aaron grunted. "I'll always remember Papa, no matter what. Me and him used to go fishin' together, and he promised to give me his harness business some day."

"When can we see our little bruder?" Joseph asked.

"After your mamm and the boppli have had a chance to rest awhile."

"Are they tired?"

Aaron punched Joseph's shoulder. "You ask too many questions, you know that?"

"Do not."

"*Jah*, you do."

"Let's not quarrel," Alice said as she reached over and scooped Barbara's youngest boy, Zachary, off his chair and into her lap. The little guy had been the baby of the family for three and a half years. She figured he would need some extra attention now that a new baby had come on the scene. Maybe the other boys would, too.

"Are Mama and little David tired?" Joseph asked again.

"Jah." Alice patted his arm. "It takes a lot of work for a little one to get born. And it was very tiring for your mamm to do her part so the little one could come into the world."

"How come?"

"Just does." Aaron grunted and nudged Joseph's elbow.

"Now quit askin' Grandma so many questions."

"Who would like some cookies?" Alice hoped a snack might put Aaron in a better mood.

Joseph bobbed his head up and down with an eager expression. "I would."

Alice placed Zachary back in his chair, then retrieved the cookie jar from the cupboard. She had just set a plate of cookies on the table when Barbara's mother-in-law entered the room.

"How's my daughter doing?" Alice asked. "Are she and the boppli sleeping?"

"She was looking pretty drowsy when I left her room. I imagine she's dozed off by now." Mavis took a seat at the table.

"I'll take the boys up to see their bruder as soon as she wakes up." Alice pushed the plate toward Mavis. "Would you like a cookie?"

"Don't mind if I do."

Mavis selected a cookie and was about to take a bite, when Joseph nudged her arm. "Want some milk for dunkin'?"

She glanced over at him and smiled. "Where's your milk?"

He shrugged. "Grandma didn't give me none. Figured if she gave you some, she might give me some, too."

Mavis chuckled, and so did Alice. "I'll see to it right away." She looked at Aaron. "Do you want some milk?"

"Jah, okay."

"I'll get all three of you some—Mavis, too, if she'd like."

Mavis nodded. "Jah, sure. Why not?"

After their snack, Alice asked the boys to play in the living room. As soon as the boys left the room, Alice turned to Mavis and said, "I'm worried about Barbara."

"I thought the birth went okay. Was there a problem I don't know about?"

Alice shook her head. "The birth went fine. It's after Barbara is back on her feet that has me worried."

"What do you mean?"

"She wants to return to work at the harness shop, and I'm not sure she should."

"That shop was my David's joy." Mavis pursed her lips. "It's my understanding that Barbara likes it, too, so it's only natural that—"

Alice shook her head. "She might like it, but it's hard work. Too hard for a woman to be doing all by herself."

"Samuel helps out. Isn't that right?"

Mavis nodded. "But his arthritis bothers him more all the time, and I don't know how much longer he'll be able to continue helping her."

"Maybe she can hire someone."

"Like who? Do you know anyone in these parts who does harness work?"

"No, but—"

"I'm wondering if she should sell the shop and live off the profits until she finds another husband."

"Another husband?" Mavis flinched. "Ach, David's not been gone quite a year. How can you even talk of Barbara marrying again?"

Alice sighed. "I'm not suggesting she get married right away. But if the right man comes along, I think she would do well to think about marrying him." She smiled at Mavis and patted her arm. "David was a fine man, and I'm sure Barbara will always carry love for him in her heart. But now she has four sons to raise, and that will be difficult to do alone, even with the help of her family."

Mavis dabbed the corners of her eyes with a napkin. "I guess we need to be praying about this, jah?"

Alice nodded. "That's exactly what we need to do."

Paul Hilty's hand shook as he left the phone shed outside his cousin Andy's harness shop, where he worked. He still couldn't believe the message on the answering machine that Dan, his oldest brother, was dead.

Dazed, Paul meandered back into the shop. "I've got to go home. My brother passed away this morning," he said when he found his cousin working at his desk.

Andy looked up from the pile of invoices lying in front of him. "Which brother?"

"Dan. I went out to the phone shed to make a call and dis-covered that Pop had left a message on your answering machine. Dan died of a heart attack early this morning."

"I'm sorry to hear that. He was helping your daed on the farm, isn't that right?"

Paul nodded. "Him, Monroe, and Elam. Now it'll just be Pop and my two younger brothers." He grimaced. "No doubt my daed will be after me to come back to Missouri so I can help him work in the fields."

"You'll be leaving Pennsylvania, then?"

"Not if I can help it." Paul swallowed hard. "I will need to go back for Dan's funeral, though. I'd like to leave right away if I can get a bus ticket."

"Of course. No problem." Andy grunted. "I'd close the shop and go with you, but I just got in several new orders, and I'd get really behind if we were both gone. Having just hired Dennis Yoder, I can't expect him to take over the shop and know what to do in my absence."

Paul shook his head. "That's okay. You're needed here. I'm sure the folks will understand."

"Please give Dan's widow my condolences."

"I will." Paul turned toward the door.

Faith Hertzler had just stepped onto the back porch to shake one of her braided rugs when she spotted her mother's horse and buggy coming up the driveway.

"*Wie geht's?*" she asked as Mom stepped onto the porch moments later.

"I'm doing all right, but Margaret Hilty's not holding up so well this morning." Mom's face looked flushed.

Faith draped the rug over the porch railing. "What's wrong with Margaret? Is she *grank?*"

"She's not sick physically, but in here she surely is." Mom placed one hand against her chest. "Dan had a heart attack this morning and died."

"Ach! That's *baremlich!*"

Mom nodded, and her blue eyes darkened. "I know it's terrible. Poor Margaret is just beside herself."

Faith drew in her bottom lip. "I can only imagine. Dan's always seemed healthy. I guess one never knows when their time will be up, so we should always be prepared."

"Jah. Always ready to meet our Maker."

Faith opened the screen door. "Won't you come in and have a cup of tea?"

"Don't mind if I do." Mom's glasses had slipped to the middle of her nose, and she pushed them back in place before entering the house.

The women took seats at the table, and Faith poured some tea. "Would you like some cookies or a slice of cake? Noah made some lemon sponge cake last night, and we still have a few pieces."

Mom gave her stomach a couple of pats. "I'd better pass on the cake. It'll be time for lunch soon, and I don't want to fill up on sweets."

Faith blew on her tea, then took a sip. "Will Dan's brother, Paul, be coming home for the funeral?"

Mom shrugged. "I don't know, but I expect he will."

"I'll try to see Margaret later today. Maybe I'll take her one of Noah's baked goods with a verse of scripture attached."

"That'd be good. Margaret's going to need all the support she can get in the days ahead."

The back door flew open, and Noah's mother, Ida, stepped into the room. "I just talked to Mavis Zook, and she told me that Barbara gave birth to a healthy little *buwe* this morning."

"Another boy?" Mom asked.

Ida nodded. "She's already tired enough trying to run the harness shop and deal with three energetic boys. Now she'll really have her hands full."

"I guess I'd better get over to see Barbara soon," Faith said. "Even though the birth of her son must be a happy time for her, she's probably feeling a bit sad because David isn't here."

The bus ride to Missouri gave Paul plenty of time to think. How was Dan's widow holding up? What kind of reception would he receive from his family? How long would he be expected to stay after the funeral?

Paul thought about that day four years ago when he'd decided to leave home. He had been farming with his dad and brothers since he'd finished the eighth grade—first when they lived in Pennsylvania, where Paul had been born, and later when Pop moved his family to Missouri. Paul had never enjoyed farming. He'd wanted to learn a trade—preferably harness making. But there was already one harness shop in the area, owned by David Zook. Paul didn't figure their small community needed another one, and he was sure David wouldn't hire him, because his wife, Barbara, already worked in the shop.

When Paul's cousin Andy, who ran a harness shop in Lancaster County, Pennsylvania, had invited Paul to come work for him, Paul had jumped at the chance. Paul's mother had said she could understand why he wanted to leave, although she would miss him terribly, but Paul's father had shouted at Paul, calling him a *glotzkeppich naar*.

I may be stubborn, but I'm sure no fool, Paul thought as he gripped the armrest of his seat on the bus. *I like my job, and I'm much happier living in Pennsylvania than I was in Missouri.*

Guilt stabbed Paul's conscience. He liked his work at Andy's harness shop, but he wasn't really happy. Something was missing, but he couldn't figure out what it was. Andy kept telling Paul he needed to find a good wife and have a passel of kinner. Andy had been married to Sharon for five years, and they had three children already. He often said how much joy he found in being a husband and father.

Paul didn't think he would ever get married. He was thirty years old and had never had a serious relationship with a woman. Truth was, Paul was afraid of marriage, because with marriage usually came children, and since Paul had so little patience with kids, he feared he wouldn't make a good father. He figured his dislike of children went two ways, because most of the kids he'd known had avoided him like he had a case of chicken pox.

Paul's thoughts shifted to his brother's untimely death. Dan's passing was only eight months after David Zook died. Mom had written to Paul about the accident that killed David, leaving his wife to raise their three sons and manage the harness shop on her own.

I wonder how Barbara's getting along. Did she hire someone to help in the shop, or could she have sold David's business by now? If she hasn't sold the place yet, maybe she's looking for someone to buy her out.

Paul stared out the bus window, barely noticing the passing scenery. *Don't get any dumb ideas. You're going back to Pennsylvania as soon as Dan's funeral is over.*

Chapter 2

There's no reason for you to stay here with me," Barbara said to her mother, who stood just inside the kitchen doorway. "You and Dad should both go to the funeral."

Mom shook her head vigorously. "And leave you here in a weakened condition with three little ones and a new boppli? I would never do that, daughter."

There was no arguing with her mother once she'd made up her mind about something. Barbara pushed a wayward strand of hair away from her face and grimaced. She hadn't done a good job of putting up her bun this morning. For that matter, she didn't feel as if she had done much of anything right since she'd gotten out of bed. She had yelled at Joseph and Zachary for being too loud, scolded Aaron for picking on his younger brothers, and dropped a carton of eggs in the middle of the kitchen floor. Maybe her weakened condition caused her to have no control over her emotions. Or perhaps it was the fact that Dan Hilty's death had opened up the wounds of losing her husband. In either case, Barbara couldn't go to Dan's funeral. And as much as she didn't want to admit it, she needed her mother's help.

She took a seat at the table. "You're right, Mom. I do need help. Would you be willing to watch the buwe at your house while I tend to the boppli?" She was glad her folks lived next door, making it easy for her to go over for lunch with the boys. She didn't want them to think she had abandoned them now that there was a baby brother in the house.

Mom sat in the chair opposite Barbara and poured some tea. "I'd be happy to look out for your boys." She handed a cup to Barbara. "Your daed's got them out helping with chores. After breakfast, I'll take the boys over to my place and find something to keep everyone occupied so you can rest awhile. You look all done in."

Barbara released a drawn-out sigh. "I'll sure be glad when little David starts sleeping more and eating less often. He woke me every couple of hours last night."

Her mother's blue eyes held a note of sympathy. "All the more reason you should rest during the day whenever possible."

The wooden chair groaned as Barbara leaned against the back. "It's not just the lack of sleep that has me feeling so down."

"What else is bothering you?"

"I'm worried about the harness shop. I appreciate that Dad's been helping me since David died, but he can't run it alone. As you know, his arthritic fingers don't work so good, and there's too much for just one person to do."

Mom tapped her fingernails along the edge of the table. "Maybe you could hire someone to help while you're getting your strength back."

"Who would I hire? No one in our community does harness work, and Dad doesn't know enough about it to teach them." Barbara sniffed. "Dad barely manages when I'm not there to oversee things."

"That's true. Maybe keeping the shop isn't such a good idea." Mom leaned slightly forward. "Have you thought about running an ad in *The Budget* to try and sell off the supplies?"

"I don't think I could part with David's harness shop. It meant too much to him." Barbara stared down at the table as a familiar lump formed in her throat. "And it means a lot to me. I enjoy working there, Mom. Can you understand that?"

"What I understand is that my daughter's been working hard in that shop ever since her husband died—even throughout most of her pregnancy." Mom released a long sigh. "I know you want to prove you can support yourself and the buwe, but you can't do it alone. Your daed will help in the shop as long as he's able, and I'm sure David's folks will help with finances if needed."

Barbara stood. "I won't have you and Dad, or my husband's parents, taking care of us until the boys are raised. That's my job, and I'll do it." She started across the room but turned back around. "I hope you know that I appreciate your concerns and all the help you've offered."

Mom nodded. "I know you do."

"I'm going upstairs to check on the boppli, but I'll be back before Dad and the kinner come in for breakfast."

Barbara was almost to the kitchen door when her mother said, "Say, I just thought of something."

"What's that?"

"I spoke with Faith Hertzler yesterday morning, and she said she'd seen Dan's brother, Paul. Guess he came home for the funeral."

Barbara faced her mother. "I suppose he would."

"Paul's been living in Pennsylvania these last four years. . . working at his cousin's harness shop."

"So I heard."

"Maybe Paul would be willing to stick around awhile and work at your shop. Would you like me to ask your daed to talk with him about it today?"

Barbara shook her head. "Not at his brother's funeral. It wouldn't be proper to discuss anything like that there."

"You're right, of course. How about tomorrow, then?"

"Maybe. Let me think on it awhile."

"You think, and let's both be praying."

Barbara smiled at her mother's exuberance. "Thanks for the reminder, Mom."

"I hope Margaret holds up during the funeral," Faith said to her husband, Noah, who stood at the kitchen counter mixing a batch of pancake batter.

"Margaret's a strong woman. I'm sure she'll do fine with the support of her family." Noah turned to Faith and smiled. His dark eyes matched the thick crop of hair on his head. "When you took the lemon sponge cake over to her the other day, did she read the copy of Isaiah 66:13 that I attached?"

Faith nodded. "She said it was a comfort and that she would save the paper so she would be reminded that the Lord says, 'As one whom his mother comforteth, so will I comfort you.'"

"I always wonder how folks who don't know the Lord make it through difficult times without His comfort," Noah said, reaching for the bottle of fresh goat's milk.

"I know, and that's why we must always pray for others." Faith removed a jug of syrup from the cupboard. "I still haven't made it over to see Barbara, but I'm hoping to do that yet this week. I spoke with Barbara's mamm yesterday, and she said Barbara's been pretty tired since the boppli was born. I guess she won't be going to the funeral today."

"I'm sure Margaret will understand," Noah said as he lit their propane stove and placed a griddle on one of the burners. "If Barbara plans to return to work anytime soon, she'll need to rest and get her strength back."

Faith grunted. "I wish she would sell that harness shop. It's hard work, and I don't think she's up to doing it on her own while she tries to raise four boys."

"Samuel still helps her, right?"

"Jah. He started running the shop by himself the last few weeks of Barbara's pregnancy, and now he'll have to continue running it by himself until she's able to return to work." Faith stroked her chin thoughtfully. "Unless. . ."

Noah quirked an eyebrow. "What are you thinking, Faith?"

"Paul Hilty came home for Dan's funeral. He does harness work in Pennsylvania, so maybe he could stay awhile and help out at Zook's Harness Shop."

Noah pursed his lips while he poured some pancake batter onto the sizzling griddle. "If he's already got a job in Pennsylvania, he'll probably have to get right back to it after the funeral."

"Maybe not. He might have taken several weeks off so he could spend some time with his family." Faith touched Noah's arm. "Would you talk to him about it?"

His eyebrows drew together. "Why me? It was your idea."

"I think it would be more appropriate if you spoke to him, don't you?"

Noah opened his mouth, but their two children, Melinda and Isaiah, scurried into the room, interrupting the conversation.

"Is breakfast ready yet, Papa Noah?" eleven-year-old Melinda asked, sniffing the air. "I'm hungry as a bear."

Noah turned and smiled at her. "What would you know of bears? You've never even seen a bear."

Before Melinda could respond, four-year-old Isaiah spoke up. "Uh-huh. She's seen one in that big book of hers."

"You must mean the one she bought with her birthday money when we visited Bass Pro Shop in Springfield," Faith said.

"That's the one." Melinda smiled, revealing two large dimples in her cheeks. "Can we go to that place again soon, Papa Noah? I sure liked it there."

Noah patted the top of Melinda's blond head. "We'll see, daughter."

Paul left the confines of his folks' house, full of people who had come to the meal following Dan's funeral and graveside service. Some milled about the living room, while others stood outside on the lawn, visiting and offering their condolences.

Paul felt as out of place as a bullfrog in a chicken coop. Mom, his sisters Rebekah and Susan, and his brothers Monroe and Elam had been friendly enough. Pop was a different story. He'd been as cold as a block of ice, and Paul knew why. Pop still resented the fact that Paul had given up farming and had moved back to Pennsylvania to learn a new trade. Since Pop had raised all four of his sons to be farmers, he seemed to think they should farm for the rest of their lives—even if they had other ideas about the kind of work that would make them happy. It wasn't fair. Shouldn't Paul have the right to work at the trade of his choice? Why should Pop expect all of his sons to be farmers just because he had chosen to be one?

Paul hurried past the tables that had been set up on the lawn, where many of the older people sat visiting, and headed straight for the barn. He had to be by himself for a while. He needed time to think. Time to breathe.

As soon as Paul opened the barn door, the familiar aroma of sweaty horses, sweet-smelling hay, and fresh manure assaulted his senses. His ears perked up at the gentle sound of a horse's whinny, and his eyes feasted on the place where he and his siblings used to play.

He glanced at the wooden rafters overhead. The rope swing still hung from one of the beams. So many times his brothers and sisters had argued over who would get the first turn on the swing that transported them from the hayloft to the pile of straw where they would drop at will. Not Paul. He had no desire to dangle from any rope suspended so high.

Paul moved away from the old swing and was about to enter one of the horses' stalls when he heard the barn door squeak open and click shut. He whirled around.

"Hope I didn't startle you," Noah Hertzler said, holding his black felt hat in one hand. "I saw you come into the barn and wanted to offer my condolences on the loss of your brother. Dan will surely be missed. I'm real sorry about his passing."

Paul reached out to clasp Noah's hand. "*Danki.* I appreciate your kind words."

"How have you been?" Noah asked.

"I was doing okay until I got the news that my brother had died."

Noah nodded. "I understand. My mamm passed on a year ago. I still miss her a lot."

Paul swallowed hard. "It's never easy to lose a loved one."

"No, it's not."

A few minutes of silence passed between them; then Noah changed the subject. "Do you like Pennsylvania? Has it changed much since you were a boy?"

"I like it well enough. But the Lancaster area is a lot more crowded than it was when I was growing up." Paul shrugged. "I put up with all the tourists so I can do what I like best."

"You mean harness making and repair?"

Paul nodded. "Andy also sells and fixes leather shoes and boots."

"I'm sure you must've heard about David Zook passing on," Noah said.

"Jah. Such a shame. How's his wife faring? Does she have

anyone to help her in the harness shop?"

Noah shook his head. "Just her daed, and his fingers don't work so good, what with his arthritis and all."

"So it's just Barbara and Samuel?"

"Right now it's only him. Barbara won't be back to work until her strength returns and the new boppli's a bit bigger."

Paul's mouth dropped open. "She's got another child? Mom never mentioned that in any of her letters."

Noah took a seat on a bale of straw, and Paul joined him. "Barbara gave birth to son number four the same day your brother died. David never knew she was in a family way." Noah shook his head. "Barbara's mother-in-law, Mavis, told Faith that Barbara's feeling real tired. That's why she's not here today."

"Wouldn't expect her to be under the circumstances."

Noah cleared his throat. "I. . .uh. . .well, Faith and I were wondering if you might want to stick around awhile. Maybe see about working at Zook's Harness Shop."

Paul felt a rush of adrenaline course through his body. Why couldn't he have been given that opportunity four years ago? "If I did offer my services, it would only be until Barbara gets back on her feet," he said.

"Does that mean you'd never consider moving back to Webster County?"

Paul shook his head. "I doubt it. I only came home for Dan's funeral. Figured I might stay a week or two so I could visit family and friends. My sisters live in Jamesport now, and they're planning to stay here a week. I'll probably stick around that long, too, and then catch a bus back to Pennsylvania."

Noah nodded, and his dark eyes revealed the depth of his

understanding. "Before Faith and I were married, she came home not planning to stay, either."

Paul opened his mouth to say something, but Noah cut him off. "After a time, Faith realized her home was here, and she knew she was supposed to stay." He smiled. "Of course, marrying me was part of the deal."

"Faith didn't have a daed who wanted her to do something she didn't want to do," Paul mumbled. "My daed wants me to farm, and if I stick around too long, he'll start pressing me on the issue."

"As I'm sure you know, Faith was away from home for ten years, telling jokes and yodeling in the English world."

"I remember."

"She and her daed didn't see eye to eye on her yodeling, but he's come to terms with it."

Paul grunted. "Even if Pop and I could mend our fences, I still wouldn't stay here."

"Why not?"

"I like working on harnesses, and there isn't room for two harness shops in this small community."

"Maybe you could work for Barbara indefinitely."

Paul's face heated up. He wasn't about to spend the rest of his life working for Barbara Zook. She shouldn't even be running the harness shop. That was men's work, plain and simple. "Unless Barbara decides to sell out, I won't be staying in Webster County." He moved toward the door, and Noah followed. "I will drop by and see Barbara, though. I need to offer my condolences on the loss of her husband."

Chapter 3

*B*arbara was napping on the sofa when a knock at the back door wakened her. "Come in!" she called. "I'm in the living room, Mom!"

Moments later, a tall, blond-haired man entered the room. He wore a straw hat, short-sleeved cotton shirt, and dark trousers held up by tan suspenders. "I'm not your mamm, but you did invite me to come in," he said, removing his hat.

Barbara's mouth hung open. "Paul Hilty?"

"Jah, it's me." He shifted his long legs and shuffled his black boots against the hardwood floor. "Sorry if I startled you."

Barbara's hand went instinctively to her hair, as she checked to be sure her *kapp* was in place. She had planned on a short rest and ended up falling into a deep sleep. The baby was sleeping in his crib upstairs, and the boys were at her folks' place. It had been the perfect time to rest. The last thing Barbara expected when she woke up was to see a man standing in her living room. "No, no, that's okay. I mean—it's good to see you."

"And you, as well."

Barbara's cheeks grew warm as she stood and smoothed the wrinkles in her long dress. "I'm sorry I couldn't make it to Dan's funeral yesterday. I had a boppli a few days ago and haven't gotten my strength back yet."

A look of concern clouded Paul's deeply set blue eyes. "I heard that. I also heard about David's death. I came by to tell you how sorry I am."

Barbara sank back to the couch. "It's been a rough eight months," she admitted.

Paul took a couple of steps forward. "I can imagine."

"I'm sorry to hear about your brother, too. It's never easy to lose a loved one."

He shook his head. "No. No, it's not."

"How's Margaret holding up?"

"It was a shock to have Dan die so suddenly, but Margaret's doing as well as can be expected." The sorrowful look on Paul's face showed the depth of his sadness. "As you know, her six kinner are raised and out on their own, but I hope one of them will take her in to live with them. It'll probably be her daughter Karen and her husband, Jake, since they live the closest."

Barbara nodded and swallowed around the lump in her throat. It was hard not to feel sorry for herself. Just thinking about David's and Dan's deaths made her feel weepy.

"Have a seat," she said, finally remembering her manners.

He seated himself in the rocker close to the sofa, looking more uncomfortable by the minute. Barbara hadn't known Paul when they were children, and then he'd moved back to Pennsylvania to work with his cousin. Barbara had heard the move was against his dad's wishes, but she couldn't fault Paul for wanting to work where he felt comfortable. She would do most anything to keep working in David's harness shop.

Only the soft ticking of the mantel clock broke the quiet in the room. Barbara sat with her hands folded in her lap. Paul moved slowly back and forth in the rocker.

Finally, she spoke again. "How have you been? Are you happy living in Lancaster County?"

He stopped rocking and sat straight as a board. "I like working at my cousin's harness shop, but Lancaster's getting a bit overcrowded for my taste."

She was tempted to ask why he stayed but figured it probably had to do with the job he enjoyed. "I hear there's plenty of English and that tourists come by the thousands to get a look at the Plain folks living there."

Paul nodded. "Not like here, where so few tourists seem to know about us."

"They probably wouldn't care anyway, since we're such a small community."

"I suppose you're right about that."

"How long will you be staying in Webster County?" Barbara asked. Should she bring up the harness shop—see if he might be interested in working for her awhile?

He twisted the edge of his hat. "Guess that all depends."

"On what?"

"I had only intended on staying a week or so, but I could stay longer if there was a need."

"You mean if your daed needed you to help on his farm?"

He shook his head. "No way! I gave up farming when I moved, and I'm not about to go back to it again."

"I see."

Paul rubbed the bridge of his nose and leaned forward. "Since David's gone and you're not able to work in the harness shop right now, I thought maybe you might be thinking of selling it."

She shook her head vigorously. "I need to keep it open as long as I'm able."

He nodded. "So would you be needing someone to run the place for you right now?"

Barbara drew in a deep breath as she thought about the verse from Ecclesiastes 4 she'd read the night before: *"Two are better than one; because they have a good reward for their labour. For if they fall, the one will lift up his fellow: but woe to him that is alone when he falleth; for he hath not another to help him up."* She wondered if Paul's showing up was a sign from God that she was supposed to accept his help.

"I could use some help in the harness shop," she reluctantly admitted. "Dad's working, but his fingers won't let him do a lot, and it's going to be a few more weeks before I can return to work."

"That's what I figured."

"What about your job? Can your cousin get by without your help for a few weeks?"

He shrugged. "Don't see why not. When I called from Seymour to let him know I'd gotten here okay, he said he'd just hired on another part-time man. Unless things get busier than they have been, I'm sure Andy won't mind if I stay here awhile and help in David's shop."

"It's my shop now," Barbara corrected.

"Right. I understand, and I—"

The sound of a baby's cry halted Paul's words.

Barbara jumped up. "That's little David. I should tend to him."

Paul stood. "I can come back some other time."

She waved her hand. "That's okay. Why don't you make yourself comfortable while I tend to the boppli? When I'm done, we can talk more about the possibility of you working in the harness shop."

He sat down again. "Sounds fine to me."

Barbara started for the stairs but turned back. "If you'd like some coffee, go on out to the kitchen and help yourself to a cup. I think there's still some in the pot on the stove." She hurried from the room before he had a chance to respond, glad for the opportunity to think more about Paul's offer.

* * *

Paul remained in his chair for several minutes after Barbara went upstairs. The baby's crying had stopped, so he figured she must have things under control.

He couldn't believe how much Barbara had changed since he'd seen her four years ago. She used to be kind of plump, but now she was much thinner—almost too thin to his way of thinking. Had the years of working in the harness shop taken their toll, or had she lost the weight after David died? He'd heard of people nearly starving themselves to death when a mate had been taken, but Barbara was a new mother. It seemed to Paul that she should weigh a lot more than she did.

One more reason I need to stick around for a while and help out. She probably doesn't eat right because she worries about the harness shop and how she'll provide for her family.

Paul stood in front of the unlit fireplace. It was late spring, getting too warm for any fires.

Barbara's a fine-looking woman. Funny I never paid much attention to her before. He shook his head, trying to get himself thinking straight again. Of course he wouldn't have eyed Barbara before. She had been married to David Zook, and it wouldn't have been right for him to pay special attention to her. David and Barbara had already been courting by the time Paul and his family moved to Webster County. Even if Paul had noticed Barbara when she was still a Raber, it wouldn't have done him any good. She'd been David's girl from the very beginning. If he had taken an interest in her back then, their courtship would have ended before either of them had a chance to get serious. That's how it had always been with the women Paul had courted. Maybe it was because they knew he was leery of marriage. Besides, Barbara was two years older than Paul and probably wouldn't have given him a second glance during their teen years.

Might as well get myself a cup of coffee, he decided. *It will give me something to do until she gets back, and hopefully it'll keep me from all this crazy thinking.*

In the kitchen, Paul found a pot of coffee warming on the stove. He located a man-sized mug and had just poured himself some coffee when he heard the back door swing open and bang against the wall.

When he turned, a young boy with brunette hair and dark eyes like Barbara's faced him.

"Who are you, and what are ya doin' with my pa's coffee mug?" The child planted his hands on his hips.

Paul forced a smile. He didn't like the way the boy was staring at him. "I'm Paul Hilty. You must be one of Barbara's boys."

The lad thrust out his chin and pushed back his shoulders, but he didn't return Paul's smile. "My name's Aaron. I'm her oldest son."

Paul opened his mouth to reply, but Aaron cut him off. "When I grow up, I plan to take over Pa's harness shop." He stared down at Paul's black boots. "My mom'll be old by then and probably won't wanna work on harnesses no more."

Paul chuckled. Aaron scowled at him. "What's so funny?"

"Nothing. I mean, it seems odd that a young fellow like you would be talking about your mamm getting old and you taking her place in the shop."

"I don't think it's funny a'tall."

Paul took a sip of coffee and seated himself at the table, but the boy didn't budge.

"You still haven't said why you're in my mamm's kitchen, usin' my daed's mug."

Paul eyed the cup in question, then nodded toward the empty chair to his left. "Sit down, and I'll tell you."

Aaron flopped into a chair.

"I came over to see how your mamm was doing, and then the boppli started fussing. So your mamm said I should help myself to some coffee while she took care of your little bruder."

"But you shouldn't be usin' Pa's cup," the child persisted.

Paul was tempted to remind Aaron that his father was dead and it shouldn't matter who drank from his cup, but he thought better of it. No use getting the boy riled, especially if Barbara decided to hire Paul in the harness shop. Aaron undoubtedly still missed his father. The idea of someone using his mug could be a powerful reminder of the boy's loss.

Paul went to the cupboard and got out a different mug; then he placed David's mug in the kitchen sink. "Better?" he asked as he returned to his seat.

The boy nodded.

For several minutes, they sat in silence. Unable to tolerate the boy staring at him, Paul finally asked, "How old are you, Aaron?"

"Almost nine."

"Guess it won't be long until you can begin helping your mamm in the shop."

The child shrugged. "Used to help my daed some when I wasn't in school."

"What grade are you in?"

"Second."

"You have six more years, then."

"Jah."

Paul took another swig of coffee, wishing Barbara would return so he'd have another adult to talk to. His uneasiness around children was intensified with Aaron looking at him so strangely.

"Want some cookies to dunk in your coffee?"

Aaron's question took Paul by surprise, and he jumped.

"What's the matter? You got a fly on your nose?"

"Huh?"

"You're kind of jumpy, wouldn't ya say?"

Paul cleared his throat. "I'm fine. Just a bit restless is all."

"Some cookies might help."

Paul studied the boy's round face. He was pretty sure the subject of cookies had come up because Aaron wanted some, not because he thought Paul needed something to dunk in his coffee.

"You're right. A few cookies would be nice." Paul glanced around the room. "You know where there might be some?"

Aaron dashed across the room. He returned with a green ceramic jar. "These are chocolate chip." He set the container on the table and headed for the refrigerator. "Think I'll have some milk so's I can dunk."

Paul remembered how he had enjoyed cookies and cold goat's milk when he was a boy. Peanut butter with raisins had been his favorite, and his mother used to make them often. He watched Aaron fill a tall glass with milk, dip his cookie up and down a couple of times, then chomp it down in two bites.

"This is sure good. Grandma made these just for me."

"Your grandparents live next door, don't they?"

Aaron grabbed another cookie. "Jah. Grandma Raber keeps an eye on me and my little *brieder* during the day. Grandma and Grandpa Zook live a couple miles down the road."

"Where are your brothers right now?"

"Still at Grandma's."

"Does your grandma know where you are?" Paul questioned.

"Of course. Told her I was comin' over here to see if Mama needed me for anything." Aaron licked a glob of chocolate off

39

his fingertips. "Sure never expected to find a stranger sittin' in our kitchen, though."

"I'm not really a stranger," Paul said. "I used to live in Webster County. I've known your folks for some time."

"It's your bruder who died last week, ain't it?"

"Jah, my brother Dan. His funeral was yesterday."

"When you said your last name, I put two and two together."

"I see." *Aaron's not only feisty, but he seems to be a right smart little fellow.*

"What'd ya come over to see Mama about?"

"He's coming to work for me starting Saturday."

Paul turned his head. He hadn't realized Barbara had entered the room. She held a baby in her arms, and her face was slightly flushed.

Aaron glared at Paul; then he turned to face his mother and gave her an imploring look. "Why do you need him, Mama?"

"Because I'm not able to work right now."

"What about Grandpa? He's still workin' in the harness shop, right?"

Barbara nodded. "But your *grossdaadi* isn't able to handle things on his own so well."

Aaron puffed out his chest. "I could help him."

"I'm sure you could help with a few things, but not nearly enough, son."

Feeling the need to make a quick escape, Paul pushed back his chair and stood. "I should head to Seymour and call my cousin to let him know that I'll be staying awhile longer." He glanced down at Aaron, then back at Barbara. "I'll be at the harness shop bright and early."

She gave him a weary-looking smile and nodded. "Danki."

Paul had just stepped onto the front porch when a horse and buggy pulled into the yard.

❧

As John Frey stepped down from his buggy, he spotted Paul Hilty leaving Barbara's house. "I wonder what he's doing here," he mumbled.

"What was that, Papa?"

John glanced over at his fourteen-year-old daughter, Nadine, who had followed him out of the buggy. He'd dropped Hannah and Mary, his two younger girls, off at one of their neighbors' so they could play with their friend Maddie. And since Betty, his oldest daughter, was working and he didn't want to make his calls alone, he had invited Nadine to join him. "I just wondered what Paul Hilty is doing here," he said.

"Probably came by to pay his respects to Barbara since he wasn't here when her husband died." Nadine smiled sweetly. "I can hardly wait to see Barbara's new boppli. Maybe she'll let me hold him awhile."

John smiled in response. He had enjoyed holding his four girls when they were babies, but they were all older now, ranging in ages from ten to sixteen. He missed having a baby around. He also needed a mother for his daughters and hoped Barbara Zook might be willing to marry him. She was still young and could provide him with more children, as well as take charge of his household and give proper womanly instruction to his girls, so he figured she was the perfect choice. John had been widowed six months and Barbara for nearly a year. It was time for them to find new mates. Besides, he didn't think Barbara could keep working in the harness shop now that she had a new baby to care for. She needed a husband to support her and the boys.

"*Guder mariye*, Bishop Frey," Paul said, as he passed John on the way to his buggy.

"Good morning to you, too." John was on the verge of asking the reason for Paul's visit, but Paul gave a quick wave and sprinted to his buggy.

John shrugged and hurried after Nadine, who was already on the porch. Moments later, Barbara opened the door.

"Bishop John," she said. "What brings you out our way?"

"Came to see how you're getting along." He motioned to Nadine. "And Nadine would like to get a look at your boppli, if that's all right."

"Jah, sure." Barbara opened the door wider and bid them in. "I just put Davey in his cradle, but he's wide awake."

John and Nadine followed Barbara to the living room, and John took a seat on the sofa while Nadine rushed over to the wooden cradle sitting near the rocking chair.

"He's so *siess*," Nadine said dreamily.

"I think he's pretty sweet, too." Barbara smiled. "Would you like to hold him?"

"Oh, jah," Nadine replied with an eager nod. She took a seat in the rocking chair, and Barbara placed the baby in her arms.

"He feels so good. I can't wait until I'm married and have some *bopplin* of my own."

"Babies are a lot of work, but they bring many joys," Barbara said as she took a seat on the opposite end of the sofa from John.

John cleared his throat a couple of times. "We missed you at Dan Hilty's funeral. How have you been getting along?" he asked.

"I'm still feeling kind of tired, but I'm doing okay."

"Would you like me to send one of my girls over to help out? Betty's taken a job at the general store, but I'm sure either Hannah or Nadine would be glad to help you."

"I appreciate the offer, but I'm managing with the help of my mamm."

"How's Samuel doing in the harness shop? Is he able to keep up with the work now that you're not there to help?"

Barbara shook her head. "Due to Dad's arthritis, he struggles to get many things done. Paul Hilty's going to be helping in the shop for a while, so between the two of them, they'll be able to keep things going until I'm able to work again."

John's eyebrows drew together. "Are you sure you ought to return to work?"

Barbara nodded. "I enjoy working in the harness shop."

"That may be so, but it's hard work."

Barbara simply watched Nadine rock the baby.

"Have you considered selling the shop?"

She shook her head. "As long as I'm able to keep it open, I won't sell the place."

Unsure of what to say, John leaned against the sofa, folded his arms, and listened to the steady *tick-tock* of the clock mingling with the rhythmic *creak-creak* of the rocking chair. Finally, John rose to his feet. "Guess we should get going. I want to pay a call on Margaret Hilty and see how she's doing."

"I was sorry to hear of her loss," Barbara said as she stood.

"Will she be moving in with her daughter and son-in-law?"

John shook his head. "From what I've heard, Karen and Jake plan to rent their house out and move in with Margaret. It'll be easier for her if she's not alone, and I don't think she wants to leave her home right now."

"I can understand that." When the baby started squirming, Barbara leaned over and took him from Nadine. "I think he's about ready to be fed."

Nadine cast a furtive glance in John's direction. "I wish we didn't have to leave so soon."

"I think we'd better," he said, moving toward the door.

Barbara walked with them, and John was about to step onto the porch when an idea struck him. "You know, Margaret could use some encouragement, and since you lost your husband and know what it feels like to be left alone, maybe you could be helpful to Margaret."

"Helpful how?"

"Well, I know you can't get out much right now, with having a new boppli and all, but would it be all right if I encourage Margaret to come by and visit?"

"Certainly."

"Margaret's really good with flowers, so maybe she'd even be willing to help weed your garden. I'll make mention of it when I get over to her house."

"Well, I—"

"I'll be back to see you again soon." John smiled, gave Nadine a little nudge, and headed for his buggy. If things went as he hoped, in a few months he'd have a new wife, and then Barbara wouldn't have to work at the harness shop anymore.

Chapter 4

*P*aul was about to enter Zook's Harness Shop Saturday morning, but he slowed his pace, still unsure if he had made the right decision. *Maybe it won't be so bad. Barbara did say she would be staying at the house to do paperwork and tend to her children.* He would pretty much be in charge of things since Samuel Raber had arthritis and, according to Barbara, didn't know a great deal about the business.

As Paul opened the door and stepped into the shop, he drew in a deep breath. The smell of raw leather, savory neat's-foot oil, and pungent dye hung in the air. He glanced around. Several harnesses and bridles were looped from ceiling hooks. Enormous sheets of loosely rolled leather, looking like cinnamon sticks, poured out of shelves along one side of the shop. Hundreds of snaps, rings, buckles, and rivets nestled in open boxes lined neatly along one wall. Piled on the cement floor were bits of leather scraps, resembling spaghetti noodles. It was a comfortable feeling to be inside the harness shop. He'd only been gone from his cousin's place a few days, and already he missed it. But Andy and his part-time helpers were doing okay without him, and Andy didn't seem to mind if Paul stayed to help Barbara in her hour of need.

Paul saw no sign of Samuel, so he headed toward the back of the building. Two oversized sewing machines run by an air compressor sat side by side on a heavy table. A row of tools spilled out of round wooden holders on the wide workbench nearby. "Hello," he called. "Anybody here?"

Barbara's father stepped out of the back room, limping slightly as he ambled toward him. When Samuel clasped Paul's shoulder, Paul took notice of the older man's red, arthritic fingers.

Paul cleared his throat. "I. . .uh. . . assume Barbara told you I'd be working here awhile."

Samuel smiled through the reddish beard that matched his hair. "It'll be good to have you helping." He held up his hands. "These fingers don't work so good anymore. And to tell you the truth, when Barbara's not here to show me what to do, I often flounder."

Paul nodded. "I'll do whatever I can to help."

Samuel made a sweeping gesture. "Assembling a harness can be complicated. It involves dozens of snaps, straps, and buckles, all connected in a particular way." He grinned, and his cheeks flamed. "Guess you already know that, what with working at a harness shop in Pennsylvania and all."

"Jah, I've been working for my cousin Andy."

"You like it better there?"

Paul shrugged. "It's okay. But Lancaster County has become awful crowded."

Samuel frowned. "I guess some folks don't mind crowded areas, but I'd never want to live anyplace but here. There's nothing like the quiet, peaceful life; that's what I've got to say."

"So what jobs are needing to be done right now?" Paul asked.

Samuel motioned toward the desk near the front door. "There's a folder with all the job orders over there, and I'm way behind."

Paul rolled up his cotton shirtsleeves, eager to get busy. "I'll take a look-see."

Alice released a weary sigh as she placed a kettle of water on the stove to heat. Zachary and Joseph were playing in the living room, but ever since the boys had arrived, Aaron had just sat at the kitchen table and doodled on a piece of paper.

"Aaron, why don't you take your brothers and go outside for a while," Alice suggested. "It's a nice day, and the fresh air and sunshine will do you all some good."

"Don't feel like playing."

"What do you feel like doing?"

Aaron shrugged.

"Would you like to help me bake some cookies?"

"Bakin' is women's work."

Alice sat down beside him. "That's not true, Aaron. Look at

Noah Hertzler; he's always helping his wife in the kitchen, and he bakes lots of tasty treats that he shares with others."

Aaron grunted. "I don't care about bakin'."

"But you enjoy eating the cookies I make."

He nodded, and his eyes brightened some. "You got any oatmeal cookies, Grandma?"

She chuckled and patted his arm. "No, but I can surely make some."

"That'd be good."

"Are you sure you wouldn't like to help?"

"Naw."

"Why don't you go out to the harness shop and see if you can help your grossdaadi and Paul?"

Aaron's nose wrinkled like some foul odor had come into the room. "If it was just Grandpa workin' in the shop, I might, but not with Paul Hilty there."

Alice frowned. "What have you got against Paul?"

Aaron shrugged.

"You know your mamm's not able to work in the harness shop right now," Alice said. "So she's hired Paul to take her place until she gets her strength back."

"Couldn't she have found someone else?"

"No one in these parts knows much about harness making, and Paul works in a harness shop in Pennsylvania."

Aaron made little circles on the paper with his pencil. Finally, he pushed back his chair and stood. "Guess I'll go see what Joseph and Zachary are up to."

"Okay. I'll call you when I've got some cookies baked."

Aaron strolled out of the kitchen, and Alice got out a box of tea for the water she'd heated. She was worried enough about Barbara these days. Now with Aaron acting so moody, she had one more thing to be concerned about.

Barbara glanced at the battery-operated clock above the refrigerator as she poured herself a cup of tea. It was eight fifteen, and she'd sent the boys over to her mother's. She hadn't slept well because the baby had been fussy and demanded several feedings. She wished she could go back to bed, but she had some bills to pay, as well as a stack of paperwork that needed attention.

Barbara yawned and moved over to the window. An open buggy sat next to the harness shop. She figured it must be Paul's. Most of their customers didn't show up this early.

Barbara felt a sense of relief knowing her father would have help in the shop, but part of her bristled at the thought of anyone taking her place. She so missed working with leather.

"I need to eat enough, rest more, and get my strength back so I can work in the shop again," she murmured as she took a seat at the table. "Then Paul will be free to return to Pennsylvania."

Barbara's hand trembled as she set down her cup. She'd been much weaker since Davey's birth than she had been after her other boys were born. Maybe she'd done too much during her pregnancy. Perhaps she'd lost more blood with this delivery and that had left her feeling so tired. Or maybe she was emotionally drained, having had to go through the ordeal without her husband by her side.

She massaged her temples, trying to keep the threatening

tears at bay. Feeling sorry for herself wouldn't help a thing. She was on her own to care for her family, and because she was so weak, she needed Paul's help.

Barbara stood. "What I need to do is go upstairs and check on the boppli. Then I'll get busy with those bills."

Paul stood at the workbench, focused on the job at hand. Connecting the breast strap of a harness to a huge, three-way snap required some fancy looping. His hand wove in and out, neatly tacking the strap at the end.

"That's some fine work," Samuel said as he peered over Paul's shoulder. "It's clear you know exactly what you're doing."

Paul shrugged. "Took me awhile to get the hang of it when I first started, but I've done this type of thing many times."

Samuel stepped over a pile of dirty leather straps and buckles. "Always got lots of harnesses people bring in to get cleaned and repaired." He grunted. "If they'd take better care of 'em, they'd pretty well last forever."

"You're right about that," Paul agreed. "Folks need to bring their harnesses in for cleaning and oiling at least once a year, but unfortunately, many don't."

Samuel bent down and picked up a leather strap. "With my arthritic hands, cleaning things like this is about the only thing I do well here in the shop. I put the dirty ones in a tub of warm water with saddle soap, then scrub 'em real good."

Paul was about to comment, but a truck rumbled into the yard and stopped in front of the shop. A middle-aged English man ambled in, lugging a worn-out saddle, which he dropped on the floor. "Need to have this gone over. Can you do that for me, Sam?"

"If it's just a good cleaning you're after, I can manage it fine. But if the saddle needs a lot of fixing, then here's your man." Samuel motioned to Paul. "Paul Hilty, meet Frank Henderson. He lives up near Springfield."

"It's nice to meet you," Paul said, extending his hand.

"Howdy." As Frank returned the handshake, he looked a bit perplexed. "Where's Barbara? Isn't she working here anymore?"

"My daughter had a baby a few days ago, so she's taking some time away from the shop. Paul's from Pennsylvania. He came here for his brother's funeral and has agreed to help out until she's able to handle things again."

Paul squatted down and studied the worn-looking saddle. It needed more than soap and water, but he was sure it could be salvaged. "We'll give it a good going-over." He looked up at Samuel. "You want to write up the work order, or should I?"

Samuel shrugged. "Makes no never mind to me. Until Barbara returns, you're the boss."

Paul thought about Barbara and how pale and thin she appeared. As far as he was concerned, a delicate woman like her ought to be at home caring for her kinner, not trying to run a business—especially one that often required heavy lifting.

"Why don't you write up the order?" Paul said to Samuel. "I'll get back to work on that breast strap." He nodded at Frank. "Nice to meet you. We'll drop a card in the mail when your saddle is done."

"Appreciate that."

Paul turned back to his job.

Two more customers showed up that morning. Paul took time out to meet them and see what they needed, but he left the paperwork to Barbara's father.

A bit later, Samuel touched his shoulder. "Aaron just popped by to say that there's food on the table. Are you coming up to the house for the noon meal?"

Paul had been so caught up in his work that he hadn't realized it was lunchtime. "How come the boy's home from school today?" he asked.

"It's Saturday. No school until Monday, and then only a few weeks until the kinner will be out for the summer."

"Oh." Paul had been out of school for so long that he'd forgotten the summer break began in early May.

"So you comin' up to the house or not?"

"I. . .uh. . .brought my lunch pail along. Figured I'd eat out here."

Samuel shook his head. "No way. You been working hard all morning and need a hot meal. Alice has probably got a place set for you at the table. Believe me when I say you don't want to disappoint that wife of mine."

"Well, I—"

"Barbara and the boys will be joining us, and I'm sure she'd like to hear how your first day has been going."

"Guess I'd better say jah, then."

Samuel grinned. "Glad to hear it."

Chapter 5

ow come such a big meal today?" Barbara asked when she saw all the food sitting out in her mother's kitchen.

Mom placed a platter of ham in the center of the table and smiled. "I figured your daed would be bringing Paul Hilty up to the house for lunch, and I know how hungry those men can be after working all morning."

An image of David popped into Barbara's head. She remembered him saying many times that the noon meal needed to be the heartiest of the day. *"Fuels the body after working all morning and gives one strength for the afternoon,"* he used to say.

Barbara's mother touched her arm. "You still look tired. Didn't you get a nap this morning?"

"Every time I tried to lie down, Davey started to fuss. Now the little fellow's fast asleep in the portable crib we set up in your spare bedroom."

Mom clucked her tongue. "Isn't that the way? As a baby, your sister Clara was always wide awake when she should have been sleeping."

"You had five daughters with completely different personalities, and I've been blessed with four boys who are equally different." Barbara sighed. "I wish my sisters still lived nearby."

"I miss them, too," Mom agreed. "But I'm glad you're close by."

Barbara smiled. "What can I do to help with the meal?"

Mom shook her head. "Everything's about ready, so sit down and relax until the *mannsleit* and buwe come inside."

"Speaking of the boys, where are my other three? Haven't seen or heard from them all morning."

"A few minutes ago, I sent Aaron to the harness shop to tell the menfolk lunch was ready. The two younger ones have been playing on the back porch."

Barbara sat down. "I hope Aaron does what you asked. He used to help his daed with little things in the shop, but since David's death, he seems to have lost interest." She sighed. "Now I can barely get him to go in the shop at all."

Mom placed a bowl of coleslaw on the table. "The boy probably misses his daed, and being in the shop is a reminder that David's gone."

"Maybe so." Tears sprang to Barbara's eyes. "Aaron reminds me of David in so many ways. He enjoys working with his hands, and he's got his daed's determined spirit."

"Maybe someday, when you're ready to give up the shop, he'll take it over."

Barbara nodded. "He's not old enough to do a whole lot out

there yet, but after he finishes eighth grade and is ready to learn a trade, we'll see if he has any interest in the harness business."

Her mother smiled. "If he takes after his mamm, he surely will."

When Paul entered the Rabers' kitchen, the first person he saw was Barbara. She sat at the table, holding the baby in her arms. He halted inside the door and stared. The sight of her kissing the infant's downy, dark head brought a lump to his throat. He'd seen plenty of women with babies, but never had it affected him like this. It made him long to be a husband—but a father? No way! He didn't have the patience for that.

What's the matter with me? I shouldn't even be thinking about marriage or children. Maybe I worked too hard this morning and it addled my brain.

"Hello, Paul," Barbara said. "How'd it go in the shop?"

He hung his straw hat on the closest wall peg. "Everything went fine. There's a lot to be done out there, that's for sure."

She nodded. "With me not being able to work for the few weeks before the baby came, we really got behind."

"We'll catch up quick with this man minding the shop," Samuel said, following Paul into the kitchen. "I've never seen anyone work as hard as him."

Paul's ears burned, and he reached up to rub them, hoping to hide his embarrassment.

"I–I'm glad to hear it." Barbara's voice wavered when she spoke, and she stared down at her baby.

Alice Raber lumbered across the room, her generous frame pushing at the seams of her long blue dress. "If you men have already washed, then sit yourselves down at the table, and I'll call the boys inside."

"We cleaned up in the harness shop," Samuel said, "so we're ready to eat."

"I'll be right back," his wife said and went out the door.

Samuel sat down at the head of the table, then motioned for Paul to take a seat.

Paul complied but shifted uncomfortably in his chair. He felt out of place.

Barbara seemed equally ill at ease. She kept her attention on the baby.

The tantalizing aroma of sugar-cured ham tickled Paul's nose and made his stomach rumble. This meal was bound to taste better than the cold sandwich and apple he'd brought to work. Struggling to come up with something intelligent to say, Paul felt relief when Alice returned with three young boys in tow.

"Paul, these are Barbara's boys," she said, tapping each one on the shoulder. "This is Aaron—he's close to nine. Joseph's nearly six, and Zachary is three and a half."

Paul nodded as the boys took their seats. "I met Aaron the other day. It's nice to meet the rest of you."

The two younger ones giggled, and Joseph nudged Aaron. Paul didn't know what they found so amusing. Could they be laughing at him? Maybe so. He remembered one of the young English boys who'd come into Andy's harness shop not long ago had laughed at him, saying he was so tall he looked like a beanpole.

As soon as Alice sat down, Samuel cleared his throat, pulling

Paul's thoughts aside. Everyone at the table bowed their heads for silent prayer. When Samuel cleared his throat a second time, it was time to eat.

⁂

"Why don't you let me put the boppli in the crib?" Barbara's mother suggested. "That way you'll have both hands free to eat."

"I'm good at doing things with one hand." Barbara glanced at Paul and caught him staring at her. *Does he think I'm overly protective?* She looked away and reached for her glass of water.

"You're not going to let me put the boppli down?" Mom persisted.

Barbara lifted the infant and placed him across her shoulder. "He's fine, and so am I."

Mom shrugged.

Barbara speared a piece of ham with her fork and realized as soon as it touched her plate that it would be difficult to cut with only one hand. Little David was almost asleep; she could feel the warmth of his head against her neck and hear his even breathing. A weary sigh escaped her lips. "Maybe I will put him down."

She sensed Paul's eyes upon her again as she stood and slipped out of the room.

When she returned a few minutes later, Dad and Paul were engaged in conversation, while Mom looked content overseeing the boys. Barbara lingered in the kitchen doorway. Everyone seemed to be enjoying the meal and the camaraderie. She knew it was silly, but Barbara felt out of place. Since she wasn't working in the harness shop, she had nothing to contribute to the conversation the men were having.

A sudden wave of dizziness hit Barbara with the force of a strong wind, and a need to sit swept over her. She had to eat something, even if her appetite was gone.

She moved slowly to the table and sat down.

"Did you get the little one settled?" her mother asked as she poured a glass of milk for Zachary.

Barbara took a sip of water, hoping to dispel the feeling of nausea she felt every time she looked at food. This was worse than morning sickness. "Jah, he's fast asleep. It's his second nap this morning," she said with a weary sigh.

Mom studied Barbara intently. "I can see by the dark circles under your eyes that you're not getting enough sleep. Would it help if I started keeping the older boys at our place during the night?"

Barbara took a bite of coleslaw, but it could have been shreds of straw for all the enjoyment she got from it. She knew why she was tired but didn't understand the depression she'd been plagued with or her lack of interest in food. It wasn't good for her or the baby.

"Daughter, did you hear what I said about keeping the boys overnight?"

"The older ones aren't keeping me awake."

Mom reached across the table and patted Barbara's hand. "This boppli sleeps less than the others did, jah?"

Barbara nodded. "I wouldn't mind being up half the night if I could make up for it during the day. But I'm way behind paying the bills and sending out orders for supplies needed at the shop."

Paul spoke up. "Is there anything I can do to help? I'd be

glad to send out the orders for you."

Barbara bristled. *He's already doing my job in the shop, and now he wants to take over the paperwork, too?* She forced a polite smile while she shook her head. "Danki for the offer, but I can manage."

Paul shrugged and took another piece of ham.

Barbara pursed her lips. Did he think she was unappreciative? Didn't the man realize how badly she needed to take part in her own business? She cut her meat. *If only I wasn't so weak. If I could work in the harness shop, I might not feel so useless.* She felt like bursting into tears for no good reason as she swallowed the ham and washed it down with a gulp of water. *Am I experiencing postpartum depression, still missing David, or just out of sorts because I'm feeling so drained?*

"Grandpa, can I help in the harness shop this afternoon?" Aaron asked.

"I reckon it would be all right, if your mamm has no objections." Barbara's dad swung his gaze over to Paul. "And if it's okay with Paul."

A muscle along the side of Paul's cheek twitched.

Barbara was happy to hear that her oldest boy had an interest in the shop again, but Paul seemed uncomfortable with the idea. "Aaron, maybe you should wait for another Saturday when I'm back working in the shop," she suggested.

The boy's forehead wrinkled. "But that might take a long time. Grandma says you're real tired, and the boppli's gonna need you for a while."

Barbara couldn't deny it. She might not be able to return to work for several weeks. She glanced at Paul again to gauge his reaction. He looked as uncomfortable as when he'd first entered the room. "If Grandpa and Paul are both okay with it, then you can help a few hours this afternoon."

Paul reached up and rubbed his jaw. "I guess we could use some help cleaning up the place."

"Is that all?" Aaron scrunched up his nose. "I'll bet if my daed was still alive, he'd let me do some fun stuff. Always did before."

"We're out there to work, not have fun," Paul said with a frown.

Barbara stiffened. "You don't have to be so harsh with the boy. He meant no disrespect."

Paul's face turned bright red. "I was just stating facts."

"I think working in the harness shop is fun," she asserted.

Mom's head bobbed up and down. "That's right. Why, I can't tell you how many times I've heard Barbara say how much fun she has in the shop. Of course, that's not to say I agree with her. Personally, I think harness making is too hard for a woman, and I've told my daughter so many times."

Obviously, neither Paul nor her mother saw things the way Barbara did. She grabbed a deviled egg and bit into it, determined to get her strength back. As soon as she was on her feet again, she would be ready to take over the shop. Then Paul Hilty could hightail it right back to Pennsylvania.

"I think I hear Davey, so I'd better go check on him." She rushed out of the room.

<hr />

Alice stared at her daughter's retreating form. Why was Barbara being so unfriendly? She seemed almost rude to Paul. Didn't she appreciate that he had agreed to take over the harness shop until she could return to work? And why did Paul seem so testy with Aaron? It was no wonder the boy shied away from him.

"So, what's for dessert?" Samuel asked, smiling over at Alice.

"I made a fresh batch of oatmeal cookies this morning, and we've got some applesauce to go with them."

"I'll have some," Samuel said with a nod.

"Me, too," Joseph put in.

Alice looked at Aaron, but he only shrugged. She turned to Paul and said, "What about you?"

"Dessert sounds good, but I think I should get back to work. Danki for inviting me to join you for the meal. It was very good." He pushed his chair away from the table, grabbed his hat, and headed out the door.

Alice looked at Samuel. "Do you want to take your dessert with you so you can get back to work?"

Samuel shook his head. "Paul's real capable. I think he can manage without my help awhile."

He looked over at Aaron. "You comin' out to the shop with me, boy?"

"Huh-uh."

"Why not? I thought you wanted to help."

Aaron shook his head. "Not today, Grandpa."

Samuel shrugged, glanced at Alice, and lifted his eyebrows. He was probably thinking the same thing she was—that it would be great when Barbara got her strength back and things returned to normal.

Chapter 6

$\mathcal{I}$'m glad Mom could watch the kinner this afternoon so we could make this trip," Faith said to Noah as they traveled down the road in their open buggy toward Barbara Zook's place. "I really need to check on Barbara."

"And I need to visit the harness shop." Noah smiled. "So it works out well for both of us."

They rode in silence awhile; then Faith spoke again. "I'm worried about Barbara."

"Why's that?"

"I talked with Alice the other day, and she said Barbara is awfully tired and acting depressed. She thinks this baby drained Barbara's strength more than the other three did and wonders if she's feeling down because it might be some time before she's up to working at the harness shop again."

"Maybe she shouldn't return to work at all. Maybe she should sell the harness shop and concentrate on raising her boys."

"I've thought the same thing." Faith sighed. "I think my good friend needs a husband."

Noah raised his brows. "Have you got anyone in mind?"

"Not really, but—"

He reached for her hand. "Now don't go trying to play matchmaker, Faith."

"Of course not. I don't know of any available men here in our community other than Bishop John. And he's much older than Barbara, so I doubt she'd be interested in him."

Noah squinted. "Do you really think age matters so much?"

"Well, no, I suppose not." She poked his arm playfully. "After all, I'm a few years older than you."

"Jah, but only a few."

"Since I don't know who would be right for Barbara, I promise I won't try to play matchmaker, but I can sure pray about the matter. She needs a husband, and her boys certainly need a daed."

Noah nodded. "Speaking of a daed, my boss, Hank, is a lot happier since he and Sandy adopted little Johnny.

She smiled, remembering how, soon after she'd returned to Webster County, she had talked to Hank's wife about her inability to have children and how pleased Sandy had been once she and Hank had decided to adopt.

Faith placed both hands across her stomach and struggled with her swirling emotions. Despite the fact that she'd been blessed with two special children, she longed to have more. But that was not to be.

For the last few weeks, Barbara had kept pretty much to herself. She was tempted to go out to the harness shop to see how things were going but didn't want Paul to think she was checking up on him. Besides, she felt uncomfortable and defensive around him.

Barbara stared out the kitchen window. Two Amish buggies and a truck were parked in front of the harness shop. Business was obviously picking up. If Paul weren't helping out, they would probably have to turn customers away.

A knock at the front door halted her thoughts. "Now who would be using that door?" she muttered.

When Barbara opened the door, her friend Faith Hertzler stood on the porch. "Guder mariye, Barbara. I brought you one of Noah's lemon sponge cakes."

"Good morning to you, too. The cake looks delicious."

Faith smiled, and her blue eyes fairly twinkled as she stepped into the living room. "I thought it might fatten you up a bit. You're looking awful skinny."

Barbara took the cake and motioned Faith to take a seat on the couch. "I'll put this in the kitchen and bring us a cup of tea," she said.

"Sounds good. Oh, and Noah attached a verse of scripture to the cake. I added a little joke on the back side of the paper."

Barbara nodded and smiled. "That doesn't surprise me at all."

A few minutes later, she returned with two cups of hot tea.

She handed one to Faith and took a seat in the rocker across from her. "How come you used the front door?"

"Noah's out in the harness shop seeing about having some new bridles made. As I was heading up to your house, I spotted your three boys playing in the front yard and went to visit with them a few minutes." Faith chuckled. "I was too lazy to walk around back after the kinner and I finished chatting."

Barbara frowned. "Aaron's home from school already? I didn't realize it was that late."

"School let out early today. It's the last day of school, you know."

"Oh, that's right." Barbara thumped the side of her head. She didn't know why she hadn't remembered. It made her feel as if she were losing control when she forgot something. "Where are your kinner? Are they outside playing with my three?"

Faith shook her head. "We left them with my folks. Noah and I are going to Seymour to shop; then he's taking me to Baldy's Café for some barbecued ribs."

"That sounds nice."

"It's been awhile since we did anything without our two young'uns along."

"Uh-huh."

"Noah left Osborn's Tree Farm a little early today, since things are a bit slow there right now."

"I see."

"Melinda was real happy about going over to her grandma and grandpa Stutzman's," Faith continued. "Her aunt Susie's cat just had a litter of kittens."

"Is Melinda still taking in every stray animal that comes

65

along?" Barbara asked, realizing that she wasn't contributing much to the conversation.

"Oh, jah. That girl would turn our place into a zoo if we'd let her."

"She's never been one to sit around and play with dolls, has she?"

"No, only the one her real daed gave her before he died. She hung on to that doll until I married Noah; then she finally put it away in a drawer." Faith shrugged. "I tried to get her to play with the faceless doll my mamm made when I was a girl, but she stuck that away, too."

Barbara sipped her tea. "I guess some girls would rather do other things than play little *mudder*."

"Like me—the girl who grew up telling jokes and yodeling and couldn't have cared less about domestic things." Faith smiled. "How's the baby? I can't wait to hold him."

"Davey's fine. He's sleeping in his crib."

Faith leaned forward and set her cup on the coffee table. "I'm glad he's doing well, but I don't think you are."

Barbara felt her defenses rise. Had her friend come over to lecture her? "I'll get my weight back as soon as my appetite improves," she said through tight lips.

"You've got to eat enough for both you and little David. Nursing mothers need plenty of nourishment, you know."

"I'm fine. Still a little weak, but that's getting better. And I make myself eat even if I'm not hungry."

Faith clasped her hands around her knees. "How's your mental health?"

Barbara blinked. "What are you getting at?"

"You're depressed. I can see it in your eyes and the way your shoulders are slumped."

Heat flooded Barbara's face. Faith knew her so well, but she hated to admit the way she felt. She thought it was a sign of weakness to be depressed. Up until David died, she had always been so strong. Even after his death, she had managed to avoid depression by keeping busy in the harness shop.

"It might help to talk about it," Faith prompted.

Barbara shuddered as tears clouded her vision. It wasn't like her to lose control. "Talking won't change a thing," she muttered.

"Maybe not, but it might make you feel better." Faith patted the sofa cushion. "Come sit by me and pour out your heart."

Barbara sighed and placed her cup on the small table to her left. Faith wouldn't let up until she got what she came for, and Barbara was pretty sure the woman's goal was to make her break down. Faith had said many times that God gave people tear ducts for a good reason, and folks shouldn't be too stubborn to use them.

When Barbara sat beside her friend, she clenched her fingers and willed herself not to cry.

"Is it postpartum depression?" Faith questioned.

"Maybe." Barbara felt her neck spasm as despair gripped her like a vise. "I think it's a combination of things."

"Such as?"

"Missing David, feeling bad because our youngest son will never know his daed, wanting to be out at the harness shop but knowing I'm too weak to do much more than care for myself and the boppli right now."

"Your mamm's looking after the other three, right?"

Barbara nodded.

"And Paul Hilty's helping in the shop, so that gives you time to rest up and get your strength back."

"Jah."

"I don't mean to lecture, but you should be grateful for all the help."

Barbara crossed her arms to dispel the sudden chill she felt. A tear seeped out from under her lashes. "I am grateful, but I feel so guilty."

"Guilty for what?"

"Because I–I'm useless."

Faith reached over and gripped Barbara's hand. "How can you say that? The boppli needs you to care for him and be strong."

"I know if I get plenty of rest and eat right, I'll regain strength physically. But I'm weak emotionally, and I don't know if I'll ever be strong again." A sob escaped Barbara's lips, and she clamped her mouth shut to keep from breaking down in front of her friend.

Faith patted Barbara gently on the back. "Go ahead and get it out. Let the cleansing tears come."

"Why do I feel guilty when I'm sad?" Barbara wailed.

"Maybe because you're used to being in control of things, and this is something you can't control."

Barbara couldn't deny that she liked to be in charge. Even when she was a girl, she'd tried to tell her sisters what to do. Not that any of them appreciated it or did all she asked, but it had given her a sense of being in control to make plans and try to get them to follow her suggestions. "I wasn't feeling sad like this before little Davey was born," she said with a sniff.

"Until now, you didn't have time to be depressed. Since you've been forced to slow down, your feelings are rising to the surface."

"Jah, maybe so."

"Did you see the verse that Noah attached to the cake?"

"I didn't take the time to look at it."

"The verse reminds us that there is a time for laughter and a time for tears."

Faith's comment unleashed the dam. Barbara wept for all she was worth. When her sobs finally tapered to sniffling hiccups, she reached for a tissue from the box on the coffee table and blew her nose. "Sorry for blubbering like that."

"It's all right. God knows your pain, and you have every right to cry."

Barbara's gaze darted to the Bible, also on the coffee table. "My faith isn't so strong anymore. Not the way yours seems to be."

Faith shook her head. "My faith wasn't always strong. It used to be almost nonexistent. Remember how I was when I came home after living among the English, thinking I wanted to be famous and make lots of money as an entertainer?"

Barbara nodded. But her friend was a different person now, and God had blessed her in many ways. Noah was a wonderful, loving husband, and they had two beautiful, healthy children. Would Faith be as secure in her beliefs if she'd lost the man she loved? It was easy to talk about having faith in God when things were going well.

"I know it's wrong for me to feel this way, but I'm jealous of you, Faith," Barbara admitted.

"Why? What have you to be jealous of?"

"Your husband is alive, and everything's going great in your life."

Faith stared at the floor. "Noah and I have our share of troubles, too."

Regret as strong as a Missouri king snake coiled around Barbara's middle. She'd been wallowing in self-pity, and here was her friend going through problems she didn't even know about. "What's wrong, Faith? What kind of problems are you and Noah having?"

Faith smiled, but her soulful blue eyes revealed the depth of her pain. "The doctor gave us some disappointing news at my last appointment. We can't have any more children."

Barbara's heart clenched. She knew how much her friend loved children and had hoped for another baby. "I'm awful sorry, Faith," she murmured.

"I've come to terms with it. At least I have Melinda and Isaiah, and I love them both very much."

"I know you do."

"If it were God's will for us to have more kinner, He would not have closed up my womb."

Barbara couldn't believe how matter-of-fact Faith was being. It reminded her of what Bishop John had said on the day of David's funeral. "Our faith teaches that when our time on earth is over, God will call us home no matter what. We just need to accept His will and move on with life."

"You've come a long way from the rebellious teenager I used to know," Barbara said. "Your strong faith and positive attitude amaze me."

Faith gave Barbara a hug. "Your friendship is one of the things that helped me grow. I want you to know that I'm here for you."

Barbara dabbed at the corners of her eyes. "Danki. I appreciate that. But once I return to work, I'll be able to make it on my own again."

"It's good to have you back in Webster County," Noah Hertzler said, returning the strip of leather for the bridles he wanted.

Paul placed it on the workbench. "I'm not here for good, you know. Just working at the harness shop until Barbara's up to taking over again." He shook his head. "It amazes me that any woman would want to do this kind of work."

Noah snickered. "I think some of the women in our community are cut from a different cloth than most."

"How so?"

"Take my wife, for instance. She loves to yodel and tell funny stories."

Paul nodded. "So I've heard."

"Not the everyday thing you'd expect from an Amish woman, mind you. But that's what makes Faith so special." Noah grinned. "Then there's my stepdaughter, Melinda. That girl takes in every stray critter that comes near our place, and some I think she goes looking for."

Paul leaned against the workbench and laughed. "Sounds like you've got your hands full."

Noah smiled. "Jah, but in a good way."

Paul could tell by the gleam in Noah's eyes that he was a happy man. He had a wife he obviously loved, a stepdaughter whose whims he catered to, a son to carry on his name, and a job that he thoroughly enjoyed. All Paul had was a job in Lancaster County, with little hope of ever owning his own business. He had no wife or children, and he wasn't getting any younger. He'd turned thirty a few months ago, and most men his age were already married with three or four children living under their roofs.

"Are you enjoying the time with your folks?" Noah asked, pulling Paul's thought aside.

Paul shrugged. "It's good to see them, of course, but Pop and I haven't seen eye to eye since I refused to follow in his footsteps as a farmer. Fact is, we can barely be in the same room without one of us snapping at the other."

"I know what you mean. My daed has never understood why I'd rather work at the tree farm than slop hogs with him." Noah folded his arms across his chest. "He's never understood my interest in baking, either. But I've come to realize that some things probably won't change, so it's best to try and ignore them."

"Guess you're right," Paul said with a nod. "If I let Pop's grumbling get to me, I'd be on the next bus bound for Pennsylvania. But I wouldn't feel right about running out on Barbara when she needs help."

"I'm glad you're here for her, because Samuel can't carry the load alone." Noah glanced around. "Hey, where is Samuel today?"

"He hired a driver to take him to Springfield for a doctor's appointment. I've been on my own all afternoon, and as you might have noticed when you first came in, the customers have kept me quite busy."

Noah nodded. "That's why I waited until the others left to start yakkin'."

Paul pointed to the stack of papers on the desk. "I work fast, but there's no way I can keep up with the orders we have right now."

"If I knew anything about what you're doing here, I'd offer to help in my spare time, but I'd only be in the way."

"That's okay. I'll be fine. Just need to keep my nose to the leather, as my cousin Andy likes to say."

Noah chuckled and turned toward the door. "Faith went up to the house to visit Barbara. Guess I'd better see if she's ready to head for Seymour. I'm taking my wife to eat supper at her favorite place—Baldy's Café."

"Have fun. I'll let you know when your bridles are ready."

"Danki."

When the door clicked shut behind Noah, Paul turned back to the workbench, wishing he had a wife to take out to supper. "What's wrong with you, Paul Hilty? Get yourself busy and quit thinking such unlikely thoughts!"

Chapter 7

*W*here are we going, Papa?" John's youngest daughter, Mary, asked as they headed down Highway C in their open buggy.

"I'm paying a call on Barbara Zook."

The ten-year-old's lower lip jutted out. "But I thought after you picked me and Hannah up from school, we'd go straight home so we could play."

"Jah, Papa." Twelve-year-old Hannah spoke up from the backseat. "This morning, you said since this was the last day of school, me and Mary could spend our afternoon playing at the creek."

"You can do that when we get home from Barbara's."

Mary nudged his shoulder. "But why do we have to go?"

"To see how she's getting along, that's why."

"Getting along with what?"

John gritted his teeth in frustration. "Why must you ask so many questions?"

She leaned away from him. "I—I just wanna know why we have to go over to Barbara's."

"She had a boppli not long ago. Don't you want to see how the little fellow's doing?"

"I'd rather play in the creek," Hannah said.

"If you don't stop complaining, you won't be playing at all today. Instead, when we get home, I'll find some work for you to do."

John glanced over his shoulder and noticed that both girls sat with their arms folded and their mouths clamped shut. Maybe now he could spend the rest of the ride in peace.

<hr>

When Barbara stepped onto the back porch, prepared to air out the quilt from her bed, she spotted John Frey's buggy pulling into the yard. His two youngest daughters were with him. John pulled up to the hitching rail close to the house.

"Wie geht's?" he called as he and the girls climbed down from the buggy.

"I'm doing all right. What brings you out our way?"

He and the girls joined Barbara on the porch. "We're calling on a few folks today, so I decided to stop and check on you." He tipped his straw hat and grinned at her in a most disconcerting way. "How are things in the harness shop?"

"Paul Hilty's helping out. As far as I know, everything's going okay."

"Will he be staying long?"

Her fingers curled around the edges of the quilt she held. "Just until I feel up to working again."

"That's good." The bishop squinted against the sun while offering Barbara another lopsided smile.

Barbara draped the quilt over the porch rail. An uncomfortable feeling settled over her. She didn't like the way John Frey was looking at her. The man was a widower nearly fifteen years her senior with four daughters to raise, and two of them were teenagers. When Jacob Martin had passed on a year and a half ago, John had taken over as the bishop for their district. Then six months ago, John's wife, Peggy, had died of cancer, leaving him to raise their girls on his own. Barbara hoped John didn't plan on her being his new wife. She had no desire to marry again. Besides, she couldn't imagine having to deal with four more children. She had her hands full taking care of her boys.

"You're looking a mite peaked," the bishop said. "If you're needing some help with the boppli, I could send one of the girls over. Betty has a job, but I'm sure either Hannah or Nadine could come." He nudged Hannah's arm. "Isn't that right, daughter?"

Her head bobbed up and down. "Sure, Papa. I'll do whatever you say."

"I appreciate the offer," Barbara said, "but my mamm's been helping with the three older boys, and I'm managing okay with the boppli."

"Looks like you could use some help outside." John glanced around the yard. "I'll mention it to Margaret Hilty the next time I see her. I'm sure she and some of the other ladies would be glad to give you a hand."

Barbara couldn't argue with the fact that her yard looked a mess. Since David had died and her responsibilities had increased, the lawn and flower beds had been dreadfully neglected. Dad wasn't able to keep up with yard work and help in the harness shop, too, so the lawn only got cut when he felt up to it and had the time. Mom had a weak back, which meant Barbara couldn't count on her help with yard work, either.

"I must admit, it is difficult to keep up with everything around here," she mumbled, feeling a knot form in her stomach. "If some of the ladies want to help, I'd appreciate it."

"I'll see that it's done real soon." John leaned against the railing opposite the quilt, apparently in no hurry to leave. "I was wondering if you and your boys would like to go on a picnic with me and the girls Saturday afternoon."

The knot in Barbara's stomach tightened, and she gritted her teeth as she concentrated on the patterns of light dappling the porch floor. "I. . .uh. . .appreciate the offer, but I don't think the boppli's ready for that kind of outing."

"Couldn't you leave him with your mamm?"

Barbara's face grew warm. She could hardly remind the bishop that she had to stay close to Davey because she was nursing.

As if by divine intervention, the little guy started to fuss. "I've got to go inside now. The boppli's crying." She turned toward the door. "It was kind of you to drop by."

"What about the picnic?"

When Barbara glanced over her shoulder, the scrutiny she saw on the bishop's face made her feel even more uncomfortable. She forced her lips into what she hoped was a polite smile. "I appreciate the offer, but it's really not possible. Good day,

Bishop John." She nodded at the girls. "It was nice seeing you, Mary and Hannah."

They nodded in return.

Barbara hurried into the house and lifted the baby from the cradle she kept for him in the living room. "The bishop probably thought I was rude, but I couldn't let you keep crying," she murmured against the infant's downy, dark head. "Besides, I'm not about to give that man any hope of my becoming his wife."

As Alice stepped away from the kitchen window, where she'd been watching Barbara talk to John Frey, she sighed. The bishop seemed to be coming around a lot lately, and Alice was pretty sure he had more on his mind than checking on Barbara's physical status. She had a hunch the bishop had set his cap for Barbara—probably because he needed a mother for his girls. She couldn't fault him for that, but she didn't think her daughter should be that wife. Barbara had enough on her shoulders, trying to raise four boys and run the harness shop. If she took on the responsibility of John's girls, too, she would never get any rest.

Alice took a seat at the table. She really hoped that Barbara and Paul might get together. According to Samuel, Paul was a hard worker and knew a lot about repairing harnesses and saddles. And the boys, except for Aaron, seemed quite smitten with the man. Truth be told, Alice thought Barbara could develop an interest in Paul, too, if she'd give the man half a chance.

God knows what my daughter needs better than anyone else, she thought as she closed her eyes and offered up a heartfelt prayer.

Heavenly Father, if it's Your will for Barbara to marry again, then let it be at the right time to the right man.

⁂

"This isn't the way to our house," Hannah said as John directed their horse and buggy farther down Highway C.

"I know. I'm making a call on Margaret Hilty, and then we'll go home," he replied.

"But I thought you were just gonna make the one call on Barbara Zook." Hannah leaned over the front seat and grunted. "Now we'll get home even later and probably won't have time to do any wading."

"If you don't get to the creek today, you can go tomorrow." John gripped the reins tightly as a car zipped past, tooting its horn. "Sure wish the Englishers wouldn't drive so fast on this narrow road," he muttered. "No wonder there have been so many accidents along here."

"I'm hungry," Mary complained. "I was hoping Barbara might give us something to eat, but she didn't offer a thing."

"And we never got to see the boppli, either," Hannah complained.

"Barbara's tired, and she's probably not feeling up to baking," John said. "Maybe she needs a couple of girls to help her."

"You volunteered me or Nadine," Hannah reminded him. "But Barbara said she was getting along fine."

He nodded. "That's true, but I don't think Barbara knows what she needs right now."

Mary nudged his shoulder. "What do you mean, Papa?"

He glanced back at her and smiled. "I believe she could use some girls of her own."

Mary's eyebrows furrowed. "But she's gotta have a husband for that, doesn't she?"

"Jah, and I've been thinking. . . ." John's voice trailed off. Should he tell the girls that he was hoping to give them a mother and him a wife, and that he hoped that wife and mother would be Barbara Zook? *Better wait awhile,* he decided. *In the meantime, I'll keep visiting Barbara and trying to gain her approval.*

"What are you thinking, Papa?" Hannah asked.

"Nothing important."

John pulled into Margaret Hilty's place a short time later.

"Can we wait in the buggy?" Hannah asked when John came around to help them down.

He shook his head. "I think it would be better if you came up to the house with me."

"How come, Papa?" Mary wanted to know.

"Because it wouldn't be proper for me to call on a recently widowed woman alone."

Mary opened her mouth as if she might argue, but he shook his head.

Both girls trudged up the path leading to the home Margaret now shared with her daughter and son-in-law, and John followed. When they stepped onto the porch, Margaret came out the back door dressed in her black mourning clothes.

"Wie geht's, Bishop John?" she asked.

"I'm doing all right."

"What brings you out my way on this warm afternoon?"

"We came to see how you're doing." He motioned first to

Hannah and then to Mary. "Isn't that right, girls?"

"Jah," they said in unison.

John smiled at Margaret. "How are you getting along?"

"Oh, fair to middlin'." She yawned. "I miss Dan something awful, and I'm still not sleeping so well, but I'm grateful that Karen and Jacob were willing to move in here with me. Otherwise, I'd be even lonelier."

"I understand. If I didn't have my girls to keep me company, I'd miss Peggy a lot more than I do."

John shifted from one foot to the other. "Say, I was wondering if I might make a suggestion."

"What's that?"

"We were over at Barbara Zook's a short time ago, and I noticed how overgrown her garden's become."

"I suppose with a new boppli and three young buwe to look after, she doesn't have much time for gardening," Margaret said.

He nodded. "I was thinking it might be good if a group of ladies got together and went over to Barbara's to work on her flower beds."

"I'm sure she would appreciate that."

He turned toward Margaret's garden and made a sweeping gesture with his hand. "Since you've done such a fine job with your own yard, I was thinking you'd be the perfect one to help Barbara get her yard looking good again."

"I do need something to keep my hands and mind busy, and there's only so much work I can do here." She nodded. "I'd be happy to help Barbara."

"That's good. I'll speak to a few other women and see what day would work best for them, and then I'll let Barbara know there's going to be a work frolic in her garden plot soon."

Margaret looked at the girls. "Would you two care for some peanut brittle? My daughter Karen and I made a big batch earlier this afternoon."

Mary and Hannah both nodded enthusiastically. "That'd be real nice," Mary said, licking her lips.

A short time later, John and his girls were headed back up Highway C toward home.

"Say, Papa, I've been wondering about something," Hannah said as they neared their farm.

"What's that, daughter?"

"How come you didn't invite Margaret to go on a picnic with us the way you did Barbara?"

"Well, I—"

"Margaret seems lonely. Maybe she would've enjoyed a day at the pond."

John's face heated up. "I. . .uh. . .as you know, Barbara has kinner, so I figured you girls would enjoy playing with her boys."

"Except for Aaron, Barbara's boys are a lot younger than us," Hannah reminded him.

"Right," he said with a nod. "And for that reason, I figure they'd be fun for you to play little mudder with."

Mary opened her mouth as if to reply, but he held up his hand and said, "Just eat your peanut brittle."

Paul hated to bother Barbara, but he needed several orders to be sent, and she'd made it clear when she hired him that she would place all the orders. He'd thought about asking Barbara's dad to take the paperwork up to the house, but Samuel had left for another doctor's appointment. Since there were no customers at the moment, Paul decided to take the information up to Barbara. He put the CLOSED sign in the shop window with a note saying they would open again after lunch and headed out the door.

Paul stepped onto the back porch of Barbara's house, and as he lifted his hand to the door, he heard a child say, "Whatcha doin'?"

Paul whirled around. Barbara's six-year-old son, Joseph, stood beside a bush near the porch, holding a metal bubble wand in his hand.

"I. . .uh. . .need to see your mamm about something," Paul stammered. He didn't know why he always felt so tongue-tied around children.

"She's in the house."

Paul nodded. "I figured she might be."

"You come over for lunch?" Joseph asked, his blue eyes looking ever so serious.

"No. I'm here on business."

Joseph stepped onto the porch. "Mama's harness business?"

"Jah."

The boy turned the doorknob and called through the open doorway, "Mama, the harness man's here to see you!"

Paul felt as though he would be intruding to step into the house without an invitation, so he waited on the porch until Barbara showed up. "Is there a problem at the shop?" she asked.

"No problem. I just wanted to give you these." Paul handed her the folder full of supply orders.

"Danki. I'll get everything sent out right away."

Joseph tossed the bubble wand onto a small table on the porch and yanked on the hem of his mother's apron. "Can the harness man stay for lunch? We've got plenty, right?"

Barbara's face flamed. "His name is Paul, and I'm sure he's busy."

Joseph shook his head. "No, he ain't. There's no cars or buggies parked in front of the shop."

A trickle of sweat rolled down Paul's forehead, and he wiped it away.

"If you haven't already eaten, you're welcome to join us," Barbara said, much to Paul's surprise.

Whatever she was cooking in the kitchen smelled mighty good. His stomach rumbled. "Well, I—"

"Mama's fixin' chicken noodle soup," Joseph said, smacking his lips. "It tastes awful good, and it smells *wunderbaar*."

Paul smiled at the boy's enthusiasm. "I'd be happy to join you for lunch if you're sure it's no trouble," he said to Barbara. "Maybe we could talk about business while we eat."

Barbara nodded. "Sounds fine to me."

Paul stepped inside. "Was that Bishop Frey I saw here earlier?" Paul asked as he followed her into the kitchen.

Barbara nodded. "He came by with two of his daughters to see how I was doing."

"Guess that's part of the man's duties."

"Jah." Barbara motioned to the table. "Why don't you have a seat? If David doesn't wake from his nap right away, I'll have the soup ready in no time."

"Is there something I can do to help?" Paul offered. Anything would be better than watching the woman bustle around the kitchen. Every time Paul saw Barbara Zook, he thought she was prettier than the time before. Gone were the dark circles under her eyes, and if he weren't mistaken, she'd put on a few needed pounds.

He sucked in his breath. *I shouldn't be thinking about her like this. She's a widowed woman with four boys, and I'm going back to Pennsylvania.*

"I suppose you could go out back and call my other two boys in for lunch. Aaron's pushing Zachary on the swing behind the barn," Barbara said, halting his disconcerting thoughts.

"I can get 'em, Mama," Joseph offered.

"If I send you, Aaron will only argue, or you'll end up getting sidetracked."

"The boys aren't over at your folks' place today?" Paul asked.

Barbara shook her head. "Mom went to Springfield with Dad." She chuckled. "I think my mamm asks that doctor more questions than my daed ever does. He tends to go along with whatever the doctor says and never thinks to voice any concerns."

"I think most men are like that," Paul said, opening the back door. "I'll go get your boys."

He'd only gone as far as the barn when he noticed Joseph trudging along beside him. "I thought you were inside with your mamm."

"Wanted to be with you."

Paul wasn't sure how to respond, so he just kept walking. Until recently, no child had ever shown an interest in him. Truth be told, it felt kind of nice—though he would never admit it to anyone.

Squeals of laughter drew his attention. Aaron was pushing his little brother on the swing.

"Your mamm wants you to come up to the house," Paul said. "She's got lunch about ready."

Aaron stopped pushing the younger boy and whirled around to face Paul. "How come she sent you?"

"The harness man's stayin' for lunch," Joseph announced with a wide grin.

Paul felt Aaron's icy stare all the way to his toes. Clearly, the boy didn't like him, though he wasn't sure why. He figured it had to be for the same reason other kids avoided him—they obviously knew he didn't care much for kids, at least not until now. Aaron had dropped by the shop a couple of times, but he only came around when his grandfather was there. When Paul was minding the shop alone, the boy stayed away. It was just as well. Paul had too much work to spend time babysitting or dealing with Aaron's nasty attitude.

Guess I'm sort of babysitting right now, he thought as he looked at Joseph, who stared up at him with eager blue eyes. *Maybe I need to reach out to Aaron, no matter how awkward it makes me feel.*

"Come on, Zachary," Aaron said as he helped his little brother off the swing. "It's time to eat." He grabbed the boy's hand, and the two scampered toward the house.

Joseph reached for Paul's hand, and they followed the other boys. Was Aaron missing his father? Could that be the problem?

"Say, Aaron," Paul said as he and Joseph stepped onto the porch. "How would you like to come out to the harness shop after lunch and help me?"

"Doin' what?" he asked without looking back. "Sweepin' the floor, I'll bet."

When Paul touched the boy's shoulder, he halted and turned around. "Thought you might like to fasten some buckles on a couple of leather straps, or maybe you could dye the edges."

A flicker of interest sparked in Aaron's eyes, but when he blinked, it disappeared. "We'll see," he mumbled.

When they entered the kitchen, lunch was ready. Barbara motioned to the chair at the head of the table. "Have a seat, Paul."

"But that's Pa's place," Aaron was quick to say. "Nobody should sit there 'cept Pa."

"Aaron, your daed's gone, and—"

Paul shook his head. "It's all right, Barbara. I can sit someplace else." He waited until Aaron and Joseph had taken their seats and Barbara had put Zachary on a high stool. After she was seated, Paul took the empty chair across from her.

All heads bowed. When the silent prayer was over, Barbara passed Paul a basket of rolls.

"These look good. Did you make them?" he asked.

"My mamm did. I haven't had the energy to do much baking since the boppli was born," Barbara said.

Paul took a roll and slathered it with butter. "You'll get your strength back soon. Already you're looking better than the day I first dropped by."

She smiled. "I'm anxious to get back to the harness shop. I surely do miss it."

Paul was tempted to ask why she felt the need to do men's work, but he thought better of it. He would be going back to

Pennsylvania soon, and what Barbara did was her own business. Besides, she needed a way to support herself, and according to her dad, she was very good at her trade.

He dipped his spoon into the soup and took a mouthful. "Mmm. . .this is mighty good."

"Danki."

Joseph smacked his lips. "Mama's the best cook in all of Webster County."

Barbara snickered. "Jah, sure."

Paul glanced at Aaron, who sat to his mother's left. The boy had his head down and seemed to be playing with his soup, stirring it over and over with his spoon.

"Aaron, you'd best eat and quit dawdling," Barbara scolded.

The child picked up his bowl and slurped his soup.

"Mind your manners and use your spoon." Barbara handed a roll to young Zachary, and he promptly dipped it in his soup.

"Would it be all right if Aaron comes out to the shop after lunch?" Paul asked. "With your daed being gone today, I could use some help."

Barbara's look of concern made him wish he hadn't said anything. "Are you getting further behind?"

He shook his head. "Just thought an extra pair of hands would be nice."

Barbara turned to face Aaron. "Would you like to help Paul this afternoon?"

He gave a slight shrug.

"I think you should give it a try. But you must do everything Paul says. Is that clear?"

"Jah."

Paul gripped his spoon. *I may regret asking the boy to help as much as I wish I hadn't accepted Barbara's invitation to lunch.* He knew it was silly, but being this close to her made him long for something he'd probably never have. He decided to forgo talking about the harness business over lunch. *As soon as I finish this bowl of soup, I'm going to hightail it right back to work.*

Chapter 8

Barbara curled up on her bed, glad that the baby, Zachary, and Joseph were taking naps. Since Aaron was out at the harness shop with Paul, she could rest. She'd felt exhausted by the time they'd finished eating lunch. Paul had offered to help her with the dishes, but since she knew he needed to get back to the shop, she'd declined, saying she could manage. She had left the dishes soaking in the sink, deciding she could do them later, when she hopefully would have a little more energy.

As Barbara burrowed into the pillow, a vision of Paul popped into her head. She had been avoiding him lately because he made her feel so uncomfortable. Today at lunch, however, she'd actually enjoyed his company.

Joseph sure seemed taken with him, she mused. The boy hung on Paul's every word.

"It's not fair, Mama," Joseph had wailed when Barbara said he needed a nap. "If Aaron gets to help in the harness shop, I should, too."

Barbara grinned. Joseph was nearly six but not old enough to help in the shop. She didn't think Aaron was all that thrilled about helping Paul, but it might be good for the boy to spend time alone with a man other than his grandpa.

Aaron misses his daed, but he can learn from Paul the way he did David. She rolled onto her other side. *If I'm feeling up to it after my nap, maybe I'll bundle up the baby and take a walk out there so I can see how things are going.*

David had enjoyed running the harness shop so much. He'd said many times that their firstborn would take over the business someday. Even when Aaron was a toddler, David had invited the boy out there just to let him hold the leather straps and "get the feel of things."

Tears welled in Barbara's eyes. How she missed working in the shop with her beloved husband. She missed their long talks after the children were put to bed, and she pined for the physical touch of the man she had loved since she was a teenager. Would she ever know love like that again? Probably not. Her focus needed to be on running the harness shop and raising her boys.

"I don't think I could ever feel for any man what I felt for David," she whispered against the Wedding Ring quilt covering her bed. It had been a gift from her mother when she and David married, and it always brought her comfort.

Heavy with the need for sleep, Barbara's eyelids closed. As she started to drift off, David's image was replaced with that of Paul Hilty. The way he'd smiled at her during lunch made her heart feel lighter than it had in weeks, and that confused her. A chunk of blond hair kept falling onto Paul's forehead, and she had to resist the temptation to push it back in place the way she often did with one of her boys. The last thing Barbara saw as she succumbed to sleep was the vision of Aaron and Paul walking side by side toward the harness shop.

Paul peered over Aaron's shoulder as the boy reached for a buckle. "Not that one, Aaron. It's too big for the strap you're working on."

The boy grabbed another buckle. As he fumbled with the clasp and tried to fasten it to the leather strap, it slipped and fell on the floor.

"Be careful now." Paul stooped to retrieve the buckle.

"It was slippery," Aaron complained.

"Maybe you've got neat's-foot oil on your hands from when you were oiling that saddle earlier."

"Nope. I washed 'em."

"Could be you didn't wash them well enough. Might be a good idea to do it again, son."

Aaron spun around, his dark eyes smoldering. "You ain't my daed."

The tips of Paul's ears warmed. " 'Course not. Never said I was."

"But you called me 'son.' "

Paul shrugged. "It was just a figure of speech."

"And you've been tellin' me what to do ever since we came out to my daed's shop."

"If you're going to be my helper, then I have the right to tell you what to do."

Aaron frowned. Then he headed for the sink at the back of the shop.

Paul shook his head. *Maybe asking the boy to help out wasn't such a good idea. Might be best if I sent him back to the house.* Paul opened his mouth to say so, but the front door swung open. Noah Hertzler stepped into the shop.

"I got off work early today and was passing by on my way home," Noah said. "Thought I'd stop and see how you're coming along with those bridles I ordered."

"They should be ready by next week," Paul answered.

Noah motioned to the back of the building. "I see you've got yourself a helper today."

Paul grimaced. "I believe he likes being in the shop, but I don't think he cottons to me so well."

"Give him time. He'll come around."

"Did he help his daed much?"

Noah nodded. "He followed David around like he was his shadow, though I'm not sure how much help he was in the shop. Never seen a father and son so close as those two seemed to be."

"Wish I could say the same for me and my daed."

"Still having problems?"

"Jah. Just last night we got into a disagreement over my returning to Pennsylvania."

Noah's eyebrows furrowed. "Will you be leaving soon?"

Paul shook his head. "Not until Barbara's back working again."

"You think it'll be much longer?"

"Don't rightly know. She invited me to eat lunch with her and the boys today, and she seemed to be doing okay." He frowned. "Come to think of it, she did look kind of tired by the time we were done."

"She's been through a lot."

Paul nodded.

"Guess your brother's widow must still be grieving, too."

"Jah. Margaret's taking Dan's death pretty hard, although she's trying to keep busy so she doesn't miss him so much."

"We've had several deaths in our community lately." Noah stuffed his hands into his pants pockets. "John Frey lost his wife six months ago."

"I heard that."

Noah's voice lowered a notch. "Word has it that he's looking for another wife already."

Paul leaned against the workbench and crossed his arms. "Is that so?"

"Jah. He's got four daughters who need a woman's guiding hand."

"I suppose they would."

"Faith thinks the bishop has set his cap for Barbara."

Paul's mouth dropped. That would explain John Frey's visit earlier in the day. Apparently, the man had more on his mind than seeing how Barbara was doing.

"You look surprised," Noah said. "It's pretty common for a widower with kinner to remarry soon after his wife's passing. Truth be told, I'm surprised Barbara hasn't remarried by now, what with her having three young'uns and a boppli to raise."

Paul gave a slight shrug. The thought of Barbara marrying

Bishop Frey made his stomach churn. She was too young and full of life to be married to a man whose hair and beard had more gray than brown. As he opened his mouth to say something, Aaron sauntered up, holding his hands out for inspection. "See, no oil."

"That's good. Why don't you get back to work on those buckles, then."

Aaron glanced up at Noah. "Did you bring any cookies today?"

"Not this time." Noah motioned toward the workbench. "Want to show me what you've been working on?"

"It's nothin' much, but if you wanna see, it's all right by me."

Noah winked at Paul. Aaron led Noah over to the bench while Paul went to work at the riveting machine. He was thankful Noah had dropped by. Aaron seemed much more comfortable with him.

⁂

When Barbara awoke from her nap, Joseph and Zachary were playing in their room. Aaron was nowhere to be found, so she assumed he was still at the shop with Paul. David was awake but not fussy. She would change his diaper and see if he wanted to nurse; then the four of them would go check on Aaron.

Half an hour later, Barbara headed to the harness shop. She held the baby in her arms while Zachary and Joseph traipsed alongside her.

"Do I get to help in the harness shop like Aaron's doin'?" Joseph asked.

She shook her head. "You're not old enough for that yet, son."

Joseph halted and dragged his bare foot through the dirt, making little circles with his big toe. "How come Aaron gets to have all the fun?"

"Working in the harness shop isn't like playing a game," Barbara said patiently. "You'll find that out in a few years when you're able to start helping there."

Joseph shrugged and started walking again.

Barbara smiled. Joseph was her most easygoing child. He would get over his disappointment quickly.

When they entered the harness shop a few minutes later, the sight that greeted Barbara sent a shock through her middle. Aaron's hands were completely black, and he had dark smudges on his face and shirt. He held on to a strap, which he'd obviously been staining, but the child had more dye on himself than anyplace else. She looked around for Paul and spotted him in front of the riveting machine, humming and working away as if he didn't have a care in the world. Didn't the man realize what a mess Aaron had made? He'd obviously not been watching the boy closely enough. Maybe Barbara had made a mistake agreeing to let Aaron help Paul. Maybe she shouldn't have hired Paul to work for her in the first place.

"What's wrong, Mama?" Aaron asked. "You look kind of grank."

Barbara moved swiftly to his side. "I'm not sick, Aaron, just a bit put out."

"How come?"

"Look at your hands."

"Jah, they're black as coal," Joseph put in.

"Black as coal," Zachary parroted.

Aaron wrinkled his nose. "Stay out of this, you two."

"There's no reason for you to be talking to your brothers like that." Barbara shifted the baby to her other arm and nodded at Aaron. "I want you to march on back to the sink and scrub your hands and face."

"But, Mama, I'm not done yet. Paul said if I finished this job by four o'clock, he'd pay me a dollar."

Barbara didn't want to say anything that might cause Aaron to dislike working in the harness shop. "All right, then. But try to be more careful. You're supposed to be staining the leather ends, not your hands and clothes."

"I'll do my best."

She moved toward Paul, but the two younger boys stayed near Aaron. That was just as well. She didn't think they should hear what she had to say.

"Did you come to see how Aaron's doing?" Paul asked when she stood beside him at the riveting machine.

Barbara nodded. "I'm not too pleased to see the mess he's making with that dye you're letting him use."

"Dying leather's a messy job."

"True, but his hands are all black, and he ended up getting dye on his shirt and face, too."

Paul kept working.

"Did you show him the right way to hold the brush and cover the edges of the leather with stain?"

"Of course."

When the baby hiccuped, Barbara put him over her shoulder and patted his back. "There's a right way and a wrong way to hold the paintbrush," she said. "The right way keeps the stain on the leather and not so much on the hands."

Paul's pale eyebrows drew together. "Are you questioning my ability to teach your son?"

She clamped her lips together, afraid she might spew some unkind words. Who did Paul Hilty think he was? He acted as if this were *his* shop.

"Well, are you questioning my ability?" he persisted.

Barbara drew in a deep breath and blew it out quickly. "I'm not questioning your ability. But I think you need to remember that this is *my* shop and Aaron is *my* son." She paused long enough to grab another quick breath. "Not only that, but I'm the one who will have to spend time trying to get the dye off his hands and face before Sunday. I sure wouldn't want him going to preaching like that."

Paul chuckled. "No, that would never do."

Barbara bit her bottom lip hard. "Are you laughing at me?"

"Not really. I was just thinking how different you look when you're mad."

Her face heated up. "I am not mad."

"You're not mad, huh? Then how come your cheeks are so pink?"

Barbara mentally counted to ten. Was he trying to goad her into an argument? "I'm upset because you haven't been watching Aaron closely enough."

"I have been watching him, and the boy's doing fine, Barbara. I know he made a mess with the dye, but how is he supposed to learn if he doesn't try?"

In her heart, Barbara knew Paul was right. Aaron would

learn best by doing, even if he did make a mess. She still felt defensive. This was her shop, and she had a certain way of doing things. That included how she would teach her son to dye leather straps.

"I'm thinking sometime next week I might come to the shop and work awhile," she blurted out.

Paul's eyebrows lifted. "You really think that's wise? It's only been a few weeks since you had the baby."

Her heart began to pound. Did he think he knew what was best for her, too? "I'm not planning to work full-time. I thought it would be good to try a few hours and see how it goes."

"What about the kinner?"

"I'm sure my mamm will watch them."

"Even the boppli? Doesn't he need to be fed regularly?"

She nodded. "I can plan my time in the shop around his feeding schedule. If he needs me, Mom can send one of the boys out to let me know."

Paul shrugged and grabbed another metal rivet. "Whatever you think best. You're the boss."

Chapter 9

Sunday dawned with a cloudless sky, and for the first time since little David was born, Barbara would be going to church. In some ways, she looked forward to it. She had missed fellowshipping with other believers. But in another way, she looked on it with dread. Paul would be there, and after their confrontation at the harness shop, she wasn't sure she could face him.

She stared out at her overgrown lawn. *He probably thinks I'm rude and controlling, but he has to understand the way things are. I own the harness shop, and that gives me the right to say how things should be done. I'm also Aaron's mother, and regardless of what Paul may think, I know what's best for my son.*

A vision of her oldest boy's dirty black hands popped into Barbara's mind. When Aaron had come home from the shop that day, she'd scrubbed for nearly an hour, trying to get the black stain off. Three days later, Aaron's hands were a dingy gray.

When Barbara's three boys came running into the kitchen, she looked away from the window.

"Is breakfast ready yet, Mama?" Joseph asked. "I'm hungry!"

She smiled. "I made blueberry pancakes."

"Yum. Those are my favorite," Aaron said as he pulled out a chair.

"Did you wash your hands?" Barbara asked.

"Didn't think I needed to this morning."

"Oh? And why's that?"

Aaron held up his hands. "Been washed so many times, there ain't much skin left."

"Don't exaggerate." Barbara nodded toward the sink. "You'd better get it done."

Aaron grunted but did as he was told.

"Me and Zachary washed our hands," Joseph said.

"That's good to hear. Now scoot up to the table." Barbara lifted Zachary onto his stool while Joseph sat in a chair. At least two of her boys were compliant. *I wonder how little David will be when he's older,* she mused. *Will he be even-tempered like these two, or will the boppli take after his oldest brother and be stubborn as a mule?*

"Margaret's yard sure looks nice," Faith commented as Noah pulled their buggy into the Hiltys' yard. "She's obviously been busy weeding."

"It probably does her good to keep busy."

Faith nodded. "Jah. It's only been a few weeks since Dan died." She looked over at Noah and smiled. "While you're getting the horse unhitched, I'll see if I can speak with her before preaching service starts."

"Okay. See you later."

Faith herded their two children toward the house and stopped to say a quick hello to her mother.

Mom smiled at the children. "Susie's out back playing on the swings with some of the other kinner. Why don't the two of you join them?"

The children didn't have to be asked twice, and as they scampered off, Faith went inside to speak with Margaret. She found her in the kitchen getting a glass of water.

"Wie geht's, Margaret?" she asked, stepping up beside the woman.

Margaret smiled, although there was no sparkle in her blue eyes. "I'm getting by. . .taking one day at a time."

"I was admiring your garden as we drove in," Faith said, glancing out the window. "Looks like you've been busy. I didn't see a single weed."

"I enjoy spending time in the garden. It makes me feel closer to God, and it keeps my hands and mind occupied."

"Speaking of gardens, did you know there's going to be a work frolic at Barbara Zook's place next week?"

"Jah. Bishop John told me. He asked if I'd be willing to go and help out since I know a thing or two about gardening."

"Are you planning to go?"

Margaret nodded. "May as well. It'll give me something meaningful to do."

Faith gave Margaret a hug. "I lost my first husband, so I know a little of what you're going through. Of course, Greg and I were never as close as you and Dan." Faith wouldn't have admitted it to Margaret, but back when she'd been living in the English world and Greg had been killed after stepping into traffic during one of his drunken stupors, she'd had mixed feelings. Greg had been harsh and abusive with her almost the whole time they were married. He'd gambled and drunk excessively and, as her agent, had forced her to do more performances than she had cared to. But Faith had been in love with Greg when they first got married, and he had been a decent father to Melinda. For that reason, Faith had grieved when he'd been killed. How grateful she was that God had brought Noah into her life and given her a second chance at being a godly wife and a good mother to her two precious children.

"I spoke with Paul the other day, and he said he's enjoying the work he does in Barbara's harness shop," Margaret said, pulling Faith's reflections back to the present.

Faith smiled. "That's what he told Noah not long ago, too."

"Do you think it'll be long before Barbara takes over the harness shop again?"

"I don't know, but I just may ask her." Faith pointed out the window. "Looks like her daed's rig pulling into your yard now."

"Well, I'll let you go so you can visit with her before preaching service begins." Margaret set her glass in the sink. "I should speak with Dan's mother."

Faith gave Margaret's arm a gentle squeeze. "I'll see you at the work frolic next week."

"You can count on it."

Faith scurried out the back door and made it to Samuel's buggy moments after he halted it near the barn. "It's good to see you this morning," she said as she helped Barbara climb down with the baby in her arms. The boys had already run off toward a group of children.

Barbara smiled. "It feels good to be out again."

Faith held out her hands. "Mind if I hold the boppli? It's been awhile since I had a newborn in my arms."

Barbara handed her son over to Faith. "I believe he's put on a few pounds since you last saw him."

"That's good." Faith scrutinized Barbara. "Looks like you've gained some weight, too."

Barbara nodded. "I believe I have. My appetite's slowly returning."

"Glad to hear it. How's the depression?"

"It comes and goes. But I'm sure it'll be gone once I'm able to work in the harness shop again."

"How long do you think it will be before that happens?" Faith asked as they walked toward the house.

"I'm hoping to work a few hours next week."

Faith's eyebrows rose. "So soon?"

Barbara shrugged. "I get bored sitting around the house."

Faith kissed the top of Davey's head. "But you have this little guy to keep you busy. Not to mention your three active boys." She motioned to the maple tree where the children awaited their turn on the swing.

"I love caring for my kinner, but I also like working in the shop. Besides, somebody's got to earn the money to support my brood."

"According to Noah, Paul's managing the harness shop just fine."

"He probably is, but he won't be here forever. I'm sure he's anxious to return to Pennsylvania." Barbara nibbled on her lower lip. "Until I'm working full-time, I doubt he'll feel free to go."

"Shows what kind of man he is, don't you think?" Faith took a seat in the rocking chair on the porch and rocked the baby.

Barbara sat in the wicker chair next to her. "Paul seems conscientious and hardworking."

"Is that all?"

"What are you getting at?"

Faith tipped her head. "I merely wondered what you think of him as a man, that's all."

"I just told you."

"Does he appeal to you?"

Barbara's mouth dropped open. "It's not proper for a newly widowed woman to think such things, and you know it."

"Barbara, it's been almost a year since David died. I've known several widows and widowers who married within the first year."

Barbara's body stiffened. "I'm not looking for a husband."

"Maybe not. But I'm pretty sure there's one looking for you." Faith nodded toward Bishop Frey. "I hear tell he's got marrying on his mind, and word has it you're the man's first choice."

John stepped onto the porch. "Guder mariye, ladies," he said with a nod in Barbara's direction.

"Morning, Bishop Frey," the women said in unison.

He gave his beard a quick tug. "You're looking tired today, Barbara. Are you sure you don't want me to send one of my girls over to your place to help out?"

She smiled, but it appeared to be forced. "I'm managing, but I'll let you know if I should need anything."

"All right, then. I'll be around to call on you again soon." He took a few steps closer to Barbara. "Oh, by the way, I spoke to Margaret Hilty the other day, and she said she'd be happy to help with your garden. She and some other women will come over next week to help."

"I appreciate that."

John shifted his weight from one foot to the other while clearing his throat. After a few awkward moments, he glanced over at Faith. "How are things with you and Noah these days?"

"We're doing fine. Noah's keeping busy with his job, and I keep busy with things at home."

"It's always good to be busy. Jah, real good." He shuffled his feet a few more times, then looked back at Barbara. "Well, I'd best be getting inside now. Service will be starting soon." With a quick nod, he left.

From where Paul sat on the men's side of the room, he had a perfect view of Barbara Zook. She looked serene, sitting on the bench, cradling her infant son. A deep yearning welled up in Paul's chest, just as it had that afternoon in Barbara's kitchen. Had he made a mistake thinking marriage wasn't for him? Should he look

On Her Own

for a wife when he returned to Pennsylvania? Only problem was, he wasn't interested in anyone back there. No other woman had affected him the way Barbara had, yet his attraction to her made no sense. Whenever they were in the same room, he either felt uncomfortable or irritated with her criticism.

Paul forced his gaze away from Barbara and tried to focus on Bishop Frey's sermon.

" 'Lo, children are an heritage of the Lord: and the fruit of the womb is his reward. As arrows are in the hand of a mighty man; so are children of the youth. Happy is the man that hath his quiver full of them: they shall not be ashamed, but they shall speak with the enemies in the gate.' Psalm 127:3–5," the bishop read from the Bible he held. "And chapter 128, verse 1, says, 'Blessed is every one that feareth the Lord; that walketh in his ways.' " He smiled. "Be fruitful and multiply and be blessed."

Paul shifted uncomfortably. Were the bishop's words directed at him? Was God speaking through John Frey, telling Paul he should get married and raise a family and that by so doing, he would be blessed? He thought about his conversation with Noah Hertzler the other day. Noah had mentioned the bishop's interest in Barbara. Maybe the man's sermon was directed at himself. Could be that John thought if he took another wife and had more children, he would be twice blessed. That wife could turn out to be Barbara Zook.

I've got to quit thinking about this, Paul reprimanded himself. *If the bishop should marry Barbara, it's none of my business. She has the right to choose whomever she pleases.* He shuddered. *Then why does the idea of her becoming the bishop's wife make me feel so miserable?*

After the noon meal, Barbara put the baby and Zachary down for naps. She stared at her youngest son, sleeping peacefully on his side, and a lump formed in her throat. She knew she was more protective of him than she had been with her other three. Maybe it was because this little guy would never know the wonderful man for whom he'd been named. Or maybe her own insecurities caused her to feel overly protective. Ever since David had been snatched away so suddenly, Barbara had been a little paranoid. What if something bad happened to one of her children? What if she died and left them with no mother? Sure, her folks would step in and raise the boys, but because they were getting up in years, it would be difficult for them to take on such a big responsibility. Her four married sisters might be willing to take the boys, but two of them lived near Sweet Springs, and the other two had moved to Minnesota. It would be hard for the boys to move from the only home they'd ever known.

Try not to worry, she admonished herself. *As the book of Matthew states: " 'Which of you by taking thought can add one cubit unto his stature?' "*

Barbara turned away from Davey's crib and tiptoed out of the room. She needed to turn the future of her sons over to God. She decided to go outside and enjoy the rest of the day.

As soon as Barbara stepped onto the front porch, she spotted Paul sitting under a maple tree with Joseph nestled in his lap. Her heart nearly melted at the sight. He looked so natural holding her son, and Joseph appeared as content as a cat lying in a patch of sun.

I need to speak with Paul, she told herself. *I need to apologize for my abruptness the other day.*

Barbara walked swiftly across the lawn before she lost her nerve.

"Hi, Mama," Joseph said with a wide smile. "Me and the harness man—I mean, Paul—we're plannin' a fishin' trip."

Paul's ears turned pink, and he gave Barbara a sheepish-looking grin. "Guilty as charged. I thought maybe next Saturday after I close the shop in the afternoon."

Before Barbara could respond, Joseph thumped the spot beside him. "Have a seat, and we'll tell ya all about it."

Barbara knelt on the grass next to her son. "I'm all ears."

"I heard there's some pretty nice catfish in the pond over by Ben Swartley's place," Paul said. "I thought it might be fun to take the boys fishing." He motioned to Barbara. "You're welcome to come along if you like."

The thought of going fishing was like honey in Barbara's mouth. She hadn't been on such an outing in over a year. Not since David had taken her and the boys to the pond for a picnic a few weeks before his death.

"It sounds like fun," she murmured. "But I couldn't leave Davey that long."

"You wouldn't have to," Paul said. "You could bring the baby along."

Joseph nodded enthusiastically. "Jah, Mama. The boppli can come, too."

Barbara shook her head. "He can't be in the sun all day."

"We could put up a little tent," Paul suggested. "We'll set his baby carriage inside, and he'll be just fine."

Barbara had some netting in her sewing cabinet. Maybe she could drape it over the carriage to keep the bugs away, and if she put the carriage under the shade of a tree, it might work out okay. It would be nice to get away and do something fun. But did she really want to spend several hours alone with Paul? *Of course*, she reasoned, *I wouldn't really be alone with him. The boys will be there, too.*

"Can we go, Mama? Please?"

She patted her son's shoulder. "I'll think on it. In the meantime, I'd like you to go find Aaron."

"What for? He don't wanna play with me; he said so."

"Tell him I want to head for home soon."

Joseph's lower lip protruded. "Aw, do we have to?"

"Jah. I'm going back to the house to get Zachary and Davey in a few minutes, and I'd like you and Aaron to be ready to go."

The boy stood and squeezed Paul around the neck. It was obvious that he'd taken a liking to the man. And from the way Paul responded by grinning and patting Joseph on the back, Barbara was fairly sure the feeling was returned.

As Joseph skipped away, Barbara searched for the necessary words. "I. . .uh. . .owe you an apology for the other day."

Paul's eyebrows rose.

"I shouldn't have been so testy about Aaron's black hands, and I didn't mean to question your judgment. I hope you'll accept my apology."

A slow smile spread across his face, and a familiar longing

crept into her heart. *David used to look at me like that. Oh, I surely do miss him.*

"No apology needed," Paul said. "Aaron's your son, and you had a right to be concerned."

"I appreciate your understanding."

He plucked a blade of grass and stuck it between his teeth. "I hope you'll consider the fishing trip."

Barbara was taken aback by the stark emotion she saw in Paul's eyes. What did it mean? Was he missing someone, too? Maybe Paul had a girlfriend back in Pennsylvania. Barbara had never thought to ask. Should she say something now? No, she'd better not; it might embarrass Paul.

"I'll give it some thought," she finally murmured.

"While you're thinking on it, I hope you'll remember how much Joseph wants to go fishing." He leaned back on his elbows and smiled. "For that matter, from the look I saw on your face when the fishing trip was mentioned, I'd say it's something you might be looking forward to, as well."

Barbara rose to her feet and hurried toward the house with her heart beating an irregular rhythm.

Chapter 10

$\mathcal{O}$n Wednesday morning, a group of women including Margaret Hilty and Faith showed up to work in Barbara's yard. Barbara felt torn between helping them and going to the harness shop. She knew it could only be for an hour or two, as she didn't have the energy to work a full day yet. Her plan was to wait until lunch was over and then take the three younger boys to her folks' place so her mom could watch them. She figured Aaron might like to help in the shop, too.

"I feel like I should be helping you with the yard work," Barbara said when Faith came up to the house to get a jug of iced tea for the women. "But I'm planning to work in the harness shop a few hours this afternoon, and if I work in the garden this morning, I won't have the energy to work in the shop after lunch."

Faith shook her head. "We don't expect you to help us in the garden." She touched Barbara's arm. "If you want my opinion, you shouldn't be working in the harness shop yet, either."

"Why not?"

"Have you looked in a mirror this morning? You've got dark circles under your eyes, and your face looks pale and drawn." Faith nodded toward the steps leading to the upstairs bedrooms. "What you should do after lunch is take a nap."

"I don't need a nap, and I don't need any lectures." Barbara gritted her teeth, and her hand shook as she pushed a strand of hair back into her bun. She wished people would stop telling her what to do.

Faith drew back like she'd been stung by a bee. "Sorry. I didn't mean to upset you."

Barbara's face relaxed some. "It's me who should apologize. I don't know why I'm so testy lately."

"You're tired and no doubt feeling a bit stressed with all the responsibilities you have."

"That's true, but it's no excuse for me being rude. Will you forgive me?"

Faith nodded and gave Barbara a hug. "Of course. And I'll keep praying for you, too."

"Danki. I appreciate that."

"Well, I'd best head back to the garden so the women can have a cold drink." Faith made a beeline for the yard, and Barbara hurried upstairs to check on little David.

"Looks like a group of women have converged on Barbara's yard today," Samuel said to Paul as he glanced out the window of the harness shop.

Paul stepped up beside Samuel. "I see that. I wonder what they're all doing."

"From what Alice told me, they came to weed the garden and get Barbara's yard in shape."

Paul craned his neck as he watched several women bent over the garden with hoes and rakes. "Looks like my sister-in-law Margaret is here."

Samuel nodded. "Alice heard that John Frey invited Margaret, thinking it would give her something meaningful to do that might take her mind off her grief."

Paul cringed at the mention of the bishop's name. He didn't care for the way that man looked at Barbara. . .like he owned her. He turned away from the window and grabbed a hunk of leather that needed to be trimmed. *Maybe I'm overreacting. Bishop John might not have a personal interest in Barbara at all. He may just be doing his job as head minister of this community when he pays her a call, same as he's been doing with Margaret.*

"Did Barbara tell you she plans to come out to the shop this afternoon?" Samuel asked.

Paul shook his head. "She never said a word. I guess it's her right to drop in and check on things, since this is her shop."

Samuel glanced out the window again as the rumble of buggy wheels could be heard coming up the driveway.

"Guess there must be more women coming to the work frolic, huh?"

Samuel shook his head. "Nope. It's John Frey's rig, and he doesn't seem to be headed to the harness shop, so he must be planning to pay another call on Barbara. Or maybe he came by to see how the yard work is coming along."

Paul clamped his teeth together. *More than likely the bishop's here to see Barbara.*

***

Knowing the three older boys were playing in the barn, Barbara opened the door and stepped outside to call them in for lunch.

"There's a buggy comin', Mama," Aaron said as he, Joseph, and Zachary hurried across the lawn.

She shielded her eyes against the harsh glare of the sun and noticed Bishop Frey's rig heading toward the house. Instinctively, she reached up to straighten her kapp.

"Wie geht's?" the bishop called as he stepped down from the buggy.

"I'm fine, and you?"

"Hot and thirsty." He swiped his hand across his forehead. "It's a real scorcher."

"It sure is," she agreed. "It makes me feel guilty to see how hard the women are working in my yard."

Bishop John glanced over his shoulder. "Have they been working long?"

"A few hours, but they'll be stopping soon for lunch. My mamm made some sandwiches, so I'll be calling them in to eat in a few minutes." Barbara nodded toward the porch swing. "If you'd like to have a seat, I'll get you a glass of iced tea."

He grinned and seated himself on the swing. "I'd be much obliged."

Barbara wasn't sure whether to leave her boys with Bishop John or take them inside with her. Seeing how much fun Zachary was having as he raced back and forth on the lawn, chasing after Joseph, she decided to leave things as they were. "I'll be right back," she said before hurrying inside.

A few minutes later, she returned with a glass of iced tea for the bishop and some crackers for her boys. She figured it would tide them over until lunch and maybe keep their mouths too busy to talk. Joseph could be quite chatty, and the last thing she needed was for him to tell John Frey any of their personal business.

She called the boys over to the porch, gave them the crackers, and instructed them to go back to the barn and play.

"How come, Mama?" Aaron asked. "You just called us out of the barn, and now you want us to go back?"

"I know I did, but I want you to play awhile longer so I can speak with Bishop John."

Joseph didn't have to be asked twice. He grabbed hold of Zachary's hand, and the two scampered off. But not Aaron. He glanced at the bishop with a strange expression, then stared at the porch floor, scuffing the toe of his boot along the wooden planks.

"Go on now," Barbara instructed. "Get on out to the barn with your brothers."

Aaron grunted and finally ambled off.

"Won't you sit with me and visit awhile?" the bishop asked.

Barbara's skin prickled as she sensed it was more than a casual visit, since he hadn't brought any of his daughters along. She sat in the wicker chair on the other side of the porch.

"I don't bite, you know," he said with a slanted grin.

She forced a smile in return. "I'm sure you don't. But I want to be close to the back door so I can hear the boppli if he starts to cry."

He shrugged and removed his straw hat, using it to fan his face. "Whew! Sure hope it cools down some. It's only the beginning of June, and already it's hotter than an oven turned on high."

She nodded. "Jah, hot and sticky."

The bishop cleared his throat. "I've been thinking about the two of us."

The speed of Barbara's heartbeat picked up. "What about us?"

"You've been widowed almost a year now, and it's been six months since my wife died." He paused and licked his lips. "The book of Ecclesiastes says, 'Two are better than one; because they have a good reward for their labour.' "

She nodded politely.

"I figure you've got young ones who need a daed, and I have four daughters who certainly could use a mother's hand. Since two are better than one, I was wondering how you'd feel about marrying me."

Barbara's mouth fell open. She'd suspected John Frey had marriage on his mind, but she hadn't expected him to be quite so direct. This proposal, if she could call it that, was much too sudden and abrupt. They hadn't courted or done anything of a social nature together, and she doubted they had much in common.

"Your silence makes me wonder if you find the idea of marriage to me objectionable." His forehead wrinkled. "Is it the thought of being a bishop's wife that bothers you, or is it our age difference?"

Barbara twisted her hands in her lap. How could she put her feelings into words and not sound as if she were being too particular or unappreciative of his offer? "There is a good fifteen years between us," she admitted. "Though I know many folks who have married people much older or younger and things worked out fine."

His lips turned upward. "That's how I see it, too."

"As far as being a bishop's wife, I don't think that's reason enough to keep someone from marrying another, either."

He jumped up and moved quickly to stand beside her. "Does that mean you'd be willing to marry me?"

Barbara cringed. She was making a mess of things and had to fix it before she ended up betrothed to this man for whom she felt nothing but respect as her bishop. "I'm not ready to commit to marriage again," she said, carefully choosing her words. "And if I should ever marry, I would want it to be for love, not merely for the sake of convenience."

A pained expression crossed his face, and she was sure she had hurt his feelings.

"You're saying you don't find me appealing, isn't that right?" The poor man looked as if he'd taken a whiff of vinegar.

"That's not it at all." Barbara sucked in her lower lip. "It's just that I'm not over the loss of David yet, and it wouldn't seem right to take another husband until the pain subsides."

The bishop paced the length of the porch several times. After a few minutes, he stopped and faced her again. "Both of us will always have love in our hearts for the ones we married in our youth. But that shouldn't stop us from starting a new relationship. Fact is, getting married again might help heal our pain."

Even if the bishop was right, Barbara didn't want or need a husband right now. She had her hands full making sure her business didn't fail. "I truly do appreciate the offer, John, but—"

He held up one hand. "I want to take care of you, Barbara. I'd like to offer you a home and provide for you and your boys."

The man sounded sincere, but what he'd said caused her spine to go rigid. "I've got my job at the harness shop, and it supports us well enough."

"I understand that, but wouldn't you prefer not to have to work in order to take care of your boys?"

"I enjoy working with leather."

"But keeping the harness shop is becoming harder for you to do now that your daed's arthritis is getting worse and you have to rely on your mamm to care for the boys. Isn't that right?"

She nodded.

John reached out his hand like he might touch her, but he pulled it back and smiled instead. "You don't have to give me your answer this minute. Just promise you'll think about marrying me, okay?"

Not wishing to hurt the man's feelings, Barbara nodded.

"I'll give you a few more months to make up your mind."

"I. . .uh. . .appreciate that," she mumbled.

He handed her his empty glass. "I think we could both benefit if we were to marry, and I believe our kinner would gain something from our union, too."

Barbara's hand shook as she lifted it to touch her flushed

face. "If you'll excuse me, I need to get my boys. It's past their lunchtime."

"I can call them for you, since I'll be headed that way to my buggy," he offered.

"That would be fine." Barbara scurried into the house. Maybe she would feel better after she'd had some lunch. She was determined to do a little work in the harness shop, no matter how drained she felt.

When John poked his head into the barn, he discovered Zachary and Joseph sitting on a pile of straw playing with two kittens. The oldest boy, Aaron, sat on a wooden stool, fiddling with an old wooden yo-yo. "Your mamm wanted me to tell you that she's got lunch ready," John said, smiling at the boys.

Zachary and Joseph set the kittens down and scampered out. But Aaron just sat twisting the string of the yo-yo around his finger.

Deciding to take advantage of the situation, John stepped up to Aaron and touched his shoulder. "I was thinking it might be kind of fun to go on a picnic and maybe do some fishing sometime. What do you think of that idea, huh?"

Aaron looked up, and his eyebrows lifted slightly. "Just you and me?"

John shook his head. "I was planning to ask your mamm and brieder to go along."

"Mama and my brothers might want to go, but I'm not interested."

"How come?"

"Just don't wanna go, that's all." Aaron shrugged. "Paul Hilty asked Mama to go fishing with him on Saturday, but if she goes, only my brothers are goin'."

John stiffened. Was Paul planning to stay in Webster County for good? Did he have his cap set for Barbara? He grimaced. Maybe the man was after Barbara's harness shop and figured the best way to get it was to marry the woman.

Well, it's not going to happen. I'll keep after Barbara until she marries me. It's my job as her bishop to see that no one takes advantage of her.

Chapter 11

Paul glanced at the clock. It was almost one, and he'd just finished eating his lunch. His mother had outdone herself when she'd packed him leftover meat loaf, tangy potato salad, and zesty baked beans. The food had gone down a lot better than two hunks of bread with a slice of ham sandwiched between, which was what he usually fixed.

As Paul slipped his lunch pail under the counter, he thought about the day he'd been invited to join Barbara and her boys for their noon meal. It had been simple fare, just soup and rolls, but he had enjoyed it immensely. The food wasn't the only thing Paul had taken pleasure in. He actually liked being around Barbara's boys. All but Aaron. He wasn't sure he and the boy would ever see eye to eye, but he hoped they could at least come to an understanding, especially if Aaron continued to help in the harness shop.

Paul was preparing to cut a piece of leather when the shop door opened and Barbara and Aaron stepped into the room. His heartbeat quickened. Every time he was around the woman, he felt more drawn to her. That scared him.

"We thought we'd help out for a few hours," Barbara said. "That is, if you don't mind."

He shook his head. "It's your shop; you can do whatever you like." Paul could have bitten his tongue. He hadn't meant for his words to come out so clipped. "Sorry," he mumbled. "I just meant—"

"Anything in particular you're needing help with?" she asked.

He nodded toward the back of the shop. "Your daed's trimming the edges of some leather. When he's done, they'll need to be dyed."

Barbara's forehead creased. "More black hands for Aaron?"

Paul shrugged. "Maybe you can show him a better way or find some rubber gloves he could wear."

Barbara nodded. "I think I may have a pair somewhere that will fit him." She moved away, and Aaron followed.

Paul went back to work on the leather strap he was planning to cut, feeling a sense of irritation he didn't fully understand. Was it the fact that this was Barbara's shop and not his that bothered him so much? Maybe his irritation stemmed from her thinking she knew more about dying leather than he did. Well, if she had a better way of doing it that wouldn't stain the boy's hands, then she was more than welcome to show him.

Paul gripped the piece of leather in his hands as the truth behind his agitation surfaced and threatened to boil over. Every time Barbara came out to the shop, even for a short visit, it was a reminder to him that she would soon be back working full-time, taking over *her* shop again. When that happened, there would be no reason for Paul to stay in Webster County. Unless, of course, he could convince Barbara to sell the shop to him. If she married John Frey, she might be willing to.

Paul dropped the hunk of leather on the workbench with a thud. *But I don't want Barbara to marry the bishop. I want—*

What did he want, anyway?

With a grunt of determination, Paul resumed his work. If he kept focused on the job at hand, he wouldn't have so much time to think about other things. Things he had no right to be thinking about.

A short time later, Barbara returned to the front of the shop. "I think Aaron can manage on his own now," she said. "So I'm available to help with whatever else needs to be done."

Paul thought. He didn't want her doing anything too strenuous, yet he was sure she wanted to feel needed. "How about pressing some grooves into the edges of the straps that have been cut and dyed?"

Barbara nodded. "I can do that. I haven't worked the pressing machine in some time, but it should feel good to get back at it."

Paul watched as she moved to the machine and took up her work. He could see by the smile on her face that she loved working in the harness shop. *And who am I to say otherwise? Just because I don't think this is the kind of work a woman should do doesn't mean it's not right for Barbara. Besides, the sooner she gets back to work full-time, the sooner I can return to Pennsylvania.*

Paul shook his head. Who was he kidding? He liked it

here and wished he could stay. He forced his gaze away from Barbara and on to the job at hand. This kind of thinking was dangerous.

Barbara straightened with a weary sigh, easing the kinks out of her back. She'd only been working an hour, and already she felt as if the strength had been drained from her body. *Maybe I wasn't ready to come back yet, not even for a short time.* Tears flooded her eyes, and she willed them away. She loved being in the shop, where the subtle smell of leather mixed with the tangy aroma of linseed and neat's-foot oil. *Just take it slow,* she told herself. *If you work a few hours each week, soon you'll be up to working full-time again.*

"Are you okay, daughter?"

Barbara whirled around. She hadn't realized her father had come up behind her. "I–I'm a bit tired," she admitted. "Maybe I should call it a day."

He nodded soberly. "I should think so. You're paler than a bucket of fresh milk. And look at your hands—they're shaking."

Barbara clasped her fingers tightly together.

"I can't believe you're out here today," he said with a frown. "You ought to be up at the house, taking care of that new boppli of yours."

Barbara's cheeks warmed. "Dad, I'm a grown woman, and I know my limitations. Mom's watching Joseph, Zachary, and Davey, and if the boppli needs me, she will send Joseph straightaway." Barbara's voice quavered, but she hoped her father wouldn't notice.

Paul stepped up beside them. "Is everything all right?"

Barbara opened her mouth to respond, but her father cut her off. "She's not ready for this yet. Just look at the way she's trembling like a baby tree in the midst of a storm."

Paul frowned. "I should have been watching closer. Sorry about that, Samuel."

Barbara stomped her foot. "I am not a little girl who needs to be pampered. No one has to watch me or tell me when I should quit working."

The men stood silently, apparently dumbfounded by her outburst.

"Your daed's right about how tired you look," Paul finally said. "But if you want to continue working, it's your right to do so. After all, this is *your* shop, and *you're* the boss."

Not this again, Barbara fumed. *Why does he feel the need to keep reminding me that I'm the boss?*

She drew in a deep breath. "Actually, I should probably check on the boppli. So if I'm not needed for anything else, I'll go on up to the house."

"I'm sure we can manage," Paul said, glancing at Barbara's father.

"Jah, with Aaron's help, we'll do just fine."

"All right."

As Barbara headed for the door, Paul tapped her on the shoulder. "Can I speak with you a minute, outside?"

Barbara nodded.

When they stood outside the shop, she asked, "What is it?"

Paul stared at the ground and pushed the toe of his boot around, making little circles in the dirt. Barbara listened to the soft swooshing sound and wondered when or if he was going to tell her what was on his mind.

"I was wondering if you've thought anymore about Saturday," he mumbled.

"Saturday?"

"Jah, my invitation to take you and the boys to the pond for a picnic and some fishing."

Barbara hated to disappoint the boys, and she didn't want to send the three oldest ones with Paul while she stayed home with the baby. What if one of them fell in the water and he didn't see him in time? A lot could happen with three little boys.

"It will be a lot of fun," he prompted.

"Jah, okay. We'll go."

His lips lifted at the corners. "That's. . .uh. . .great. I'll check with my brother and see if he has a pole I can borrow."

Barbara thought about loaning him David's pole, but that idea didn't sit well with her. It wouldn't seem right to see someone else using her husband's fishing rod. "See you Saturday if not before," she said with a nod.

He turned back to the shop. "You can count on it."

Chapter 12

Barbara didn't go out to the harness shop the rest of the week. She needed to rest as much as possible if she was going to feel up to going on the picnic. Despite her misgivings about spending time with Paul outside the harness shop, she looked forward to taking the boys to the pond. She had packed some food they would eat for supper. Paul had promised to come by the house as soon as he closed the harness shop at three.

Barbara glanced at the kitchen clock, and a sense of apprehension crept up her spine. Should she have accepted Paul's invitation? She'd gone to bed early the night before, but she was exhausted. Maybe a little time spent at the pond would do her good. She used to like going there when David was alive. The children deserved to have a little fun at the pond, and maybe she did, too.

She opened the back door and spotted Aaron and Joseph sitting on the top porch step with a jar full of ladybugs. "You two need to go out to the barn and look for your fishing poles," she said.

Joseph jumped up, but Aaron sat unmoving.

"Aaron, did you hear what I said?"

"I don't wanna go fishing."

"Why not? You love to fish."

"Only with Pa when he was alive." Aaron's shoulders trembled.

She took a seat on the step beside him. "Grandpa's busy today, and Paul was nice enough to invite us. Don't you think you should go?"

He shook his head.

"It might hurt Paul's feelings if you don't come."

"I don't care."

"But you can't stay home alone."

"I can go over to Grandma and Grandpa's."

She took hold of his hand. "You'd rather be with them than fishing?"

"Jah," he said with a sober nod.

"We won't get home until after supper."

Aaron shrugged.

Barbara gave a weary sigh. "All right, then. If it's okay with Grandma and Grandpa, you can stay at their place."

Paul couldn't remember the last time he'd been this enthused about going fishing. Was it the anticipation of catching a mess of catfish, or was it the idea of spending time with Barbara and her boys? A *little of both*, he admitted as he shut down the gas lantern hanging above his workbench.

He reached under the bench and grabbed the fishing pole his brother Monroe had loaned him, then headed out the door.

When Paul reached the house, Zachary and Joseph were sitting on the porch, each holding a small fishing pole. He grinned at their enthusiasm. *Those two must like fishing as much as I do.*

"We've been waitin' for you," Joseph said eagerly. "Want me to call Mama?"

Paul stepped around them and onto the porch. "Sure, if you don't mind."

"Don't mind a'tall." Joseph jumped up, leaned his pole against the porch railing, and scurried into the house. A few minutes later he returned, lugging a wicker picnic basket. Barbara followed, holding the baby.

"Are you sure you don't mind me bringing David along?" she asked. "I just fed him, so he could be left with my mamm for a few hours."

Paul shook his head. "I think he'll be fine under the makeshift tent I've got stashed in my buggy. Besides, if you bring the boppli along, we won't have to hurry back if the fish are biting real good."

She smiled. "That's true, and I appreciate your making a little tent for the carriage." She nodded at the baby carriage on one end of the porch.

Paul reached down and scooped up the carriage, then glanced around. "Say, where's Aaron?"

"He ain't comin'," Joseph announced.

Paul glanced at Barbara.

"He said he'd rather stay with his *grossmudder* today," she said.

"*Ich wolle mir fische geh,*" Zachary said, looking up at Paul with wide eyes.

Paul smiled and started for the buggy. "I'm glad you want to go fishing, Zachary." If Aaron didn't want to go, Paul couldn't do much about it.

He loaded the carriage and Barbara's two boys into the backseat. Then he helped Barbara and the baby get settled up front with him.

As they pulled out of the yard, Paul caught a glimpse of Aaron heading for the barn. Barbara waved, but the boy didn't look their way.

"Aaron's missing his daed," she said. "They used to go fishing together every chance they got."

He nodded. "I figured as much."

"I guess going to the pond today would be a painful reminder that his daed's not here anymore."

"He'll come around in time." Even as the words slipped off Paul's tongue, he wondered if they were true. Aaron might never completely get over his father's death, and he would probably never take a liking to Paul.

Barbara kissed the top of her baby's head. "At least Aaron will have some memories of David, which is more than this little guy will have." She glanced over her shoulder. "For that matter, Zachary probably won't remember his daed at all. I'm not even sure about Joseph."

Paul wished he could say or do something to ease the pain on Barbara's face. It wasn't fair that she had to bear the loss of her husband and try to raise four boys on her own. It didn't seem right for Margaret, his brother's widow, to go through life on her own, either. At least Margaret and Dan's four children were grown, so she didn't have the responsibility of caring for little ones. Even so, Margaret must be lonely without Dan.

Paul's thoughts turned to John Frey. Had the man considered Margaret as a candidate for marriage? She was closer to his age than Barbara. But she'd only been a widow a few weeks. It wouldn't seem proper for the bishop to court a newly widowed woman. Would the man consider someone else in this small Amish community for a wife?

When Barbara's baby gurgled, Paul set his thoughts aside. He glanced over at Barbara. "Is the little fellow doing okay?"

She nodded. "I think he's enjoying the ride."

Paul looked over his shoulder. "The boys in the back must be, too. They're fast asleep."

Barbara chuckled. "As soon as we pull up to the pond, they'll be wide awake and raring to go."

"I sure hope the fish are biting today," he said. "Wouldn't want to disappoint the kinner."

"Zachary's not old enough to do much fishing yet, so I doubt he would care whether or not they were biting."

"Joseph might, though."

"Maybe. But he's so taken with you, he'd probably be happy just sitting on the grass by your side."

"Sure don't know why. I've never been that comfortable with little ones. I think most of 'em feel the same way about me."

"What makes you think that?"

"Don't rightly know, but I am sure of the reason I'm leery of them."

"Why's that?"

"I dropped my brother Elam when he was a boppli, and it left him with a fat lip and a lump on his forehead." He blew out his breath. "I was afraid of holding any bopplin after that."

"That must have been scary for both of you. But you were only a boy, and what happened was just an accident."

"Jah, well, I still get *naerfich* around kinner—especially little ones. I never know what to say to them." He grunted. "Take your boy Aaron, for example. He doesn't like me; that's obvious enough."

"Don't take anything Aaron says or does personally, Paul. He's still struggling with his daed's death."

He shrugged. "Guess you might be right about that. Even so—"

"I believe Joseph sees something you don't," she said, reaching over to touch his arm.

The feel of Barbara's slender fingers on his bare skin made Paul's arm tingle. He inhaled deeply, searching for something else to talk about. "We're getting close to the pond. I can smell it. Can you?" he asked as she pulled her hand away.

"Jah, I believe I can."

A short time later, they pulled onto a grassy spot. Paul had no sooner secured the horse to a tree than the boys woke up and clambered out of the buggy. "Here, let me help you down," Paul said, offering Barbara his hand.

She leaned forward and gave him the baby. "If you'll take Davey, I can get out of the buggy a little easier."

"After what I said about dropping my little bruder, are you sure you trust me to hold him?"

She nodded. "I'm sure you'll do fine."

Reluctantly, Paul took the infant. He'd never held a baby this young before and wasn't sure if he was doing it right. He laid the baby against his shoulder, then patted the little fellow's back, feeling more awkward and nervous by the minute.

As soon as Barbara stepped down, she took her son. Paul felt a rush of relief. He'd seen many fathers hold their babies and look perfectly comfortable, but he doubted he ever would if he became a father.

Paul reached under the front seat and grabbed an old quilt. He handed it to Barbara. "If you and the boys want to get settled, I'll get the rest of the stuff unloaded."

"Joseph can help," she said.

Paul nodded toward the shoreline. The boys were already romping back and forth, throwing rocks into the water. "Let him play. I can manage."

"All right." Cradling little David, Barbara headed for a grassy area not far from the water.

In short order, Paul had a little tent set up for the baby carriage. Barbara put the infant inside and draped the piece of netting she'd brought over the sides. After Paul got the boys' fishing poles ready, he baited Barbara's hook and handed her the pole.

"Danki." She placed it on the ground and took a seat on the grass. "I'm not used to having someone wait on me, you know."

He grinned and sat next to her, noticing that she looked more rested. "It feels nice to be taking the time to go fishing."

She nodded, then leaned forward and cupped her hands around her mouth. "Joseph, Paul has your pole ready! Bring Zachary over here, and let's do some fishing."

The boys came running, and soon all four of them had their lines in the water. The sound of the children's laughter rippled over Paul like a bubbling brook, and he was amazed at how comfortable he felt. Savoring the moment, Paul closed his eyes and allowed himself to fully relax.

"Would you like to have some cookies and milk?" Alice asked Aaron when she opened the back door and found him sitting on the top porch step with his shoulders slumped and his head down.

"Naw. I ain't hungry."

She resisted the urge to correct his English and instead seated herself beside him. "Are you wishing you'd gone to the pond with your mamm and brieder?"

He shook his head vigorously. "Paul's there, too, and I don't want to do anything with him."

"Not even help in the harness shop?"

"I only go there 'cause it's my daed's shop, and he promised it'll be mine someday. Otherwise, I'd never go anywhere near Paul Hilty."

"What have you got against Paul?"

Aaron shrugged.

"Your grandpa says Paul knows a lot about harness making. I'm sure he could teach you plenty of things."

"Mama can teach me when she starts workin' full-time again."

"Even so, it's good for you to be around a man," Alice said.

"I'm around Grandpa a lot. At least he doesn't think he knows everything."

Alice placed her hand on Aaron's knee. "I'm sure Paul doesn't think he knows everything."

"Jah, he does. He acts like he's the boss of me and everything in my daed's harness shop." Aaron grunted. "You should see the way Joseph and Zachary hang all over him—like he's somethin' real special."

"They like Paul. He seems to like them, too."

"Humph!" Aaron folded his arms and stared straight ahead. "I think he's only pretendin' to like 'em."

"Why would he want to do that?"

A horse and buggy rolled into the yard just then, interrupting their conversation.

"That looks like Faith Hertzler's rig," Alice said. "She must be looking for your mamm."

Aaron stood. "Think I'll go out to the barn awhile and see what Grandpa's doin'."

"If you change your mind about having some milk and cookies, give a holler."

As Faith stepped down from her buggy, she noticed Barbara's oldest boy dart into the barn. She glanced up and saw Alice standing on the porch.

"I came to see how Barbara's doing. Is she at home?" Faith called.

Alice shook her head. "She and the three younger ones went to the pond with Paul Hilty for a picnic and to do some fishing."

"Really?" Faith asked as she joined Alice on the porch.

"Jah. I was surprised that she agreed to go, but I'm glad she did. My daughter needs to get out more. Maybe some fresh air and sunshine will perk her up a bit."

"I totally agree." Faith glanced at the barn. "How come Aaron didn't go?"

"That boy's been acting moody as all get-out ever since Paul began working for Barbara. He was invited to go fishing, but he didn't want to go."

"That's too bad. I'm sure he would have enjoyed spending the evening at the pond with a fishing pole in his hand. I know Isaiah sure would have." Faith chuckled. "For that matter, Melinda would rather be at the pond or in the woods than doing anything at home."

Alice smiled. "Is she still taking in every critter that comes along?"

"Jah, as many as we'll allow."

"At least she has something that holds her interest. That's more than I can say for Aaron these days. All he seems to want to do is sit around and mope." Alice motioned to the wicker chairs sitting near the front door. "Would you like to have a seat and visit awhile?"

"I don't mind if I do." Faith sank into one of the chairs with a weary sigh. "I spent most of the day helping Noah bake, and my feet are tired from standing so long."

"That man of yours is a wonder to me," Alice said. "Most men don't go near the kitchen unless it's to fill their bellies with food, but he actually enjoys being there."

"That's true. According to Noah's mamm, he started helping her in the kitchen when he was just a boy. I feel fortunate to have him."

"I hope Barbara finds another husband someday. She deserves to be happy, and it's getting harder for her to run that harness shop by herself." Alice gave a gusty sigh. "Of course, she thinks she can do everything on her own."

"Has she started working in the shop again?"

"Just a couple of hours here and there, but as soon as she regains her strength, she'll be back working full-time. Then Paul Hilty will probably be on his way back to Pennsylvania."

"Paul seems like a nice man," Faith said. "From what Noah's told me, Paul's real good at what he does, too."

Alice nodded. "I don't think he would have left Missouri if he'd been able to do harness work here."

Faith popped a couple of knuckles as she contemplated the best way to say what was on her mind. "I was wondering. . . ."

"What's that?"

"If Paul invited Barbara and her boys to go to the pond with him, do you think he might be interested in Barbara?"

Alice blinked. "Is that what you think?"

Faith's face heated with embarrassment. "I didn't say that. I just meant—"

Alice waved her hand. "It's all right. To tell you the truth, I'm hoping things work out so Barbara and Paul can be together.

After all, they both enjoy the harness business, and Barbara's boys—all but Aaron—seem to like Paul a lot."

"Maybe in time, Aaron will come around." Faith smiled. "Now we just have to hope and pray that Barbara will see that she needs another man, and that if it's meant to be Paul, they'll both realize it before Bishop John convinces her to marry him."

Barbara couldn't get over how relaxed she felt as she fixed her gaze on Paul. For one crazy moment, she was hurled into a whirlwind of conflicting emotions as she wondered what it would be like if Paul were to stay in Missouri and—

Barbara shook her head. She couldn't allow herself the luxury of thinking about Paul as anything other than her temporary employee. She had a business to run, not to mention four boys to raise. There wasn't time for romantic notions or even a close friendship with someone who would be leaving Webster County soon.

She nibbled on her lower lip. *Even if I did feel free to begin a relationship with Paul, and I knew he wanted one, he's never been married. He wouldn't want to take on the responsibility of raising another man's children, especially when one of them doesn't seem to like him much.*

"Hey! I've got me a bite!" Joseph hollered, pulling Barbara's musings aside. "I think it's a big one!"

"Hold on tight," Paul instructed as he sprang to his feet.

"Would ya help me reel him in?"

Paul grabbed Joseph's pole and held it steady.

"Don't let him get away, okay?"

"I won't." After several tugs, a nice big catfish lay flopping at the boy's feet.

Zachary squealed and jumped up and down. *"Fisch! Fisch!"*

Barbara laughed. It felt nice to see her boys having such a good time.

Joseph pointed to his trophy. *"Es bescht,"* he said with a wide grin.

Paul nodded. "Jah, the best." He removed the hook, then placed the catfish in a bucket of water.

For the next hour, they continued fishing. With Paul's help, they each caught at least one fish. The boys vied for Paul's attention, plopping down beside him and taking turns crawling into his lap. It pleased Barbara to see them so happy and carefree. If only Aaron hadn't been too stubborn to come. He would have enjoyed himself as much as his younger brothers.

After a while, the baby woke up and started to howl.

Zachary and Joseph covered their ears. "Make him quit, Mama," they pleaded in unison.

"There's only one way to stop his crying," Barbara said. "I'll need to feed him." Feeling the heat of a blush cover her cheeks, she looked over at Paul. "Would you mind if I take the boppli to your buggy?"

Paul shook his head, and she noticed the blotch of red covering his face. "Sure, go ahead. Maybe when you're done, we can eat our picnic supper," he said.

A short time later, the baby was fed and settled back in his carriage. Barbara spread the contents of their picnic basket on the quilt, and they bowed for silent prayer. Following the prayer, they dug into the fried chicken, baked beans, carrot sticks, and rolls. Paul brought out a batch of peanut butter cookies Noah had given him.

"Everything tastes great," Paul said, smacking his lips. "Especially the chicken."

"It's a recipe my mamm and her mamm used to make," she said with a smile. "I call it Webster County Fried Chicken, and it used to be David's favorite meal."

Paul smacked his lips again. "I can see why. It's *appeditlich*."

She smiled and pushed the container of chicken closer to him. "Since you think it's delicious, would you like to have some more?"

"Don't mind if I do," he said, reaching for another drumstick.

"Have you gone on many picnics in Lancaster County?" Barbara asked.

He shrugged. "I've gone on a few with my cousin's family."

"How about a girlfriend?"

He shook his head. "Don't have one of those right now."

"Oh, I see." Barbara handed Paul a glass of lemonade, and when their fingers touched briefly, a strange sense of warmth crept through her body. She hadn't felt this giddy since her courting days with David. It was more than a bit disconcerting.

Paul smiled. "Danki, Barbara."

She returned his smile, realizing that despite her best intentions a special kind of friendship was taking root in her heart. She didn't need love or romance to enjoy the company of a man—especially this man.

Chapter 13

Paul was glad to have an off Sunday, when there would be no church. It wasn't that he disliked the services. He just wanted some time alone. After yesterday's trip to the pond with Barbara and three of her boys, he needed to think and pray. He'd had a good time. *Too good, maybe,* Paul thought as he headed for his folks' barn. Since he wouldn't be doing any work that wasn't absolutely necessary on this day of rest, a little getaway might do him some good.

As soon as Paul entered the rustic building, he took a seat on a bale of straw. He had come here countless times when he was a boy, and it had always been a good place to think and pray.

Heavenly Father, I don't know why I'm so drawn to Barbara, he prayed. *Mom told me how hard Barbara mourned when David was killed, and I have an inkling she might still be grieving.*

A vision of Barbara's pretty face popped into his head. *Despite my attraction to her, Lord, I know it's not likely she would ever be interested in me. She's got the bishop after her, and I suspect she'll consider marrying him.*

The barn door creaked, and Paul's eyes snapped open.

"Paul?"

"Jah, Pop, I'm over here."

His father removed his straw hat, revealing a thick crop of nearly gray hair, and plopped the hat over a nail protruding from a nearby beam. "What are you doing in here?"

"Just sitting, thinking, and praying."

"Always did like to hide out in the barn, didn't you?"

"Jah."

"I would like to talk to you for a minute if you're done praying."

"Sure, what's up?"

Pop leaned against a wooden beam as he studied Paul. "Your brothers and I could use some help in the fields next week. We were hoping we could count on you."

Paul shifted uneasily on the bale of hay. "Sorry, but I can't."

"Why not?"

"I can't leave Barbara in the lurch."

Pop squinted his pale blue eyes. "She's not back to work yet?"

Paul shook his head.

"When will she be?"

"I don't rightly know. She tried working a few hours one day last week, but I think it took its toll on her."

Pop crossed his arms. "Your mamm tells me Barbara and a couple of her kinner went fishing with you yesterday afternoon.

Doesn't sound to me like she's feeling so weak if she can fish all afternoon."

Paul's defenses rose as his face heated up. "Sitting on a grassy bank with a fishing pole is relaxing. It's not hard work like the things we do in the harness shop."

His father's face contorted. "Jah, well, it makes me wonder if there isn't more going on with you and Barbara than just you working for her."

Paul clenched his fists. Pop had no right to be saying such things, but there had been too many harsh words between them in the past. He didn't want to respond disrespectfully.

"There's nothing going on between me and Barbara," Paul said slowly. "I promised to help her until she's back on her feet, and I aim to do just that."

Pop grunted. "And then what?"

"Then I'll be on my way back to Lancaster County to work in Andy's harness shop. Fact is, I went to Seymour the other day and phoned Andy to see if my job's still waiting."

"And?"

"He's got a couple of fellows working there now, but he said my job will be waiting for me when I go back to Pennsylvania."

"Didn't figure it would be any different." Pop grabbed his hat and stalked out of the barn, letting the door slam shut behind him.

Paul shook his head. "I guess some things will never change."

Barbara stood on the front porch of her house. As she watched her three boys play in the yard, her thoughts took her back to the pond, where she had enjoyed herself so much yesterday. Paul had shown a side of himself she hadn't known existed. Usually serious, he had joked with her, frolicked with Zachary and Joseph, and seemed genuinely relaxed. He'd even commented on how much the baby was growing and said he was a cute little guy. As long as they stayed away from the topic of the harness shop, Barbara and Paul got along quite well.

"Mama, Aaron's bein' mean."

Barbara whirled around at the sound of Joseph's voice. "What's the problem, son?" she asked, leaning over and wiping away the tears glistening on his cheeks.

"Aaron says Paul's tryin' to be our new daed."

Barbara's mouth dropped open. "Where did he get such a notion?"

"I was tellin' him how much fun we had at the pond yesterday and how Paul said he wished he had a son like me." Joseph's lower lip quivered slightly. "Aaron said Paul was just tryin' to butter me up. He said that Paul's a mean man."

"And what has Paul done to make Aaron think he's mean?"

Joseph sniffed. "He says Paul's real bossy and is always givin' him crummy jobs in the harness shop."

Barbara pursed her lips. Paul had given Aaron menial jobs to do. But her son was too young to do anything complicated or that required heavy lifting. She also knew the child wanted to help in the shop and figured he would appreciate any job, no matter how small. Aaron had never complained when his father had given him easy chores to do. Barbara suspected Aaron's dislike of Paul had more to do with not wanting anyone to take his father's place.

She tousled Joseph's curly, blond hair and gave him a hug. "I'll speak to Aaron about his attitude. In the meantime, why don't you take Zachary inside? There's a jar of chocolate chip cookies that Grandma made yesterday on the cupboard. You two can have some with a glass of milk, if you like."

Joseph smiled, and his blue eyes brightened considerably. "Okay. I'll climb up on a stool and get us some." He turned around and motioned for Zachary. "Come inside and have some cookies and milk."

Zachary darted across the grass like a colt kicking up its heels and bounded onto the porch. When Joseph jerked the screen door open, both boys scampered into the house.

Barbara glanced across the yard. Aaron was seated on the swing hanging from the maple tree, kicking at a clump of grass with his bare toes.

Lord, please give me the right words, Barbara prayed as she headed for the swing.

Aaron looked up. "I suppose that tattletale Joseph told you we was sayin' things about Paul Hilty," he said with a lift of his chin.

She nodded. "Did you tell your brother that Paul was mean and trying to butter him up?"

He nodded. "Jah, and I meant it, too."

"That wasn't nice, and it's not true."

He grunted. "You haven't seen the way that bossy fellow treats me whenever I'm in the harness shop. He acts like I'm *dumm* or something."

"I'm sure Paul doesn't think you're stupid, Aaron."

"Jah, he does."

"Are the jobs Paul has given you any different from the ones you did for your daed?"

He dropped his gaze to the ground. "Not really, but—"

"Then why do you think Paul's treating you differently?"

He shrugged.

"You're still young, Aaron, and Paul's giving you jobs you're able to do. If you keep doing them well, I'm sure Paul will give you other jobs as he sees that you're capable of doing them."

Aaron stared straight ahead.

"You need to give Paul a chance to get to know you better," Barbara said. "Maybe you should have gone fishing with us. Then you'd have seen for yourself that he's not mean."

"Humph! All Joseph's been talkin' about since Saturday is that dumb old fishin' trip and how much fun he had with Paul." Aaron wrinkled his nose. "Paul favors my little brothers—that's for certain sure."

Barbara knelt and touched Aaron's knee. "That isn't true, son. Paul has reached out to Joseph and Zachary, but they'd also reached out to him. If you would give the man half a chance, you and he could become friends, too."

Aaron started pumping the swing. "I don't care if he takes 'em fishin' every day of the week. I'm never gonna like him!"

Barbara wanted to say more, but the words wouldn't come. It wasn't likely anything she had to say would change Aaron's mind. That would have to come from Paul, and since he wouldn't be staying around Webster County much longer, she doubted there could be a resolution. All the more reason she had to get back to work as soon as possible. If Aaron helped her instead of Paul, he would be more agreeable.

"Your brothers are having cookies and milk up at the house," she said. "If you've a mind to join them, I'm sure there's plenty left."

Aaron kept swinging. Barbara walked away with a sick feeling. Her oldest boy was becoming more belligerent all the time. If he didn't come to grips with his father's death soon, would he carry the resentment clear into his adult life? She had to find some way to help him. Maybe if she spoke to her father, he could get through to Aaron.

Barbara headed for the house. When she stepped into the kitchen, she was greeted with a mess. Joseph and Zachary sat at the table with chocolate all over their faces and crumbs covering their light blue cotton shirts. The cookie jar was nearly empty, and an empty bottle of milk sat beside it. The milk was on the floor.

"What happened?" Barbara yelled. "Just look at the disaster you two have caused!"

Joseph gave her a sheepish look. Zachary continued to munch on his cookie.

"Sorry, Mama," Joseph said. "The milk spilled on the floor."

Barbara grabbed a sponge from the kitchen sink. So much for the quiet Sunday morning she'd hoped to have. First Aaron's impossible attitude, and now this!

The baby started to howl from the crib in the next room.

"The boppli's awake," Joseph announced.

"I can hear him." Barbara tossed the sponge onto the kitchen table. "Here, Joseph. Please get things cleaned up while I tend to Davey." She marched out of the room before he had a chance to respond. Tomorrow she would work in the harness shop no matter how tired she felt. At least that might bring some sense of normalcy to her life.

Chapter 14

For the next several weeks, Barbara forced herself to get out of bed early, feed the boys, and send them to her folks' house. With a renewed sense of determination, she worked in the harness shop three days a week, taking breaks only for lunch and to feed the baby. On the days her father had physical therapy, she took Aaron to the shop so he could help. Dad's hands had become stiffer, but the therapy and wax treatments seemed to help some.

At Barbara's request, her father had spoken to Aaron about his attitude. The boy wouldn't open up to his grandpa, but he seemed a little more compliant while working at the shop. Barbara suspected it might be because she was there, too.

As Barbara cleared the breakfast table, she noticed for the first time in many weeks that her energy level was actually up.

Maybe it's because my appetite's back, she mused. *Or it could be because I'm back doing what I love best—making and repairing leather items. Maybe I can start working full-time soon.*

She placed a stack of dishes in the sink and ran water over them. It wasn't easy being a full-time mother and running a business, but she enjoyed the work and it did support her family.

"I'm ready to go when you are, Mama."

Barbara turned at the sound of Aaron's voice. "I've still got to feed the boppli. Why don't you head out to the shop. Zachary and Joseph are already at Grandma's, so I'll be along shortly."

Aaron's dark eyebrows drew together. "I'd rather wait for you."

"But Paul might need you for something."

Aaron stared at the floor. "Do I have to go now?"

"Jah."

Aaron huffed and turned toward the door. "Don't be too long, okay?"

"If I can get your wee bruder to cooperate, I shouldn't be more than half an hour or so." Barbara's heart went out to her melancholy son. "*Naemlich do,* Aaron," she called.

"I love you, too."

The door clicked shut, and Barbara hurried into the next room to get the baby. She prayed things would go all right between Aaron and Paul today. She prayed that her full strength would return soon, too.

"Here's that bread you wanted, Papa," Nadine said, as she handed

John a loaf of bread with an overly browned crust.

He grimaced. "What happened? Did you forget to check on it while it was baking?"

"Papa, I—"

"You're fourteen years old, daughter. You ought to be able to bake a loaf of bread without burning it."

Nadine's chin quivered, and her blue eyes filled with tears. "I'll make another batch, and I promise I won't leave the kitchen until it's done baking."

He shook his head. "Never mind. I need to call on Barbara Zook so I can get back to work here." He held up the bread and studied it intently. "Only the crust is overly brown; I'm sure it'll taste okay."

"Papa's right," Betty put in as she put away the orange juice. "Some of the bread I've made has been overly brown, but it tasted fine and dandy just the same."

"How come you're calling on Barbara again?" Nadine asked. "Didn't you, Mary, and Hannah go there not long ago?"

"That's right, we did," Mary said as she washed dishes. "Doesn't Barbara have time to make bread?"

"I—I don't know if she's had time for baking or not," John sputtered. "She's got her hands full taking care of the boppli right now, and she's still looking pretty tired, so I'm sure she would appreciate the bread." He took a seat at the table. *Maybe now's the time for me to tell the girls what's on my mind.*

"How come you're sitting down, Papa?" Nadine asked. "I thought you were in a hurry to get to Barbara's."

"I am in a hurry, but it can wait a few minutes." He motioned to the four empty chairs across from him. "Why don't you all have a seat? I'd like to say something to you."

"But I'll be late for work," Betty said as she reached for her lunch pail sitting on the counter near the door.

"This will only take a minute."

Betty and Nadine took a seat, and the two youngest girls dried their hands and did the same.

John cleared his throat a couple of times.

"What's wrong, Papa? Have you got something caught in your throat?" Mary questioned with a worried frown.

"Do you need a drink of water?" Nadine asked.

He shook his head. "I'm fine. Just trying to think of the best way to say what's on my mind."

The girls stared at him with curious expressions.

He drew in a sharp breath and released it quickly. "The thing is. . .your mamm's been gone over half a year now, and things have been kind of confused around here without her."

The girls nodded soberly.

"And I've concluded that I need another wife—someone who'll make a good mudder for all of you."

Betty's eyebrows shot up, Nadine's mouth dropped open, and the two youngest girls stared at him with wide-eyed expressions. Betty spoke up. "I don't think we need a new mother, Papa. Me and the sisters are getting along just fine."

The other three girls nodded.

"No one could ever take our mamm's place," Nadine put in.

John gripped the edge of the table. He was botching things up badly and needed to think of something to say that would smooth things over with his girls. "Of course no one could ever take your mamm's place. She was a loving mudder and a faithful *fraa*. Your mamm will always be with us in here," he said, touching his chest with the palm of his hand.

The girls' heads bobbed up and down in agreement.

"Even so," he continued, "I think it would do well for me and be good for you if I got married again."

Betty leaned forward, her elbows on the table, as she gazed at him. "Have you got someone in mind?"

He nodded. "Barbara Zook."

"What?" Betty and Nadine said in unison.

"I said—"

"But, Papa, Barbara's a lot younger than you, and—"

John held up his hand to halt Betty's words. "Your mamm wanted to give me more kinner, but that didn't happen because we lost her to cancer." He drew in another quick breath. "Barbara's still in the childbearing years, and she's got four kinner of her own, so she would not only be a suitable wife, but she could give me those kinner your mamm wanted me to have."

The girls' mouths dropped open, and they stared at him as if he'd taken leave of his senses.

He shifted in his chair. The air had become so thick he thought he could have sliced right through it if he'd had a knife in his hands. Maybe he'd said too much. It might have been better just to state the obvious—that he needed a wife and they needed a mother.

"Have you already asked Barbara to marry you?" Nadine questioned.

His face heated up. "Well, I did make mention of it."

Betty's pale eyebrows drew together. "Don't you think we should have some say in this?"

He puffed out his cheeks. "That's why we're talking about it now."

Betty shook her head. "But we're not really talking about it, Papa. You're telling us what we need and saying you've already spoken to Barbara about marrying you. It doesn't sound to me like our opinion matters much at all."

John opened his mouth to reply, but Hannah cut him off. "Has Barbara agreed to marry you?"

He shook his head. "She said she'd think on it, that's all."

"Do her boys know about this?" The question came from Mary.

"I don't think so. . .unless Barbara decided to mention it to them after I left her place the other day." John reached out and touched the plastic wrap surrounding the loaf of bread sitting in front of him. "Barbara's been trying to run her husband's harness shop for nearly a year now—ever since he died. And it's getting harder for her to keep up with things, which is why she had to hire Paul Hilty to help out. What Barbara needs is a husband to care for her and the boys. She needs someone to protect her from. . ." His voice trailed off, and he turned to look at the clock on the far wall. It was past time for Betty to leave for work. He needed to wrap this conversation up so both he and she could be on their way.

"Protect her from what, Papa?" Nadine asked.

"From anyone who might want to take advantage of her." John pushed away from the table and stood, snatching up the loaf of bread. "I'd better get going, and so should Betty. If Barbara has an answer for me today, then tonight I'll let you all know what she said."

Paul had just entered the back room and was looking over an old saddle when he heard the front door of the shop creak open and then click shut.

"I'm back here, Barbara," he called.

A few seconds later, Aaron came into the room. "It's me, not my mamm," he said with a frown.

"Guder mariye," Paul responded, hoping the greeting would wipe the scowl off the boy's face.

"Mornin'," Aaron mumbled.

"Where's your mamm?"

"Had to feed the baby. Said she'd be here soon."

Paul reached for a clean rag and handed it to Aaron. "Why don't you rub this saddle down with some neat's-foot oil while I take care of a few other things?"

Aaron responded with a muffled grunt, but he did take the rag.

"If you need me, I'll be up front at my desk looking over some work orders."

"It ain't *your* desk," Aaron muttered. "It belonged to my daed."

Paul blew out an exasperated breath. Wouldn't the boy ever lower his defenses? Couldn't he see that Paul wasn't his enemy?

"I know it's not my desk," Paul said. "It was just a figure of speech."

No reply.

Paul stood there a few seconds; then he shrugged and went

to the desk. *I sure hope Barbara gets here soon. Then she can deal with Aaron.*

Forty-five minutes later, Barbara finally showed up. "Sorry I'm late," she said breathlessly. "I got the boppli fed okay, but then he wouldn't burp."

"No problem," Paul replied, barely looking up from the papers on the desk.

"Is everything going okay?"

"I guess so."

"What have you got Aaron doing?"

"Oiling a saddle in the other room." Paul craned his neck in that direction. "It sure is taking him awhile to get it done, though."

"Maybe he finished up and found something else to do."

"I didn't give him any other chores."

"Would you like me to check on him?" Barbara asked.

"Sure."

She took a step toward the back room but turned around and leaned over the desk. "Are there any new work orders I should know about?"

When Paul brought his head up, it connected with Barbara's.

"Ouch!" they said in unison.

"Sorry." Paul rubbed his forehead; then instinctively, he placed his fingers against her head. "Are you okay?"

"I think so."

"I don't feel a lump anywhere," he said, swallowing hard. Being this close to Barbara made his heart pound and his hands sweat.

She stared at him with an anxious expression; then she

reached out and touched his forehead. "You, on the other hand, do have a little bump."

Barbara's fingers felt cool, and Paul's heart pounded even harder when he noticed the tender look in her eyes. An unexpected flame ignited in his chest, and he fought against the sudden urge to kiss her. "I. . .uh. . .it's nothing to worry about," he mumbled.

Barbara pulled her hand away, but her touch lingered in his mind. His arms ached to hold her. His lips yearned for the touch of hers. This wasn't good. Not good at all.

Paul grabbed a work order off the top of the pile. "This one's the most recent," he said, handing the piece of paper to Barbara and hoping his trembling hands wouldn't betray his feelings.

She pursed her lips as she studied it. "Is this one for the saddle Aaron's working on?"

He nodded.

Her eyebrows drew together. "But this says Harold Shaw wants the saddle repaired, not oiled or cleaned. Haven't you got Aaron doing something completely unnecessary?"

Paul sat up straight as the feelings of tenderness he'd had for Barbara dissolved like a block of ice left sitting in the sun. What right did she have to question him like this? Didn't the woman realize it was good business to clean and oil a saddle that had been brought in for repair? He opened his mouth to say so, but she spoke first.

"David always asked the customers if they wanted something cleaned or oiled. If they did, he wrote it on the work order so I would know. If not, then we didn't do it." She blinked a couple of times. "I don't see any point in doing something not asked for when there's lots of other work to be done."

A muscle in Paul's cheek quivered, and he reached up to massage the spot.

Barbara placed her hand on her hip and stared at him. "Your silence makes me wonder if you disagree with that practice."

He shrugged. "This is *your* harness shop. Who am I to say anything about the way you do business?"

She tipped her head. "After working together these past few weeks, I think we know each other well enough to be honest. I'd like it if we could express our thoughts and concerns, not clam up or become defensive."

He pushed the chair away from the desk and stood. "I'd say you've expressed your thoughts clear enough for the both of us."

When he started to walk away, she stepped in front of him. "I think we need to talk about this."

"I don't think there's much to be said." He grunted. "You see things one way, and I see them another. You're the boss. I'm just helping out until you're back working full-time."

"I would like to hear your reason for oiling the saddle without Harold having asked to have it done."

Paul reached up to rub his forehead. That bump from their heads colliding hurt more than he realized. Either that or he was getting a headache caused by stress.

"Paul?"

"Jah?"

"Are you going to share your thoughts on this or not?"

"I don't see how it'll do much good."

"Please."

He motioned for her to sit in the chair at the desk. When she complied, he leaned over and pointed to the stack of work orders. "If you'll look through these, you'll see that some of them are from customers who have returned more than once since I started working here."

"And?"

"After their first order, they found other things for me to do. Things they said they'd originally planned to do themselves."

"Then why didn't they?"

"Some said I had done such a thorough job on their previous order, they decided to bring in a second or third item."

She turned in her chair and nodded slowly. "I see what you mean."

"My cousin Andy taught me that doing a little something extra for a customer makes for good business."

"I guess you're right. I should have realized that." Barbara's dark eyes took on a faraway look. "I'm sure David tried to please our customers. But sometimes, when we got real busy, he might not have thought to do the little extra things."

Paul smiled, feeling somewhat better. "I'm sure David was good at his job. He and you made this business succeed."

She returned his smile. "Danki."

Paul touched her shoulder. "Barbara, I—"

His words were cut off when the front door opened and in walked Bishop John Frey.

"Guder mariye, John," Barbara said when the bishop entered her shop. "What brings you here today? Did you need a new harness made, or do you have one that needs to be repaired?"

Paul stepped aside as the bishop walked up to the desk and offered Barbara a wide smile. "Came to see about getting a new bridle for one of my driving horses." He held out the paper sack he had in his hand. "Also wanted to give you this."

Barbara took the sack and peered inside at a loaf of bread that appeared to have a very dark crust. She guessed it must have been baked too long. Certainly not the kind of baked goods she was used to getting from Noah Hertzler.

"Betty made it," John said with a crooked grin. "I figured with you back here working again, you probably wouldn't have much time for baking."

"I'm managing with my mamm's help, but I appreciate the gesture. Tell your daughter I said danki."

Paul cleared his throat, and she turned toward him.

"Why don't you check on Aaron?" she suggested.

"You're the boss." He gave the bishop a quick nod and headed for the back of the shop.

Barbara set the bread aside, pulled out her order pad, and grabbed a pencil. "Let's see now. . . . You said you wanted a new bridle?"

"Jah, that's right."

"It shouldn't be a problem." Barbara scrawled the bishop's name at the top of the page and wrote down the order. "Do you want it to be black or brown?"

"Black. And nothing fancy added." He shook his head. "Wouldn't do for the bishop to be driving around using a worldly-looking bridle on his buggy horse."

"No, of course not."

When Barbara finished writing up the order, she tore off the top sheet and handed it to John, placing the carbon copy in the metal basket with their other orders. "If you'd like to drop by in a few weeks, we'll have the bridle ready for you."

His forehead wrinkled. "I was kind of hoping to come by sooner than that."

She tapped the tip of the pencil against the desk. "I don't think we can have it ready any sooner."

He grunted. "That's not what I meant."

"Oh?"

"I was planning to come calling on you. Maybe take you and the boys for a drive or on a picnic."

Barbara gulped and tried to keep her composure. If the bishop had heard she'd gone fishing and shared a picnic supper with Paul a few weeks ago, there was no way she could tell him she wasn't up to such an outing yet. Besides, it would be a lie, and her conscience wouldn't let her knowingly tell an untruth.

"How about it, Barbara? Can I come by on Saturday and pick you and the boys up?"

She nibbled on the inside of her cheek, searching for the right words. She didn't want to offend the man, but she didn't want to lead him on, either. "Well, I. . .uh. . .appreciate the offer, but—"

"She's made other plans."

Barbara dropped the pencil and whirled around in her chair. Paul stood slightly behind her, off to one side. She opened her mouth to ask what other plans she had for Saturday, but the bishop cut her off.

"Is that so? What kind of plans?"

"She and the boys are going fishing with me." The look of

determination on Paul's face made Barbara wonder what was going on. He hadn't said a word to her about going fishing again, but the idea did sound rather appealing, especially if it gave her an excuse to turn down the bishop's invitation.

A warm rush spread through Barbara. She struggled to hide the unexpected pleasure of knowing Paul had spoken on her behalf.

John took a few steps in Paul's direction and scowled at him. "I hear from your daed that you're planning to return to Pennsylvania soon."

Paul shrugged. "When Barbara doesn't need me anymore."

The bishop turned his gaze on Barbara. "How long will that be?"

Her face heated up, and she pressed both hands against her cheeks, hoping to cool them. "Really, Bishop John, I don't think—"

Before Barbara could finish her sentence, Paul jumped in. "We haven't set a date for my leaving, but since you're so interested, I'll be sure to let you know when it's time for me to go."

Barbara couldn't believe Paul's boldness or the way his eyes flashed when he spoke to John. What was he thinking, speaking to their bishop that way? *Of course, he's not Paul's bishop,* she reasoned.

John shook his finger in Paul's face. "I'll have you know, I've asked Barbara to be my wife. Has she told you that?"

A vein on the side of Paul's neck bulged. Violence went against their teachings, yet Barbara worried he might be about to punch the bishop right in the nose.

"Mama, are you gonna marry the bishop?"

Barbara whirled around. She hadn't realized Aaron had come onto the scene.

She reached for her son's hand. "I've made no promises to marry anyone. I only said I would think on it."

Aaron stared up at the bishop. "My mamm doesn't need another husband. She's got me to help out." Then he looked at Paul. "Someday this harness shop will be mine, and then nobody can tell me what to do!" Aaron rushed out the door. Barbara just sat there, too stunned to say a word.

Chapter 15

"I still don't see why I have to go fishing," Aaron complained when Paul pulled up in his buggy on Saturday. "You let me stay home with Grandma and Grandpa before. Why can't I stay with them again?"

"Because Grandma's going to visit her friend Ada, and Grandpa's got a cold and needs to rest." Barbara ruffled his hair. "Besides, a day of fishing will be good for you."

He gave a muffled grunt as he climbed into Paul's buggy behind his brothers.

"Looks like a good day for fishing," Paul said after he'd helped Barbara and the baby into the front seat.

She smiled. "Jah, there's plenty of sunshine."

As they traveled down the road, Barbara couldn't believe she had let Paul talk her into going fishing again—this time with all four boys in tow. She hoped today would be as pleasant as their other fishing trip had been.

It's strange, she thought as she cast a sidelong glance at Paul. *We get along fine at certain times, but other times, we're at odds with each other.*

She wished she understood what attracted her to him. Other than their love for harness making and their commitment to God, they were as different as north from south. Of course, they did both enjoy fishing.

"I do love it here in Webster County, especially the warm days of summer," she said, lifting her face toward the sun.

Paul grunted. "I'm not really partial to hot, muggy weather."

"Doesn't it get humid in Pennsylvania?"

"Jah."

"But you still like it there?"

"I like my job."

"Wasn't it hard to leave your family and friends and move so far away?"

"It was, but I didn't want to farm. I wanted to work in a harness shop. Since you and David owned the shop here, I didn't see a need for a second one in our small community. So going to Pennsylvania to help my cousin was the only way I could do what I wanted."

Barbara could see by the wistful expression on Paul's face that he would have preferred to open a harness shop here rather than move to Pennsylvania. A sense of guilt stabbed her, but she realized it wasn't her fault Paul had chosen to move. If he'd wanted to work in a harness shop that badly, he could have talked to David about working for him. Maybe Barbara never would have become interested in working with leather if her husband had hired a helper.

"Did you ever talk to David about going to work for him?" she asked.

"By the time I figured out what I wanted to do, you were already his partner, and I didn't think he'd need anyone else in the shop."

"He could have used you part-time."

He shook his head. "I didn't want to work part-time. Pop would have expected me to farm when I wasn't helping David."

She could understand why he felt forced to leave Webster County. But from the tone of Paul's voice, Barbara sensed bitterness in his heart toward his dad.

"I sure hope the fish are biting today," he said. "I'd like to catch some nice big bass."

"I think my boys would agree." Barbara shifted the sleeping baby in her arms and glanced over her shoulder. Joseph and Zachary were drawing on their tablets. Aaron sat with his arms folded, looking straight ahead. She hoped that once they got to the pond and he saw how much fun the others were having, his attitude would improve.

A few minutes later, Zachary leaned over the seat and tapped her on the shoulder. "Mama, I'm hungry."

"We'll eat when we get there." She touched Paul's arm lightly. "Would you mind if we have supper before we fish?"

He patted his stomach. "That's fine by me. I'm always ready for good food."

When they pulled into the grassy area by the pond, Barbara noticed another open buggy parked there. She thought she recognized it, and her suspicions were confirmed when she saw Bishop John sitting on a large rock holding a fishing pole.

"What's he doing here?" Paul mumbled. "I'll bet he only came because he knew we were coming."

"He has as much right to be here as we do," Barbara reminded him. "Why would you care, anyway?"

"I just do, that's all." When Paul came around to help Barbara and the boys down from the buggy, Barbara noticed deep furrows in his forehead. He was obviously not happy about having to share their fishing spot.

"It might be better if we go to the other side of the pond," Paul said with a frown. "Wouldn't want to scare away any fish the bishop might want to catch."

Before Barbara could reply, her three boys took off on a run, heading straight for the area where the bishop sat.

"Yippee!" Zachary shouted. "Fisch! Fisch!"

"I hope I get me some big ol' bass!" Joseph hollered.

Barbara grasped Paul's arm. "So much for not disturbing the bishop."

Paul's skin prickled under his short-sleeved cotton shirt. Every time he and Barbara made physical contact, his insides turned to mush.

If I had a lick of sense, I'd catch the next bus heading for Pennsylvania and let Barbara marry the bishop. Paul grimaced. *Of course, she might become the man's wife even if I were to stick around.*

"Would you mind holding the boppli while I get the picnic

basket out of the buggy?" Barbara asked.

He blinked. "Huh?"

"I said—"

"I heard what you said, but don't you think it would be better if I got the basket and you kept the boppli held securely in your arms?"

She grinned at him, and his heart did a little flip-flop. "Davey won't bite, you know. He has no teeth yet."

Paul's face heated up. What if the little guy started to howl or spit up all over him? What if he dropped the baby?

"I think you're blushing, Paul Hilty," Barbara said with a smirk. "A big man like you isn't afraid of a baby, I hope."

Regaining his composure, Paul held out his hands. "I'm not afraid of much. Leastways, not a little scrap of a guy like Davey."

She chuckled and reached into the buggy to grab a quilt, which she tucked under Paul's arm. "Why don't you ask Aaron to spread this on the grass? You and Davey can have a seat, and I'll be there soon with our picnic supper."

"What about the boppli's carriage?"

"We can get it later."

"Okay." Paul glanced over at Aaron and forced a smile. "Are you looking forward to putting your line in the water, Aaron?" he asked, hoping the idea of fishing might put a smile on the boy's face.

Aaron grunted.

"You've been grunting an awful lot lately," Paul said as they strode to the pond. "I'm wondering if you're spending too much time with your grandpa's pigs, because you're beginning to sound like one of them."

"I ain't no pig," Aaron said with a frown.

Paul bit back a chuckle. "Let's get that quilt put on the ground like your mamm asked us to do."

The boy complied, but not without first giving Paul another disgruntled look. To make matters worse, he placed the blanket not three feet from where the bishop sat fishing.

"Good day to you, Paul," John said with a slight nod. "Looks like you've got your hands full."

Paul's face flooded with warmth again. "How's the fishing?" he asked.

"Got myself a couple bass and a nice fat catfish." The man nodded toward his cooler sitting nearby. " 'Course, with the way Barbara's boys are running around hollering like that, it'll be harder to lure the fish now."

If the bishop was looking for an apology, or even an offer to move, Paul wasn't about to provide him with one. He was pretty sure the man had come here on purpose. Well, two could play that game. If Bishop John wanted to marry Barbara, he'd have to earn the right. But the man hadn't won Barbara's hand or her heart yet. At least not as far as Paul knew.

The baby started to cry, and Paul shifted uneasily on the quilt. *Sure hope Barbara shows up soon, or the bishop will have one more thing to razz me about.*

Paul watched in horror as Zachary picked up a flat rock and pitched it into the pond—right in front of John's fishing line. *Splat!* Drops of water splattered everywhere, some landing on the man's shirt and trousers. A few even made it to the quilt Paul sat on. At least he and the baby hadn't gotten wet.

"Hey, watch what you're doing!" The bishop's face turned

red, and a vein on the side of his neck stuck out like a noodle boiling in a pot.

"What's going on here?"

Paul cranked his head. Barbara stood nearby, holding the picnic basket and tapping her foot.

"Your boy Zachary is throwing rocks into the pond," John said before Paul could open his mouth.

Barbara's brows furrowed. "Is that so, Zachary?"

"He only threw one," Paul said in the boy's defense.

"Jah, and it splashed water all over me." The bishop held up his arm, but there was barely a sign of the water droplets left.

Barbara took a step toward her son. "Zachary, tell Bishop John you're sorry."

The boy's lower lip quivered, and he stared down at the grass. "S-sorry, Bishop."

"Jah, well, don't let it happen again." The bishop smiled up at Barbara. "It's good to see you. Even though your boy tried to drown me."

She nodded but didn't return his smile. Paul felt a sense of relief.

"Come now, boys," Barbara said, grabbing Zachary's hand. "Let's see about eating our supper."

Aaron, Joseph, and Zachary followed her to the quilt, and in short order, she had the food set out.

"Yum, this looks good," Joseph said, licking his lips.

"Let's pray, and then we'll eat," Paul said, handing Barbara the baby.

She turned to face the bishop, who was watching them like a hungry cat ready to pounce on its unsuspecting prey. "Would you care to join us, John? That is, if you haven't already eaten."

"Haven't had anything since lunch, so I'd be much obliged." John quickly reeled in his line and set the fishing pole aside. Then he took a seat beside Barbara.

Paul gritted his teeth. It didn't surprise him when the bishop accepted her invitation, but did he have to plunk down right beside Barbara, as though he was the one who'd brought her and the boys to the pond?

The bishop cleared his throat. "Shall we pray?"

All heads bowed. When he cleared his throat a second time, they opened their eyes.

"Everything looks mighty good," the older man said as he reached for a piece of Barbara's fried chicken.

"I hope it tastes as good as it looks." Barbara handed the container to Paul, who took a drumstick. Then he passed it to each of her boys.

"Want me to get the boppli's carriage from the buggy so you can eat with both hands?" Paul asked, looking at Barbara.

She nodded. "That would be nice."

Paul set the drumstick on his paper plate and stood. When he returned a few minutes later, he set up the carriage and took the baby from her. After the little guy was settled, he draped the netting across the top and sides of the carriage. He sat back down and was about to reach for his piece of chicken when he noticed Aaron's plate still had most of his food on it.

He tapped the boy on the shoulder. "You haven't eaten very much."

Aaron shrugged. "I ain't all that hungry."

"Well, I sure am. Guess a few hours of fishing gave me a

hearty appetite." John chomped down the last hunk of white meat he'd taken and licked his fingers. "Your mamm is one fine cook, Aaron." He turned to Barbara. "Got any corn bread or baked beans?"

"As a matter of fact, I do." Barbara handed the man the bowl of baked beans, followed by the basket of corn bread.

"Danki."

"You're welcome."

It was all Paul could do to keep from telling the bishop what he thought. He had wanted to spend the evening with Barbara and her boys, do a little fishing, and hopefully work on his relationship with Aaron. Instead, he was being forced to sit here and watch the bishop eat the choicest pieces of meat, listen to the man praise Barbara for her cooking skills, and worst of all, watch John make cow eyes at her. Paul was beginning to wish he had never suggested this outing.

He gritted his teeth. *It's only natural that Barbara would be interested in a man like the bishop. He has the respect of those in the community, he plans to stay in Webster County, and he has the smarts to outwit me.*

Paul leaned back on one elbow and took a bite of chicken. *Might as well make the most of the evening, because if John has his way, this will probably be the last time I take Barbara and her kinner anywhere.*

John studied Paul as he ate his chicken. He couldn't figure out why the man would be showing such an interest in Barbara and her boys when he didn't plan to stay in Webster County—unless Paul planned on staying with the hope of marrying Barbara and taking over her harness shop. If Barbara accepted John's proposal, then Paul would know he didn't have a chance and would soon be back in Pennsylvania, where he belonged.

"How's Margaret doing these days?" Barbara asked, looking over at John. "I've only seen her at church since the day she came to help with my yard work, and we haven't had much chance to talk."

"She's getting along all right, but of course, she still misses Dan." He smiled. "I think it did her some good to help with the work frolic, so maybe if you've got more work that needs to be done, you might see if she's free to help."

"I'll be going back to work in the harness shop full-time soon, I hope," Barbara said. "It'll be even harder for me to keep up with things around the house and yard, so I might have to ask for more help."

John was tempted to tell Barbara that if she married him she'd have all the help she needed from his daughters and that she wouldn't have to work in the harness shop at all because he would suggest that she sell it. But it would be out of place to mention his marriage proposal in front of Paul, so he merely nodded and said, "Anytime you need some help, just let me know, and I'll spread the word."

"Danki." Barbara lifted the container of chicken and held it out to him. "Would you care for another piece of chicken?"

He nodded and licked his lips. "Don't mind if I do."

Chapter 16

On Sunday morning, Barbara awoke with a headache. Church would be held at her in-laws', and as much as she enjoyed visiting with Mavis, she dreaded going. It wasn't merely the constant pounding in her head that made her want to stay home in bed. After yesterday's picnic supper and fishing, she wasn't looking forward to seeing either Paul or Bishop John. They had acted like a couple of little boys the whole time, causing Barbara to wonder if they both might be vying for her attention.

Barbara swung her legs over the edge of the bed and rubbed her temples. She knew the bishop wanted to marry her, if only to help raise his girls. But why would Paul try to gain her attention? He would be going back to Pennsylvania soon and surely had no interest in her. So why had he seemed irritated because the bishop had been at the pond?

She padded across the room to check on the baby. *Maybe I'm imagining things. It could be that Paul was just worried the bishop would take all the good fish, like I'd suspected in the first place. Paul is a strange man—sometimes friendly and relaxed, other times distant and uptight. I wish I could figure him out.*

Barbara stared down at her son sleeping peacefully in his crib and thought about the baby's father. "Oh, David, why did you have to die and leave me with four boys to raise and a business to run on my own? I feel so helpless and confused. I miss you so much. If only you were here to tell me what to do."

Barbara glanced around the room she had shared with her husband for ten years. Everything looked the same—their double bed and matching dresser made by David's father, the sturdy cedar chest at the foot of the bed given to Barbara by her parents when she'd turned sixteen, and the beautiful Wedding Ring quilt her mother had made as a wedding present.

Her gaze came to rest on the Bible lying on top of the dresser. It had been David's, and she always found a measure of comfort by simply holding it in her hands. Not because it was God's Word, but because it had belonged to her husband and she knew how much the Bible had meant to him. Truth was, Barbara had been neglecting her Bible reading lately. She was too busy during the day and too tired at night.

Barbara left the crib and made her way across the room. As she picked up David's Bible, tears coursed down her cheeks. The feel of the leather cover made her think about the harness shop. Should she sell the business and hope to make enough money so they could live off it? She certainly couldn't rely on her folks to support her and the boys. It was all Dad could do to help part-time in the shop. But the wages she gave him were a much-needed supplement to the meager income he and Mom made selling some of their garden produce and the quilts Mom made. Dad's arthritis had kept him from farming for quite a spell, and even though Barbara's sisters sent money to their folks whenever they could, Barbara still felt the need to assist her parents as much as possible.

"Of course, I could sell the shop and marry the bishop," she said with a weary sigh as she sat on the edge of her bed. "Maybe Paul would be interested in buying it." She opened the Bible to a place marked with a slip of paper. In the book of James, David had underlined the fifth verse of chapter one. " 'If any of you lack wisdom, let him ask of God, that giveth to all men liberally, and upbraideth not; and it shall be given him,' " she read aloud.

Setting the Bible aside, Barbara closed her eyes. "I'm so confused, Lord. I need the wisdom of Your words found in this *Biwel*. I need to know what to do about the bishop's offer of marriage, the harness shop, and my befuddled feelings toward Paul."

She released a sigh as she thought about the verse from Ecclesiastes that John had quoted to her awhile back, about two being better than one. Maybe she did need someone to share her life with. But could she ever be truly happy married to the bishop, for whom she felt no love? Could she take on the responsibility of raising the bishop's four girls plus her boys? She would have to give up the harness shop unless she could count on the girls to watch the boys.

Barbara rubbed the bridge of her nose. There was so much

to think about—so many conflicting thoughts whirling around in her head. Truth be told, she was falling in love with Paul, but she couldn't let him know that. If they were meant to be together, he would have to make the first move and let her know he felt the same way.

With another long sigh, she stood. It was time to set her thoughts aside and turn things over to God. She needed to wake the boys up, start breakfast, and get ready for church. "I'm going to pray for wisdom and leave my future in God's hands, just as David always did. And I'm not going to let a little old headache keep me from worshipping the Lord today."

⁂

Paul had a hard time keeping his thoughts on the preaching service and not on Barbara, who sat directly across from him on the women's side of the room, holding her baby. On one side of Barbara sat her mother. The bishop's oldest daughter, Betty, occupied the other spot. Paul wondered if it was merely a coincidence or if John Frey might have asked Betty to sit beside the woman he hoped to marry.

It was all Paul could do to keep from staring at Barbara's dimpled cheeks, which were slightly pink, no doubt from the heat of this warm summer morning. He wished he were free to fall in love with her and stay in Webster County. But there were too many complications to prevent them from having a relationship—his insecurities about becoming a husband, her possible marriage to the bishop.

Paul thought about yesterday's trip to the pond. Despite

his irritation over the bishop's presence, he had enjoyed being with Barbara and her boys. With the exception of Aaron, who'd remained aloof all day, Barbara's children had really warmed up to him. Even the baby had seemed content when Paul held him, and the little guy sure was soft and cuddly. When the infant had nestled against Paul's chest, it made him feel loved and appreciated. It had also caused him to wish for something he felt sure he would never have.

The bishop's booming voice drove Paul's thoughts to the back of his mind. "The Bible says, 'For the Lord God will help me; therefore shall I not be confounded: therefore have I set my face like a flint, and I know that I shall not be ashamed.' Isaiah chapter fifty, verse seven."

John Frey was preaching on challenges, and Paul wondered if the verse he'd just quoted was an announcement of the man's personal challenge to win Barbara's hand in marriage.

At the moment, Bishop Frey's face looked like it was set in flint. He pursed his lips and held the Bible in front of him as though it were a weapon.

Paul stared at the floor. *Maybe his message is directed at me. Could be he wants me to realize how determined he is to make Barbara his wife.*

He grimaced. It didn't seem likely that the bishop would bring his personal life into the sermon. But the man was only human. And he obviously needed a wife to help him raise his four girls.

Paul was pretty sure John had God on his side, him being a spiritual leader and all. Still, that shouldn't give him an edge with Barbara, at least not to Paul's way of thinking.

Forcing his thoughts aside so he could concentrate on the rest of the service, Paul reminded himself that he needed to keep his focus on God.

When church was over, Paul headed quickly for the door. It was stuffy inside the house, and he needed some fresh air.

❦

"I still don't understand why you're chasing after Barbara Zook, Papa," Betty said, stepping up to John as he headed toward the barn.

He halted his footsteps and turned to face her. "What are you talking about, girl?"

"I saw the way you were looking at Barbara when she was helping the other women serve lunch. It was probably obvious to all the other men sitting at your table."

"I am trying to find you and your sisters a mudder," her father said impatiently. "Barbara would make a good mother, don't you think?"

"Maybe so, but as far as I can tell, we've been getting along fine since Mama died."

"You might believe that to be so, but the truth is, things aren't done around the house the same as your mamm used to do them."

She tipped her head and stared at him as if he didn't have a lick of sense. "What makes you think Barbara would do things the way Mama used to do them?"

He shrugged. "Maybe she wouldn't, but I'm sure things would go better than us trying to fend for ourselves."

"I think we're doing all right on our own."

He folded his arms and stared hard at her. "Oh, jah, right. . . overly done bread, tasteless stew, and arguments over who does what chores and when. Does that sound like you girls are doing all right on your own?"

"Things might go better if my sisters would listen to what I tell them." Betty grunted. "And don't you think adding four boys to the family would make things more hectic and stressful?"

"I rather like the idea of having a couple of buwe around," he said with a nod. "It would be kind of nice to have a few sets of strong hands in a couple years to do some of the harder chores. I could use some help with my business, too."

Betty cleared her throat. "Papa, I just want to know one thing."

"What's that?"

"Do you love Barbara?"

"Well, I—"

"You don't love her, do you?"

"There's a lot more involved in marriage than a bunch of romantic nonsense. Besides, love can be learned."

"Did you love Mama?"

"Of course I did. Loved her from the first moment I laid eyes on her."

There was a brief pause before Betty spoke again. "Papa, I hope you do remarry someday. But it needs to be for love, not convenience, or even to have a mudder for me and my sisters."

"Guess I'll have to think on that awhile." He started walking again, hoping she would take the hint and realize the subject was over. Being the oldest, Betty had begun to act a bit bossy toward her sisters since Peggy had died, and there were times, like now, when she said more than she should to her father.

"Where are you going?" she asked.

"Out to the barn to visit with some of the men."

"Oh, okay." Betty turned toward the house, and John breathed a sigh of relief. Obviously, Betty didn't want him to remarry. He hoped if he did talk Barbara into marrying him, all four of his girls would accept it and be kind to Barbara and her boys.

When John entered the barn a few minutes later, he discovered Barbara's father petting one of the horses. Deciding to take this opportunity to speak with Samuel about Barbara, he stepped up to the man.

"Wie geht's, Samuel?"

Samuel offered John a smile. "Except for the pain and stiffness of my arthritis, I'm doing all right. How about you?'

John shrugged. "Can't complain, I guess."

"Are you keeping busy with your seed and garden supply business?"

"Jah. That and making calls on people in our community who are sick or hurting."

"I heard you've been by to see Barbara a few times since the boppli was born."

"That's right," John said with a nod. "I saw her and the boys at the pond the other day, too."

"Heard that, as well. Guess they went there with Paul for some fishing and a picnic."

John cleared his throat a couple of times, searching for the right words to say what was on his mind. "I'm. . .uh. . .concerned for Barbara's welfare."

"You mean because she's been so tired since the boppli was born?"

"That and a few other things."

Samuel tipped his head. "Such as?"

"Well, for one thing. . .I think she needs to consider selling the harness shop. It's too much for her to run on her own, and I know you're not able to help as much as you'd like."

"That's true, but Paul's there helping out now, and he does the work of two good men."

John held up one hand. "Which brings me to my next point."

"And that would be?"

"Paul Hilty."

"What about Paul?"

"I don't trust the man." John lowered his voice. "I think he's out to get the harness shop any way he can."

A muscle on the side of Samuel's cheek quivered. "What's that supposed to mean?"

"It means, I think Paul might be trying to woo Barbara so she'll marry him." John grunted. "As her husband, he would have full run of the harness shop, you know."

Deep creases formed in Samuel's forehead. "I don't know what would make you think such a thing, but I'm sure it's not true. Fact is, I've been working with Paul for several weeks now, and he's been nothing but helpful and hardworking."

"That doesn't prove he's not trying to gain control of the harness shop without having to buy it."

Samuel turned his hands palm up. "Doesn't prove he's trying to get it, either."

John pulled his fingers through the ends of his beard and grimaced. "If you would have seen the way he acted around Barbara when they were at the pond the other day, you might understand what I'm saying."

"How'd he act?"

"He said some goofy things and looked at her like a horse eyeing a tree full of ripe apples."

Samuel chuckled. "Are you sure it wasn't all that good food Barbara prepared that he was eyeing?"

John shook his head. "You can laugh all you want, but I'm sure of one thing—Paul's trying to win Barbara's heart, and I think he's using her boys to do it!"

Samuel's eyebrows rose. "How so?"

"He's got those boys—well, two of them, anyway—wrapped around his long fingers."

"I've seen the way Paul acts around Zachary and Joseph, and I don't think he's using them to get to my daughter." Samuel pursed his lips. "What I think is that Barbara's boys, with the exception of Aaron, enjoy spending time with Paul because they see the good in him."

John opened his mouth to respond but was interrupted when Moses, Paul's dad, showed up.

"Are you two talking about something private, or can anyone join the conversation?" the man asked.

"We weren't discussing anything important," Samuel said with a shrug. "Matter of fact, I was just petting one of the horses when John showed up."

Moses smiled. "How are things going in the harness shop these days? Is my son Paul really as much help to you as he says?"

Samuel nodded vigorously. "Oh, jah. Paul does the work of two men. His cousin must have taught him well, because he really seems to know what he's doing."

John ground his teeth together. The way Samuel talked, one would think Paul was some kind of a saint. He was good with Barbara's boys, he did the work of two men, and he knew a lot about the harness business.

Moses gave his left earlobe a quick pull. "Paul used to help me and the boys in the fields until he got it into his head to move to Pennsylvania and learn the harness trade from Andy. Now all he talks about is leather straps, silver rivets, and the smooth feel of a well-made harness." He grunted. "If there wasn't already a harness shop in Webster County, I believe he'd open one of his own."

Hmm . . . John folded his arms and contemplated Moses's statement. If Paul wanted to open his own harness shop, maybe his suspicions about the man wanting to get his hands on Barbara's shop weren't so far-fetched, after all. Now John was even more determined to get Barbara to marry him. She needed someone to watch out for her and protect her interests.

Soon after lunch, Barbara left the baby with her mother-in-law and allowed the three boys to play with their friends. When Barbara spotted her friend Faith on the other side of the yard, she headed that way.

"You're looking a bit down in the mouth today," Faith said as she and Barbara took a seat on the grass under the shade of a hickory tree. "Are you still feeling *hundsiwwel?*"

"No, I think I'm done with the postpartum depression."

"Then why the long face?"

"I'm struggling with several issues," Barbara admitted. "Things I really need to talk about if you're willing to listen."

Faith nodded. "Of course I'll listen. What issues are you struggling with?"

"Bishop John and Paul."

"What about them?"

"John wants me to marry him."

"Ah, I suspected as much."

"He's been over to my house a couple of times, asking me to go places with him, but I've always turned him down."

"So he knows you're not interested?"

"I'm not sure, but John was at the pond yesterday when Paul and I arrived with the boys, and he acted like a jealous little boy."

Faith's mouth dropped open. "You went there with Paul again?"

"Jah."

"I should have guessed what was going on."

"What's that supposed to mean?"

"I can see by the look on your face that you're smitten with the man."

"Paul and I don't see eye to eye on some things concerning the harness shop," Barbara said. "But I must admit I'm attracted to him, though I can't figure out why."

Faith leaned her head back and laughed.

"What's so funny?"

"Don't try to figure out love, my friend. When two people

fall for each other, they can be as different as sandpaper and polished cotton—yet the feelings are there, and you can't do a thing to stop them."

Barbara moaned. "I don't know how Paul feels about me."

"He's invited you to go fishing with him twice. I'd say that says something about his interest."

"It's really strange, but there are times when Paul acts friendly and nice, and other times when he seems distant and almost as if he's angry about something. I think he wants to do things his own way in the harness shop, and he gets irritated when I want things done my way." Barbara frowned. "To tell you the truth, I don't think he likes me very much."

Faith clicked her tongue. "Ever since Adam met Eve, there has been trouble between men and women. Just because Paul doesn't always see things the same as you doesn't mean he dislikes you."

Barbara shrugged. "I think he believes my place is in the house with the kinner, not running a harness shop."

A ruckus on the lawn interrupted their conversation, and Barbara turned to see what was going on. She was taken by surprise when she heard Joseph hollering and saw him running after Faith's son, Isaiah, with a squirt gun.

"Now, where in the world did he get that?" she muttered as she scrambled to her feet.

"Guess we'd better put our conversation on hold and see about our boys before one of them ends up crying." Faith shook her head. "Most likely it'll be Isaiah unless his big sister comes to the rescue."

Barbara marched across the yard, planted herself in front of

Joseph, and reached for the squirt gun.

Swish! A spurt of water hit her right in the face.

"Give me that!" she ordered. "What's gotten into you? And where did you get this squirt gun?"

Joseph's brows furrowed, and he pointed across the yard. "Paul Hilty gave it to me."

Barbara hurried across the lawn to where Paul stood talking to Faith's husband. "Excuse me, Noah," she said, "but I need to speak with Paul."

"No problem." Noah smiled and moved off in the direction of his wife.

"What's up?" Paul asked with raised eyebrows.

She handed him the item in question. "Would you mind telling me why you gave my son a squirt gun?"

He shoved the toy inside his shirt pocket and looked at her as though she were daft. "Didn't see any harm in it. The boy said he was hot, so I got the squirt gun out of my buggy, figuring it would help cool him off."

"What were you doing with a squirt gun in your buggy?"

"It was mine when I was a kinner, and I found it in my daed's barn the other day. So I decided to bring it today to see if one of your boys might want it."

Barbara wrinkled her nose. "I don't cotton to the idea of my boys pointing a gun at anyone—not even a toy one."

Paul's ears turned bright red. "Sorry," he mumbled. "At least this time you're not chewing me out for something related to the harness shop."

His statement caught Barbara off guard. Was she always chewing him out? Did Paul think all she ever did was nag? She had to admit that she had been pretty testy of late, but he seemed to know just how to get under her skin.

Unable to look him in the eye, she lowered her gaze. "I–I'm sorry for snapping. It's just that I would have preferred it if you'd checked with me about the squirt gun. Then I could have explained my reasons."

"You're right. I shouldn't have given Joseph the toy without first asking you."

Shivers shimmied up Barbara's spine as Paul stared intently at her. Did he really agree with her on this, or was he merely giving in to avoid an argument?

"Mama?"

Barbara glanced down when she felt a tug on her dress. Aaron stared up at her with a curious expression. "Is it all right if I spend the night at Gabe Schwartz's?" he asked. "Gabe's daed has hired a driver to take 'em to Springfield tomorrow morning. They're going to Bass Pro Shop, and I think they plan to do some other fun stuff, too."

"Oh, I don't know, Aaron. Paul might need you in the harness shop tomorrow."

Paul shook his head. "Your daed said he's free to help in the morning, so I think we can manage okay without Aaron."

Barbara deliberated a few seconds. Her oldest child had been moody and sad ever since David died. This was the first spark of the old Aaron she'd seen in a long time. Maybe she should let the boy have a good time with his friend.

Finally, she nodded. "Jah, okay. You can go."

Aaron clasped her hand. "Danki. I'll ask Gabe's daed to stop by our house when they head for home today so I can get a change of clothes."

Barbara smiled at her son's enthusiasm. "Don't forget your toothbrush and comb. I wouldn't want my boy going off to the big city looking like a ragamuffin." She bent down and gave him a hug. "You be good now, you hear?"

"I will, Mama." The child scampered off toward Gabe.

Paul smiled. "Seemed real eager, didn't he?"

Barbara nodded. "Aaron and Gabe have been good friends since they were little fellows."

"Sure wish he'd see me in a friendlier light."

"Give him time, Paul." As the words slipped out, Barbara wondered why she had bothered to say them. She would be back working full-time soon, and it would only be a matter of days before Paul would announce his intention to return to Pennsylvania. Then everything would be back to normal.

Chapter 17

On Monday morning as Barbara headed to the harness shop, she decided to tell Paul that she could manage on her own now. If she gave him the option of leaving and he took it, she would know he had no interest in developing a relationship with her. If he hesitated and said he wanted to stay, then maybe he could take Dad's place permanently.

Barbara shook her head, hoping to get herself thinking straight again. Having Paul working in the shop with her alone six days a week wouldn't seem proper when they weren't married or even related.

As Barbara drew closer to the shop, she noticed that Paul's buggy wasn't parked outside. *Strange,* she thought as she opened the front door. *He's always here early—usually before Dad or me. Surely he wouldn't have gone back to Pennsylvania without telling me first.*

When Barbara entered the shop, she spotted her father working at the riveting machine. He smiled and nodded in her direction. "Guder mariye, daughter."

"Good morning, Dad. I'm surprised to see you pressing rivets. Paul usually does that, and it's not like him to be late for work."

Dad stepped away from the machine and placed the leather he'd been holding on one of the workbenches. "Paul dropped by a little bit ago. He wanted me to let you know that he wouldn't be in today."

She wrinkled her forehead. "He's not sick, I hope."

"*Nee.* His daed fell off a ladder in their barn this morning. An ambulance had to be called to take him to the hospital, so Paul and his brothers hired a driver to take them there."

Barbara's breath caught in her throat. "How bad was Moses hurt?"

Dad shook his head. "Paul didn't have any information yet. He said he would let us know as soon as he could what the doctors had to say."

"I hope it's nothing serious." Barbara sighed. "We've had enough tragedy in our community lately."

Barbara's father patted her shoulder. "And that's why we need to pray."

❦

Paul paced the length of the hospital waiting room, anxious for some report on his father's condition. The doctors had been running tests on him for the last couple of hours, and Paul worried that might mean something was seriously wrong.

"Won't you please stop that pacing?" his mother said from the bench where she sat. She blinked her dark eyes and patted the sides of her grayish-brown hair, which she wore parted down the middle and pulled tightly into a bun.

He came to a halt in front of the window and stared out at the cloudy sky. They might be in for some rain, which seemed fitting for an already gloomy Monday morning.

"I wonder why Monroe and Elam aren't back yet. It shouldn't take them this long to get a few cups of coffee." Mom shifted restlessly on the bench. "I sure could use some about now."

Paul clenched and unclenched his fingers. How could Mom be worried about coffee when Pop was in the emergency room and they didn't know how badly he'd been hurt? *Maybe it's just Mom's way of trying to take her mind off the situation,* he concluded. *I know how much she loves Pop.*

"Maybe you should head down the hall and see what's taking your brieder so long," she said.

Paul turned to face his mother. "I'm sure my brothers will be back in due time. They don't need me to go traipsing after them."

Mom grabbed a magazine from the table in front of her. "I just figured it would give you something to do besides wear down the soles of your boots as you pace back and forth."

A middle-aged nurse stepped into the room. "Joann Hilty?" she asked, looking at Paul's mother.

Mom nodded and stood.

"Your husband has been moved to a private room now, so if you wish to see him, please follow me."

Mom's face looked pinched, and deep lines etched her forehead. "Is Moses going to be all right? What did the tests reveal?"

The nurse offered a reassuring smile. "The doctor will fill you in on all the details."

Paul started to follow his mother, but she stopped him with a raised hand. "I think it would be better if you waited here for your brothers so they won't worry when they return."

Paul looked at the nurse. "What room is my dad in?"

"Second floor, room 202."

"Okay." Paul offered his mother what he hoped was a reassuring smile. "Monroe, Elam, and I will be up to see Pop as soon as they get back."

⁂

As soon as Alice stepped into the harness shop, she spotted Barbara bent over a huge metal tub filled with neat's-foot oil. Holding a leather strap in each hand, she dipped them up and down in the savory-smelling oil. Samuel stood in front of the riveter, punching shiny silver rivets into a leather strap. "I heard about Paul's daed and knew Paul wasn't helping today," Alice said, stepping up to him. "How are things going here without his help?"

"We're managing okay," Barbara said before Samuel could respond. She hung the straps overhead to dry, then stood.

"Are you sure? You looked awfully *mied.*"

Barbara arched her back and rubbed a spot near her right hip. "I'm not really tired. Just feeling a little stiff is all."

Alice glanced over at Samuel to gauge his reaction. He merely shrugged.

"I've got lunch ready, so if you'd like to come up to the house, I'll put it on the table."

"Sounds good to me. I'm hungry as a mule." Samuel moved away from the riveter and toward the door.

Alice looked back at her daughter. "Are you coming?"

"I'll be there shortly," Barbara said, motioning to the pile of leather strips lying at her feet. "I want to get these oiled and hung before I eat."

Alice's forehead wrinkled. "Can't it wait until you've had some lunch?"

"I need to get this done so I can work on some orders this afternoon."

"But you need to keep up your strength, and you can't do that unless you eat," Alice argued. "Besides, the boppli will be waking from his nap soon, and you'll need to feed him, as well."

Barbara released a sigh. "There's so much work to do, and it seems there's just not enough of me to go around anymore."

"Which is exactly why you should think about giving up the harness shop."

"But the harness shop is all I have left of David."

"That's not true. You've got four of David's buwe to raise." Alice looked over at Samuel, who stood near the door with his arms folded. "Can't you talk some sense into our daughter?"

"I've tried, but she won't listen to anything I have to say concerning the shop." He held up his hands. "She knows that I'm not much help to her, what with these old gnarled hands that don't work so well. Yet she's determined to keep the shop going, and I guess I can't fault her for that." He smiled at Barbara. "So I'll continue to help as long as I can."

Barbara's chin quivered, and her eyes filled with tears. "I love working here, Mom. I love the feel of leather beneath my fingers, and I love knowing that this shop is mine and will be passed on to my oldest boy someday."

Alice moved over to Barbara and patted her gently on the back. "Be that as it may, you still need to take care of yourself. So I insist that you come up to the house with your daed and have some lunch."

Barbara blinked a couple of times, and then her lips curved into a smile. "Guess I should know better than to argue with my mamm when she's determined to make me do something."

Alice gave Barbara's arm a gentle squeeze. "Well, at least I get my way on some things."

⁂

"Papa, I don't see why Mary and I couldn't have stayed home and baked some cookies this afternoon," Hannah complained from her seat at the back of John's buggy.

John grimaced. Not this again. It seemed like all his girls ever did anymore was whine. "It's not proper for me to call on Margaret alone when she's newly widowed. I've told you that before." He glanced over his shoulder. "Besides, the last time I left you two at home alone, you ended up arguing all day."

Hannah poked Mary's arm and glared at her. "Papa wouldn't have known that if you hadn't blabbed."

"And if you hadn't been tryin' to tell me what to do, we

wouldn't have had a *dischbedaat* that lasted most of the day," Mary shot back.

John ground his teeth together. "You're having an argument now, and if you don't stop it, you'll both end up with double chores for the rest of the week."

The girls sat back in their seats and clamped their mouths shut. John breathed a sigh of relief.

At this point, he wondered if he shouldn't have left them home. Maybe it wouldn't be so bad if he called on Margaret by himself. In times past, either her daughter, son-in-law, or one of the grandchildren had been around, so they hadn't really been alone. Well, it was too late to turn back now.

When he pulled into Margaret's yard, John spotted Margaret filling one of her bird feeders from a large sack that sat near her feet. "Why don't you girls go out to the barn to play while I visit with Margaret awhile?" he suggested as they clambered out of the buggy.

"Okay," the girls said in unison. They scampered off and disappeared inside the barn before John could get the horse tied to the hitching rail.

"Hello, John. It's good to see you again," Margaret said when John stepped up to her.

"Good to see you, too. You must like feeding the birds," he said, nodding at the wooden feeder that was shaped like a covered bridge and had been nailed to a sturdy post.

She nodded and smiled. "I've enjoyed bird-watching ever since I was girl."

"Me, too." His face heated up. "I mean, since I was a boy."

Margaret chuckled, and a flash of light seemed to dance in

her pale blue eyes. It was good to hear her laughing again. She'd been so somber on John's other visits.

"Would you like to sit on the porch and have a glass of iced tea with me?" she asked. "We can watch the birds eat at the feeders."

John nodded enthusiastically. "That'd be real nice." He pointed to the sack of birdseed. "Would you like me to carry this for you?"

"Danki, I'd appreciate that. Jacob carried it out to the yard after lunch, but he had to head back to the fields. Karen took the two little ones to town to do some shopping, so I figured I'd be stuck lugging it back to the house."

John hoisted the sack into his arms and placed the birdseed on one end of the porch.

"If you'd like to have a seat, I'll run into the house and get the tea," she said, motioning to the porch swing.

"Sounds good."

She reached for the screen door handle and was about to open it when she turned back around. "I saw Mary and Hannah go into the barn. If you'd like to call them, I'd be happy to fix them each a glass of iced tea, too."

"I think I'll let them play awhile," he said, lowering himself to the swing. "It would be nice for us to visit without any interruptions."

She tipped her head in question.

"They've been arguing a lot lately and asking too many questions."

"Ah, I see. Maybe it would be best if we had our tea first; then I'll offer some to the girls." Margaret gave him another smile and disappeared into the house.

John leaned his head against the back of the swing and closed his eyes. It was peaceful here with the birds singing in the yard and a slight breeze blowing against his face. Soon fall would be upon them.

"Are you sleeping, John?"

His eyes snapped open, and he sat up straight. Margaret stood in front of the porch swing holding two glasses of iced tea. "Uh. . .no. I was just thinking, is all."

"They must have been good thoughts, because I saw a smile on your face."

"I was enjoying listening to the birds and thinking about the nice weather we've been having."

She handed him a glass and took a seat on the swing beside him. "With all the sad things that have gone on in our community the past year or so, it's nice to have something good to think about, jah?"

John nodded. "Hopefully nothing else will happen for some time. We need a break from tragedy."

Margaret's forehead wrinkled as she frowned. "Guess you haven't heard about my father-in-law's accident, then."

His eyebrows lifted. "No, I haven't heard. What happened to Moses?"

"He fell off a ladder in his barn early this morning."

"Sorry to hear that. Was he hurt badly?"

She shrugged. "I haven't had any word since he was taken to the hospital, but from what Paul told me this morning, his daed had complained that his back hurt really bad."

John slowly shook his head. "Moses sure doesn't need that

kind of thing happening to him right now. Especially with the harvest about to begin." He took a sip of his tea. "Think I'll see about hiring a driver to take me to the hospital later this afternoon so I can see how Moses is doing."

"I'm sure Moses and his family will appreciate having you there with them."

Chapter 18

$\mathcal{B}$arbara had just closed up shop for the day when Paul Hilty pulled into the yard. Anxious for news of his father, she hurried out to him.

"How's your daed?" she asked when he got down from the buggy.

"He broke a couple ribs, bruised his left elbow real good, and pulled a muscle in his lower back." Paul slowly shook his head. "He'll live, but he'll probably be in traction for the next few days."

Barbara breathed a sigh of relief. At least Moses Hilty's wounds would heal, and they wouldn't have to face another death in the community right now. "I'm sorry about your daed's accident, but I'm glad it wasn't any worse."

"So am I."

"I guess he'll be laid up awhile, huh?"

Paul nodded soberly. "I'm sure Pop won't be able to farm for several weeks." He shifted his weight in an uneasy manner. "I. . . uh. . .was wondering if you'd be able to get by without my help at the harness shop. I promised Pop I'd help Monroe and Elam in the fields until he's back on his feet."

"Oh, of course, we'll get by here." Barbara hated to admit it, but she would miss Paul's help—and seeing him every day.

Paul grunted. "You know things haven't been good between my daed and me for some time, and I want to show him I care by helping out in this time of need."

"I understand. I'm feeling stronger now, so I think Dad and I can manage okay on our own."

She wondered if she should tell Paul he was free to return to Lancaster County after his father's injuries were healed. *I'd better not say anything just now,* she decided. *It can be said after Paul's done helping his brothers.*

Paul shuffled his boots and stared at the ground. "Well, I guess I'd better be going."

Barbara couldn't help but notice his forlorn expression. He was probably worried about his father and not looking forward to working in the fields.

Impulsively, she touched his arm. "How would you like to join the boys and me for supper tonight? We're planning to eat outside at the picnic table with my mamm and daed."

Paul hesitated, but only for a moment. His lips curved into a wide smile. "Sounds real nice."

Barbara motioned to the house. "Come along, then. You can relax on the porch swing with a cold drink while I go next door to my folks' place to get the kinner."

On Her Own

Paul leaned against the cushion on the back of the porch swing, sipping the lemonade Barbara had given him before she went next door. It felt nice to sit a spell and enjoy the cool evening breeze. He drew in a deep breath and savored the varied aromas of country air. Soon fall would be here, with its crisp fallen leaves and bonfires to enjoy. He'd always liked autumn, especially here in Webster County where life was easygoing and much more unhurried.

Paul closed his eyes and let his imagination run wild. In his mind's eye, he saw Barbara sitting in the rocking chair on her front porch. In her lap was a baby, but it wasn't Davey. The baby he envisioned was a dark-eyed little girl with shiny blond hair.

Instinctively, he reached up and touched the side of his head. *Hair just like mine. What would my life be like if I could stay right here, marry Barbara, and have a few kinner of my own?* Was it a foolish dream, or could Barbara possibly open her heart and home to him? With each passing day, Paul had fallen harder for her.

"You sleepin', Paul?"

Paul jerked upright and snapped his eyes open. He'd had no idea Joseph was standing there, and he wondered how long the boy had been watching him.

"I was resting my eyes, son," he said with a smile. "It's been a long day."

Joseph's forehead wrinkled. "I heard Mama tell Grandma you've been at the hospital with your daed."

"That's right. He fell off a ladder in the barn this morning

203

and banged himself up pretty good."

"Sorry to hear that. I'll say a prayer for him."

"That'd be nice. I'm sure he'll appreciate all the prayers he can get."

Joseph's eyes brightened. "Mama also said you'd be joinin' us for supper tonight. I'm real glad 'bout that."

"Me, too." Paul patted the empty spot on the swing beside him. "Want to join me awhile?"

The boy scrambled onto the swing and cuddled against Paul's side.

"You miss your daed?" Paul asked.

"Jah."

"That's understandable. I'm sure your mamm and brothers miss him, too."

"I know Mama does. She cries when she's alone in her room sometimes. I think it's 'cause she's pinin' for Papa."

Paul's heart clenched. *It's a shame for Barbara to have lost her husband and for such a young boy to lose his father. But then, many things happen in life that aren't fair.* He thought about his brother dying so unexpectedly and how sad it was to see Margaret all alone and missing Dan so much.

They sat in silence awhile, Paul pumping the swing back and forth, and Joseph humming softly.

"Sure wish you were my daed now," the boy blurted out.

"That's a nice thought, but I don't know if it's possible," Paul said, giving the child's hand a squeeze. "I hope I'll always be your friend, though."

Joseph leaned away and stared up at Paul. His blue eyes were wide and his face ever so solemn. "Aaron says Bishop John is after Mama to marry him."

"And what do you think about that?"

Joseph shook his head. "Don't like it. Don't like it one little bit." He pushed his weight against Paul again. "It's you I want as my new daed. Nobody else."

A lump formed in Paul's throat. In all his grown-up years, he'd never had a kid take to him the way Joseph had. It made him long to be a father—Joseph's father, anyway.

"Can you marry my mamm and be my daed?"

Paul patted the boy's knee. "It's not that simple."

"Seems simple enough to me. You just go right up to her and ask. That wouldn't be so hard, now, would it?"

The back door of the Rabers' house opened, and Barbara stepped out, carrying the baby, with Zachary and Aaron at her side. Paul welcomed the interruption. At least he didn't have to come up with an answer for Joseph. That question had been rolling around in Paul's head for the past couple of days, and he had found no satisfactory answer.

Paul stood and followed Barbara and the boys into her house. When they entered the kitchen, Barbara placed little David in his baby carriage, instructing Zachary to push it back and forth if the infant got fussy. Aaron and Joseph were asked to haul pitchers of lemonade and iced tea out to the picnic table, while Barbara busied herself at the counter slicing thick hunks of juicy ham.

Paul's stomach rumbled. He'd spent most of the day at the hospital and hadn't taken the time for anything other than a few cups of coffee and a stale doughnut from the cafeteria. Since Mom had decided to stay at Pop's side awhile longer, Paul figured he'd have to manage on his own for supper. Barbara's invitation had been a pleasant surprise. Not only would his hunger be satisfied, but he was being offered an opportunity to spend time with Barbara again, even if they would have her parents and the boys as chaperones.

"Is there anything I can do to help?" he asked. "I'm sure you're tired after a long day at the shop."

She shook her head but kept her back to him. "Dad and I managed okay, and I'm not feeling too done in."

"Even so, I'd like to do more than stand here by the wall and watch."

"If you really want to do something, you can check the boppli's *windle*."

Paul's eyebrows shot up. Did she really expect him to change a diaper?

"Just kidding," she said with a muffled snicker. "Mom made sure Davey's diaper was clean and dry before I showed up to get the boys."

"Alice has been a big help to you since David died, huh?"

"Jah. I don't know what I'd have done without her or Dad." Barbara turned to face him. "I don't want to be dependent on their help forever, though. Sooner or later, I'll have to make it on my own."

For want of anything better to do, Paul pulled out a chair and took a seat at the table. "Guess you could always take the bishop up on his offer of marriage."

Barbara dropped the knife to the counter with a clatter and spun around. "You—you really think I should?"

Paul wanted to tell her right then that it was him she should marry, but she'd never given any indication that she cared for him that way, and unless she did. . . He pushed the thought aside and shrugged. "It's really none of my business."

Barbara studied him as if she were waiting for him to say something more. Was she hoping he would tell her that marrying the bishop wasn't a good idea? Or maybe she wanted his approval. Did his opinion matter?

She reached for her knife again and started cutting the meat.

"Are you considering it, then?" Paul had to know. If she were the least bit interested in the bishop, he would back off, plain and simple.

"Told him I'd think on it, that's all."

Paul leaned both elbows on the table. "And have you?"

"Jah."

"He's some older than you."

"That's true enough. A good fifteen years, at least."

"And being married to a bishop could put an extra burden on you."

"Maybe so."

"What of the harness shop?"

"What about it?"

"Would you sell the place if you were to marry John?"

"Guess I'd have to, seeing as how I'd be taking on the responsibility of helping raise his four daughters plus my boys."

Paul grabbed a napkin from the basket in the center of the table and wadded it into a tight ball. The thought of Barbara marrying the bishop was enough to make him lose his appetite. Still, he couldn't seem to muster the courage to speak on his own behalf. Besides, what if she rejected him?

"I thought you loved running the harness shop," he said. "How could you give up something you enjoy doing so much?"

Barbara shrugged her slim shoulders. "One does what one has to do in a time of need." She sliced the last piece of ham and placed it on the platter. "But I haven't decided yet."

Paul breathed a sigh of relief. Maybe he still had a chance with Barbara. At least he hoped he did.

As John entered Moses Hilty's hospital room, he prayed that God would give him the right words to say. He knew it had to be hard for Moses to be lying flat on his back in a hospital bed when he wanted to be at home working in the fields with his sons.

"Wie geht's?" John asked, stepping to the end of Moses's bed.

"Not so good." Moses groaned. "That fall really messed up my back. Don't know how long it'll be before I'm on my feet again and can return to farmwork."

"It's never easy to be laid up." John moved over to the side of the bed and lowered himself into a chair. "Elam and Monroe are pretty capable, though. I'm sure they'll keep things going until you're able to work again."

"Jah, but they can't do all the work alone. Thankfully, Paul's agreed to help 'em until I'm healed up."

"You mean after he gets done working at the harness shop each day?"

Moses shook his head. "He quit helping Barbara so he could help his brothers."

John's eyebrows drew together. "Does that mean he's not going back to Pennsylvania, after all?"

"Not right now, but I think he's planning to return as soon as the harvest is done."

"What about helping Barbara?"

"Don't know. But from what Paul said, she's back working full-time in her shop, so I doubt she'll be needing him from now on."

"I see." John gave his beard a couple of sharp pulls. If Paul was being kept busy in the fields and he wouldn't be returning to work for Barbara, then he would probably leave for Pennsylvania in just a few weeks. Unless, that is, he decided to stick around and try to win Barbara's hand so he could take control of the harness shop.

"You'd think you were the one in pain," Moses said.

"What makes you say that?"

"You ought to see the creases in your forehead. That worried-looking frown on your face makes me think something's wrong. Is there a problem?"

John fought the temptation to share his suspicions about Paul with Moses. No point in upsetting the man more than he already was. Besides, he might be worried for nothing. Maybe Paul would hightail it out of Missouri as soon as Moses was able to return to work. Then Barbara would be fair game. "It's nothing for you to be concerned about," he said with a smile. "I'm sure everything will work out fine—according to God's will."

Chapter 19

Paul wiped the sweat from his forehead with the back of his hand as he stopped working to catch his breath. He couldn't believe he had been helping his brothers in the dusty fields for a whole week already. Every evening, he trudged back to his folks' house, sweat-soaked, dirty from head to toe, and exhausted, while Monroe and Elam went home to their own families.

Pop had been released from the hospital three days ago, but due to the pain in his ribs and back, he was pretty much confined to bed. He was also as cranky as a mule with a tick in its backside.

Due to his father's condition, Paul tried hard to be kind and patient. However, his patience had been tested yesterday when Pop summoned him to his room and proceeded to tell Paul that if his back didn't heal up right, he might never be able to work in the fields again. That being the case, Monroe and Elam would need another pair of hands on a regular basis—namely, Paul's hands. Then he said he hoped Paul might consider giving up his job at Andy's harness shop in Pennsylvania and help on the farm permanently.

Seeing how much pain his father was in, Paul had merely said he would think on it. But after he was done working for the day, Paul was prepared to state his case before he lost his nerve. He just hoped Pop would be willing to listen.

As John pulled his rig out of Margaret's yard, his heartbeat picked up speed. He'd been calling on her ever since her husband died, and the more time he spent with her, the more he enjoyed her company. Despite the fact that Margaret was a few years older than he and her children were already grown and married, they had a lot in common. They both enjoyed looking at flowers, liked working on puzzles, took pleasure in feeding and watching birds, and had an interest in playing board games. Not only that, but John had discovered that Margaret was a kind, pleasant woman, easy to talk to, and a great cook. She'd had John and his daughters over for supper last night, and the meal had been delicious. An added benefit was that John's daughters seemed to enjoy Margaret's company, too.

"Margaret's probably past her childbearing years, so she couldn't give me any kinner," he mumbled. But that didn't seem to matter so much anymore. If only he felt free to ask her to marry him.

I might feel free if Paul Hilty were out of the picture and I knew Barbara wouldn't be in jeopardy of losing her harness shop. Maybe I need to stop and see Moses again. If I can convince him to talk Paul into going back to Pennsylvania, I'd know that Barbara wouldn't lose her harness shop and would be able to support herself and the boys if I don't marry her.

A short time later, John turned his buggy up the Hiltys' driveway. After he'd tied his horse to the hitching rail, he headed for the house.

Moses's wife, Joann, greeted John at the door. "Did you come to see Moses?" she asked with a friendly smile.

John nodded. "Is he up and about yet?"

"Only for short periods." Joann shook her head. "His back still hurts whenever he moves around too much, so he spends most of his time lying in bed complaining about his pain and mumbling that he needs to get back to work." She released a sigh. "I guess a complaining husband is better than no husband at all."

"I'm sure Margaret Hilty and Barbara Zook would agree with you on that point."

Joann motioned to the bedroom just down the hall from the living room. "Moses is in there. Do you want me to see if he feels up to coming out, or would you rather go to his room to visit?"

"I'll go to Moses." John winked at her. "No point in giving him one more thing to complain about."

"That's true enough." She smiled and turned toward the kitchen. "When you're done visiting, stop by the kitchen, and I'll have a cup of hot coffee and a hunk of apple pie waiting for you."

"Danki, I just may do that."

Joann disappeared into the kitchen, and John headed for the downstairs bedroom, where he found Moses lying on the bed, his head propped up on two thick pillows.

"It's good to see you," Moses said.

"Good to see you, too. How are you feeling these days?"

"I'm doin' some better but still not able to be working in the fields."

"Give it some time, and try to be patient." John lifted his straw hat from his head and moved closer to Moses's bed.

Moses grimaced as he pushed himself to a sitting position. "That's a lot easier said than done."

"Jah, I know."

"So how are things going with you? Are you keeping busy with your business?"

"That and making calls on ailing members of our community," John said.

Moses motioned to the chair beside his bed. "Have a seat so we can visit awhile."

"Don't mind if I do." John sat down, flopped his hat over one knee, and cleared his throat a couple of times.

"You gettin' a cold?"

"No, I was just getting ready to say something."

"What's that?"

"I was wondering if Paul's still planning to return to Pennsylvania."

Moses grimaced, and a muscle on the side of his face twitched like a cow's ear when it was being bothered by a pesky fly. "I had a talk with Paul the other day, and when I asked if he'd consider staying here and working on the farm permanently, he said he'd think on it."

John's face flamed. "But—but I thought he didn't like farmwork. That day I came to see you at the hospital, you said Paul would be going back to Pennsylvania as soon as you were on your feet again."

Moses nodded. "That is what I said, but things have changed."

"How so?"

"The day I was released from the hospital, the doctor told me that my back was weakened by the fall and that I might never be able to do any heavy lifting again." Moses released a deep moan. "Being a farmer means doing heavy work—lifting bales of hay, sacks of grain, and the like."

"Can't you hire someone to take your place?"

"I suppose I could, but—"

John touched his friend's arm. "Is it really fair to force your son to do work he'd rather not be doing? I mean, if Paul was happy working for his cousin in Pennsylvania and he stays here only as a favor to you, resentment might creep in, and then—"

"Paul's and my relationship would become even more strained than it is," Moses said, finishing John's sentence.

"Jah." John twisted the brim of his hat a couple of times. "Do you want my advice?"

Moses nodded.

"Tell Paul you'll hire someone to take your place and give him the freedom to return to Pennsylvania where he belongs."

Moses compressed his lips as he squinted. "I'll think about what you've said."

John smiled. "You should think about it and ask God what would be best for both you and Paul."

❧

When Paul entered the kitchen, Mom turned from her place at the stove and shook her head. "You surely do look a mess. Hardly a speck of skin showing that's not covered with dust."

He nodded. "I'm heading to the bathroom to wash up now. Then I need to speak to Pop before we eat our supper."

"Take your time," she replied. "The meal won't be ready for another thirty minutes or so."

Paul left the room. After he'd cleaned off most of the field dirt, he went straight to his parents' room. Pop was sitting up in bed reading from the Bible.

"How are you feeling today?"

"How'd it go in the fields?"

They'd spoken at the same time. As Paul stepped to the side of the bed, he said, "You go first."

His dad set the Bible aside and motioned to a nearby chair. "Have a seat and tell me how your work's going."

Paul did as Pop requested. "It's coming along okay. We should be ready to harvest the hay and corn in a few more weeks." Paul clasped his hands tightly together. "How's your back doing?"

"Feels fine as long as I don't move." Pop grimaced. "I'm supposed to start physical therapy tomorrow morning. Sure don't relish that."

"It should help your muscles relax."

"Jah, well, I don't much like the idea of anyone pushing and shoving on my spine." Pop shifted on the pillow and groaned. "I have to wonder if I'll ever get back to working in the fields."

Paul felt as if a heavy weight rested on his chest. The thought of giving up work in the harness shop to farm made his heart ache. When he'd left Missouri to learn the harness business, he'd never expected to move home again, much less return to farming.

He leaned forward, resting his elbows on his knees. "I've been thinking on the things we talked about yesterday and doing some praying, too."

Pop turned his head and looked directly at Paul. "Jah?"

Paul swallowed hard. He hated to upset Pop when he was hurting, but the things that weighed heavily on his mind couldn't wait forever. There was no use getting his father's hopes built up over something that wasn't going to happen.

"I know you're not able to work right now, and I said I'd help in the fields until you're better, but—"

Pop narrowed his eyes. "Are you backing out of our agreement?"

Paul shook his head. "I'll help Monroe and Elam until we get caught up and the harvest is in. But after that, I'll be returning to Pennsylvania. I've been gone a lot longer than I'd planned, and if I don't go soon, there might not be a job waiting for me at Andy's shop."

"What about Barbara Zook?"

"What about her?"

"I thought you were needed to help in her harness shop."

"I was. But her daed's doing some better, and she's back at work full-time, so she doesn't really need me anymore." *But I would stay if she asked me to,* Paul thought. *I'd proclaim my love for her and stay on as her husband if there was any indication that she loved me and would agree to become my wife.*

Pop blew out his breath. "So you're saying you'll hang around until the harvest is done; then you plan to head back to Pennsylvania?"

"That's right."

"And nothing I can say will change your mind?"

Paul shook his head. "I enjoy working with leather and never have cottoned to farmwork."

"How well I know that," Pop agreed with a nod. "Even when you were a boy, you complained about all the dust and long hours in the fields."

"You understand the way I feel, then?"

"I recognize your desire to do what makes you happy, and after some thinking and praying of my own, I've come to the conclusion that it's not fair of me to try and force you to stay." Pop swallowed a couple of times. "If I'm not able to return to farming because of my back, then I'll hire someone to help your brothers in the fields."

Paul clasped his dad's hand as a sense of gratitude welled in his soul. The change in Pop's attitude was a miracle. An answer to prayer, that's what it was. "Danki," he murmured. "I appreciate that."

"You'll be missed when you leave Webster County," Pop added.

Paul nodded. "I'll miss you all, too."

Barbara stared out the shop window, watching Aaron and Joseph head toward the one-room schoolhouse down the road. Today was the first day back to school after summer break and Joseph's first time to attend.

"Are you worried about the boys?" her father asked as he stepped up behind her.

Barbara turned. "Just Joseph. He's so young. I hope he does okay and doesn't give Ruthie Yoder a hard time." She sighed. "I wish Sarah still taught school here. He might feel more secure having his aunt as his teacher."

"I hear tell Ruthie's done a fine job of taking over for my daughter. I'm sure Joseph will do all right." Dad chuckled. "I remember when I attended school for the first time. I didn't like first grade and didn't care much for my teacher, but I sure enjoyed playing on the teeter-totter out behind the schoolhouse during recess."

Barbara smiled. Dad was probably right; Joseph would do okay. He was an easygoing, obedient child and should get along fine with the teacher as well as with the other scholars. Aaron, however, could be a real handful at times.

He's stubborn, just like his father, she mused. *But I'm sure he'll manage okay on this first day. Leastways, I pray it's so.*

"Sure seems different around here without Paul Hilty, don't you think?"

Barbara nodded. She hated to admit it, but she missed Paul coming to work every day. She missed his friendly banter, sparkling blue eyes, and lopsided grin. He'd been a big help and knew a lot about running a harness shop, even if they didn't see eye to eye on everything. Paul must be working hard at his father's farm. She'd thought about inviting him to join them for supper one night after work but had set that idea aside, fearful he might get the impression she was interested in him. She was, of course, but didn't want him to know that since he hadn't revealed any feelings for her other than friendship.

And then there's Aaron, she thought as she turned away from the window. *He finally seems to be adjusting to his daed's death. But if Paul starts coming around when it's got nothing to do with work, Aaron might become upset again.*

Barbara wasn't sure why, but Aaron seemed to consider Paul a threat. The other children liked the man real well. In Joseph's case, maybe a little too much. The last Sunday they'd had church, the boy had hung around Paul all afternoon. Barbara had noticed him clinging to Paul's hand and enjoying the piggyback rides Paul had graciously given to both Joseph and Zachary.

Paul will make a good daed someday. But I'm afraid it's not going to be my boys he'll be fathering.

Barbara grabbed some leather and dropped it into the washtub filled with dye. "I guess it's time to get something constructive done."

"Jah," Dad agreed. "Sure won't happen on its own, no matter how much I might wish it could."

Barbara's conscience pricked her heart. She knew the harness business wasn't Dad's true calling. Fact was, he'd much rather be tending his garden or relaxing on the porch than helping her keep the place running. But with Paul gone off to help his brothers, Barbara couldn't make it on her own without Dad's help. So she would take one day at a time, thanking the Lord for each hour that her father felt well enough to lend a hand. She tried not to think about the day when he could no longer hold a piece of leather in his hands. How would she manage? Aaron would help during his breaks from school, but to be on her own all the time would be nearly impossible.

Maybe I do need to give the bishop's offer of marriage more thought. I'd better pray harder about this, she decided.

"Are you sure you don't mind me quitting work early today?" Barbara's father asked as he headed toward the shop door.

She shook her head. "I don't mind at all. I know your fingers have been aching all day, and I think you might feel better if you go home and soak your hands in some Epsom salts."

"I believe you're right." He had just reached the door when he turned back around. "Don't you work too late now, you hear?"

"I won't. It'll be time to feed Davey soon, so I'll be closing shop and coming up to the house before you know it."

"Okay." Dad stepped outside and closed the door.

Barbara had just sat down when the shop door opened. Bishop John stepped into the room. Her heart thudded in her chest. Was he here to get an answer to his proposal? Was she prepared to give him one?

Maybe I should marry him and sell the harness shop. Maybe Paul would buy it if he knew he wouldn't have to put up with me working

your boys." John grunted. "It's more than obvious to me that he's been after you so he can get his hands on your harness shop."

Barbara gasped. "Is that what you really think?"

He nodded. "Paul would have liked to have opened a harness shop here in Webster County some years ago, but he couldn't do it because you and David had already opened up one."

"That's true, but Paul moved to Pennsylvania to work in his cousin's harness shop. As far as I know, he's been happy working there."

John shifted his weight again. "Well, none of this is a problem now, because I spoke with Paul's daed. He's going to hire someone to take his place in the fields so Paul can go back to Pennsylvania where he belongs."

Barbara's heart sank. If Paul planned to leave, he obviously didn't have any feelings for her. It had just been wishful thinking on her part. All his friendliness to the boys must have just been an act, too. *Can what the bishop said about Paul be true?* she wondered. *Does Paul wish this shop could be his? Is it possible that he's acted like he cares for me and the boys in order to get his hands on my harness business?*

"What does all this have to do with you asking Margaret to marry you?" she asked, looking up at the bishop.

"After spending quite a bit of time with her since Dan died, I've come to realize that I love her and would like to make her my wife." He paused and swiped at the sweat rolling down his forehead. "I'm just waiting for the right time to ask Margaret to be my wife, but I didn't want to speak of marriage to her until I knew if you were okay with the idea and didn't need me to marry you."

Barbara's spine went rigid. "I don't *need* anyone to marry me. I'm doing fine on my own."

He blanched. "I—I didn't mean for it to sound as if. . ."

Her face softened as she realized she was being overly harsh. A short time ago, she had actually been considering his proposal. "I have no objections to your marrying Margaret. In fact, I wish you both well."

Bishop John released an audible sigh. "I appreciate that." He shuffled his feet, then turned toward the door. "I know you have your hands full taking care of the shop and your boys, so if there's anything I can do to help, please let me know," he called over his shoulder.

"I appreciate the offer, but I'm sure we'll be fine."

The door clicked shut behind the bishop, and Barbara let her head fall forward onto her desk. *Dear Lord, please let us be fine.*

Paul hadn't been back to Zook's Harness Shop since he'd said that he would be quitting to help on the farm. But today he needed to go there. One of their mules had busted its bridle, and it needed to be repaired right away.

Part of Paul dreaded seeing Barbara again. Being around her evoked emotions he'd rather not deal with. Yet another part of him looked forward to seeing her beautiful face and dark eyes that made him want to shout to the world that Barbara Zook had captured his heart. Of course, he would never do anything so foolish. If Barbara was considering marrying the bishop, then

Paul had no right to be thinking such thoughts about her. But if Barbara had decided not to marry John, then maybe Paul had a chance. He just needed to get up the nerve to ask her.

Paul took the time to clean up before heading over to Barbara's place. He didn't want her to see him looking like a mess or smelling like a sweaty old mule. As he pulled into the Zooks' driveway sometime later, he cringed when he saw John Frey standing beside his buggy outside Barbara's shop.

"Doesn't that man ever give up?" he muttered.

Paul pulled his buggy alongside the bishop's and climbed down. "Afternoon, Bishop," he said, hoping his voice sounded more relaxed than he felt. "You here on business?"

John gave his beard a couple of tugs. "I was, but the business has been concluded. I'm on my way home."

Good. I wasn't looking forward to watching you flirt with Barbara. Paul hurried toward the harness shop.

"See you on Sunday if not before," the bishop called.

Paul nodded as he turned the doorknob and stepped inside the building. He didn't see anyone at first and wondered if Barbara might have gone up to her folks' house to check on the boys. Even if she had, her father should be around. The shop was still open for the day.

Paul cupped his hands around his mouth. "Anyone here?"

"Be right with you."

He smiled at the sound of Barbara's voice coming from the back room. He'd really missed her, and no matter how much he tried to fight the feelings, Paul didn't think he would ever meet another woman who made him feel the way Barbara did.

A few minutes later, she headed his way, carrying a chunk of leather that looked much too weighty for her to be lugging.

Paul stepped quickly forward and held out his hands. "Here, let me help you with that."

She hesitated a moment but finally turned the bundle over to him. "Danki."

"You're welcome." Paul placed the leather on the closest workbench. "Is this okay?"

She nodded. "What brings you by this afternoon? I figured you'd still be hard at work in the fields."

He pointed to the broken bridle draped over his shoulder. "We had a little accident with the mules. This snapped right in two."

"I can try to get it fixed first thing in the morning," she said. "Will that be soon enough?"

"We really need to have it when we start work tomorrow. I was hoping you wouldn't mind if I did the repairs myself."

Her eyebrows lifted. "You mean now?"

"Jah. If it's okay with you." He paused and licked his lips, which seemed awfully dry. "I'll pay for any supplies I use, of course."

Barbara waved her hand. "Nonsense. Just help yourself to whatever you need. It's the least I can do to say thanks for helping me out in my time of need."

"But you paid me a fair wage for that," he reminded her.

She shrugged. "Even so, that doesn't make up for the fact that you stayed here helping me when you wanted to get back to your cousin's harness shop in Pennsylvania."

He was tempted to tell her that he really wasn't in a hurry to return to Pennsylvania, but what reason could he give? He couldn't just blurt out that he had fallen in love with her and wished he could stay right here in Webster County and marry her.

"How are you managing now?" he asked instead. "Is your daed able to be here all the time?"

She shrugged and released a noisy sigh. "He comes in every day but doesn't always work the whole time. His hands are bothering him again, but he keeps at it the best he's able."

Paul's heart clenched, and he felt like he was being ripped in two. Pop needed him to work in the fields, but it was obvious that Barbara could still use his help. Then there was his cousin Andy, who'd written and said he was getting really busy and wondered when Paul planned to return to Pennsylvania. Paul wasn't sure where he belonged or who needed him the most. The only thing he knew for certain was that he loved Barbara Zook. But what, if anything, should he do about it?

Chapter 20

"Would you like to join us for supper?" Barbara asked as Paul was about to get into his buggy. "It'll just be me and the boys," she added with a look of uncertainty. "Mom and Dad are going into town to eat."

"I'd be happy to join you for supper," Paul said as a shiver of enthusiasm tickled his spine. This was the opportunity he'd been waiting for. With any luck, after Barbara's sons were finished eating, he'd have some time to be alone with her, to tell her how he'd come to care for her, and to hopefully discover how she felt about him. He didn't want to leave Webster County until he knew. Maybe, if his prayers were answered, he wouldn't have to leave at all.

He smiled to himself. *She must care a little, or she wouldn't have invited me to stay for supper.*

At Barbara's suggestion, Paul waited on the back porch while she went next door to get her brood. He took a seat on the top step and stared into the yard, overgrown with weeds again and direly in need of a good mowing. He figured Barbara was probably hesitant about asking some of the women to do more yard work for her, but he was surprised that the bishop hadn't thought to ask someone to do it. If Paul didn't forget, he might speak with Margaret about helping Barbara again. She was good with flowers and probably wouldn't mind helping out. Paul figured his widowed sister-in-law most likely needed something to do.

His thoughts returned to Barbara. *Lord, give me the courage to open my heart to her tonight. I need to know if she's going to marry John or whether she might have an interest in me. If it's Your will for us to be together, help her to be receptive to the idea.*

When Paul heard a door open, he glanced over at the Rabers' place. Joseph was the first to exit his grandparents' house, and he bounded across the lawn like an excited puppy.

Waving at Paul as if he hadn't seen him for several weeks, the child leaped into Paul's arms. "Mama said you're here for supper again!"

"That's right." Paul ruffled the boy's blond hair.

"I'm ever so glad." Joseph nestled against Paul's chest, and once more, Paul was filled with a strong desire to marry and raise a family. Never had he felt so much love from a child.

Barbara showed up then with Aaron, Zachary, and the baby. "Let's go inside, shall we?" she said with a smile that warmed Paul's heart.

"Sounds good to me." Paul stood, and Joseph latched onto his hand.

"How was school today, Aaron?" Paul asked as the boy tromped up the steps behind his mother.

"Okay."

"Have you been helping your mamm in the harness shop after school and on Saturdays?"

"Sometimes."

Paul sighed. So much for trying to make small talk with Barbara's oldest. It was apparent the boy wasn't near as happy to have Paul staying for supper as his younger brother seemed to be.

As soon as they entered the house, Aaron took off upstairs. Joseph pulled Paul into the kitchen and pointed to the rocking chair. "Why don't ya set a spell, and I'll sit with you?"

Paul looked at Barbara. When she nodded, he took a seat. Without invitation, Joseph crawled into his lap, and Zachary did the same. As Paul balanced the little guys on his knees, he wondered how it would feel to come home every night after work and be surrounded by his boys.

He began to rock, hoping the action would get him thinking straight again. These were Barbara's boys, not his.

Barbara placed the sleeping baby in his carriage on the other side of the room and donned her choring apron. "Would soup and sandwiches be okay? I've got some leftover bean soup in the refrigerator." When she glanced at Paul, he noticed how tired she looked—even more tired than when they'd been in the harness shop earlier. Dark circles hung beneath her eyes, her cheeks were flushed, and her shoulders drooped with obvious fatigue.

"How can I help?" he asked. "Would you like for me to set the table or make the sandwiches?"

Barbara presented Paul with a smile that let him know she was grateful for the offer. "The boys can set the table. If you've a mind to make the sandwiches, there's some barbecued beef in the refrigerator. Maybe you could get the container of leftover soup out for me, too."

"Sure, no problem."

She looked at Joseph. "Take Zachary to the bathroom and see that you both get washed up. Tell Aaron to do the same. When you're done, I'd like you to set the table."

Joseph leaned heavily against Paul's chest. "Promise you won't leave?"

Paul tweaked the boy's nose. " 'Course not."

The children climbed down and scampered out of the room.

Paul retrieved a platter of shredded beef and the bowl of bean soup from the refrigerator. After Barbara lit the propane stove, Paul poured the soup into a pot and set it on the burner. Then he grabbed the sandwich rolls and filled them with barbecued beef. He licked his lips as the tantalizing aroma of bean soup permeated the kitchen. His stomach rumbled, reminding him how hungry he was.

Should I say something to Barbara about the way I feel or wait until after supper? In spite of the sense of urgency that pulled on Paul's heart, he decided it would be better to wait until the boys were finished eating so he could speak to her without interruption.

All during supper, Barbara sensed Paul wanted to say something to her. Maybe it was something important. He seemed kind of edgy, toying with his napkin and staring at her in an odd way.

Does he care about me? Should I allow myself to have feelings for him in spite of Aaron's negative attitude? Would it be possible for us to have more than a working relationship or friendship?

Determined to set her troubling thoughts aside, Barbara finished her last bite of soup and pushed her chair away from the table.

Paul did the same, placing his empty bowl and eating utensils in the sink. "Barbara, I'd like to speak to you alone, if it's all right. Maybe we could sit outside on the porch awhile—just the two of us?"

"That sounds nice, but I need to do up the dishes first."

"Why not let Aaron and Joseph do them? They're old enough, don't you think?" He turned to face the boys, who still sat at the table. "Maybe even little Zachary could help by clearing the rest of the table."

Joseph grinned as though he considered it a compliment that Paul thought him big enough to do the dishes. Aaron, however, glared at Paul with a look of defiance glinting in his dark eyes.

"You've got no right to be tellin' me or my brieder what to do," Aaron mumbled.

Paul stepped forward and turned his palms up. "It was only a suggestion to your mamm."

Joseph grabbed his plate and scrambled out of his chair, hurrying toward the sink. "Boost me up, Mama, so I can do these dishes."

Barbara leaned over and tickled her son under the chin. "If you're going to be washing dishes, then you'll need a chair to stand on."

Joseph turned to face Aaron. "Bring me a chair, would ya please?"

Aaron folded his arms in a stubborn, unyielding pose. "Get it yourself!"

"What's gotten into you?" Barbara shook her finger and gave the boy a stern look. "Bring a chair over to the sink now, and apologize to your brother for the way you spoke to him."

Aaron stared straight ahead, not budging from his seat. Zachary kept eating his soup, apparently unaware of the tension that permeated the room.

Barbara grimaced. She'd thought her oldest boy was doing better lately, but apparently she'd been wrong. She opened her mouth to reprimand Aaron, but Paul spoke first.

"Your mother's right. You do owe your brother an apology. And you owe your mamm one, too, for not doing as she told you."

Aaron compressed his lips into a thin line as he sat in his chair, unmoving.

Paul crossed the room, pulled out a chair beside the boy, and sat down. "This is not acceptable behavior. What have you got to say for yourself?"

Aaron's shoulders slumped as he stared at the table.

Paul glanced at Barbara with a questioning look. He seemed to be asking for her permission to handle the situation.

"Go ahead, if you don't mind," she said, grabbing the closest chair and pushing it over to the sink. Joseph climbed onto the chair, and she helped him fill the dishpan with soap and water.

Silence reigned at the table, and Barbara wondered if she'd made a mistake letting Paul take charge of things. When she was certain Joseph could handle the dishes on his own, she took a seat across from Aaron.

"I don't know why you're acting this way," she said sternly, "but I will not have you disobeying or spouting off like this; is that clear?"

The boy nodded soberly.

Paul touched Aaron's arm, but he jerked it away and glared at Paul. "You ain't my daed."

Paul opened his mouth, and so did Barbara, but before either could speak, Aaron pushed his chair aside and raced out the back door.

Chapter 21

Paul stared out the kitchen window. "My mamm always said I ought to learn to keep my big mouth shut. Now I've made the boy real mad."

"It's not your fault," Barbara said, joining him at the window. "Aaron started acting moody and belligerent after David died. I thought he was getting better." She shrugged and sighed. "Guess I was wrong."

"Maybe I should go after him."

Barbara shook her head. "I think it's best if we let him be by himself awhile."

"But who's gonna help me with the dishes?" Joseph spoke up from his place at the sink.

Paul crossed the room and patted the boy's shoulder. "You wash, and I'll dry. How's that sound?"

Joseph grinned up at him. "I'd like that." He looked over at Zachary, still sitting at the table, dawdling with his bowl of soup. "Hurry up, ya slowpoke. We need them dishes."

"Let's get the ones in the sink done first," Paul suggested. "By then, maybe your little brother will be finished."

"Okay."

If only my oldest son would be so compliant, Barbara thought. *Is it Aaron's personality to be so negative and defiant, or have I failed him somehow? If David were still alive, would things be any different? Probably so, since Aaron and his father were always close, and Aaron was willing to do most anything his father asked of him.*

Just then the baby began to cry. Barbara turned her attention to the precious bundle lying in the carriage across the room. "I need to feed and change Davey," she said to Paul. "If you'll excuse me, I'll be upstairs for a while."

He nodded as he took another clean dish from Joseph. At least Barbara hoped the boy was getting them clean.

"Maybe by the time you come back to the kitchen, Aaron will have returned," Paul said in a reassuring tone.

Barbara felt his strength and kindness surround her like a warm quilt. For one wild moment, she had the crazy impulse to lean her head against his chest and feel the warmth of his embrace.

Pushing the ridiculous notion aside, she scooped the baby into her arms. "I shouldn't be gone too long."

Paul glanced at the clock on the wall above the refrigerator. It was almost seven. He really should be getting home so he could do any final chores for the day. Barbara had been gone nearly an hour, and so had Aaron. It was possible that she might have fallen asleep while feeding the baby, but why wasn't that insolent boy back yet?

"Hey, watch what you're doin'!" Joseph shouted.

Paul turned just in time to see Zachary chomp down on a piece of puzzle, leaving an obvious tooth mark on one end.

"Give me that!" Joseph reached across his little brother and snatched the puzzle piece from his mouth.

"You're not supposed to eat the puzzle," he said with a grunt.

"*Hungerich,*" Zachary whined.

"I don't care if you are hungry," Joseph grumbled. "You should have eaten more of your supper."

Zachary's lower lip quivered, and his eyes pooled with tears.

Joseph shot Paul a beseeching look. "Can he have a cookie?"

Paul shrugged. "I—I guess it would be all right. Where does your mamm keep the cookies?"

Joseph pointed to the cupboard across the room.

"Okay. I'll see if there are any." Paul made his way across the room and opened the cupboard door. Inside, he found a green ceramic jar with a matching lid. He opened it and discovered a batch of chocolate chip cookies. He set the jar on the table, dipped his hand inside, scooped out four cookies, and set two in front of each of the boys. Then he opened the back door and stepped onto the porch. He saw no sign of Aaron.

He stuck his head inside the kitchen doorway. "Joseph, I'm going to run over to your grandma and grandpa's place a minute. Will you and Zachary be all right?"

The boy's head bobbed up and down. "We'll be fine. Mama's just upstairs, ya know."

"Okay. I'll be back quick as a wink." Paul bounded off the porch and raced over to the Rabers' house. He pounded on the door several times, but no one answered. Then he remembered that Barbara had said her folks were going out for supper. They probably weren't back yet.

Paul thought about looking for Aaron in the barn or harness shop, but he didn't want to leave Zachary and Joseph alone that long.

"I'd better get back inside," he muttered, turning toward Barbara's house. "No telling what those two little boys are up to."

When he entered the kitchen again, Paul discovered the children had helped themselves to more cookies and a glass of milk. Joseph had a white mustache on his upper lip, and Zachary's face was dotted with chocolate. Cookie crumbs were strewn all over the table, and a puddle of milk lay under Zachary's chair.

Paul grabbed a dishrag from the kitchen sink and tossed it to Joseph. "You'd better get this mess cleaned up before your mamm comes downstairs."

While Joseph sopped up the milk, Zachary continued to nibble on his cookie.

Paul pulled a towel off the rack under the sink, dampened it with water, and sponged off the younger boy's face. He'd just finished when Barbara entered the kitchen.

"The boppli's asleep in his crib, and—" She halted and stared at her sons. "Looks like you've had yourselves a little party while I was gone."

"*Kichlin,*" Zachary announced, licking his fingers.

"Jah, I see you've been eating some cookies."

"I gave them two apiece when Zachary said he was hungry, and I made the mistake of leaving the cookie jar on the table while I went outside to see if Aaron had gone over to your folks' place," Paul explained. "Guess they must have helped themselves to a few more after I left the house."

Barbara glanced around the room. "Aaron's not back yet?" A look of alarm showed clearly on her face.

Paul took the dishrag and towel back to the sink and turned to face her. "I thought about going out to the barn or harness shop to look for Aaron, but I didn't want to leave the younger ones alone that long."

Barbara's gaze went to the window. "I'm worried."

"Tell me where his favorite places are, and I'll see if I can find him," Paul said. His chores could wait. Right now, finding the boy was more important.

"Let's see. . . . He likes to play in the barn." Barbara massaged her forehead, making little circles with the tips of her fingers. "He enjoys being in the harness shop, of course."

"I'll look around the yard real good, head out to the shop, and then check the barn." Paul moved toward the back door. "Try not to worry. I'm sure he's fine."

As Paul made his way across the yard, he thought about his plan to speak with Barbara about their relationship. It didn't look like he was going to get that chance. Not tonight, anyway.

Barbara had been pacing the kitchen floor for the last half hour.

Where was Aaron, and why wasn't Paul back with a report? She was tempted to gather up the boys and go looking herself, but the baby was asleep, and the other two needed to be put to bed, as well.

She glanced out the window one more time. It was getting dark, and since no gas lamps glowed in any of her folks' windows, she assumed they still weren't back from town. She had been watching for them, hoping her father could join Paul in the search for Aaron. Or maybe Mom could stay with the children while Barbara helped the men look.

Barbara closed her eyes and clasped her hands tightly together. *Please, Lord, let my boy be okay.*

"Mama, Zachary's hidin' pieces of puzzle on me," Joseph whined.

"Nee," Zachary retorted.

"Jah, you are so."

"Nee."

"Uh-huh. I seen you slip one onto your chair. And you tried to eat a puzzle piece awhile ago."

Zachary shook his head.

"Jah, you sure did. Ya left a tooth mark in it, too."

Zachary opened his mouth and let out an ear-piercing screech.

"Stop it!" Barbara's hands shook. She forced herself to breathe deeply and count to ten. No good could come from yelling at the boys just because she was upset over Aaron's disappearance.

This is my fault, she thought miserably. *I should have sent Aaron to his room as soon as he started mouthing off. I'll never forgive myself if anything bad has happened to him.*

Paul closed the door of the harness shop. Aaron wasn't in the shop, and as far as he could tell, the boy wasn't anywhere in the yard. Paul had checked every conceivable hiding spot outdoors, so he decided that his next stop would be the barn. If Aaron wasn't there, he didn't know where else to look.

Maybe he wandered off the property and headed down the road to his friend Gabe's. If he's not in the barn, I'd better hitch my horse to the buggy and go there.

Paul entered the barn. It was dark and smelled of hay and animals. He cupped his hands around his mouth. "Aaron, are you in here?"

The only response was the gentle nicker from the buggy horses.

Paul located a lantern and struck a match. A circle of light encompassed the area where he stood. He held the lantern overhead and moved slowly about the building. "Aaron!" he called several times.

No answer.

As he continued to circle the barn, looking in every nook and cranny, Paul noticed the door to the silo was open. On a hunch, he stepped through the opening.

"Anybody here?" he hollered.

"Help!"

Paul cocked his head and listened.

"Help me, please!"

"Aaron, is that you?"

"Jah. I'm up here."

Paul held the light overhead and looked up into the empty silo. His heart nearly stopped beating when he saw Aaron standing on the top rung of the ladder.

"What are you doing up there? Don't you know how dangerous that is?"

"I climbed up to be by myself, but I got scared and couldn't get back down."

Paul gulped as a familiar feeling of terror swept over him. He hated high places—had ever since he was a boy and had gotten himself stuck in a tree. He hadn't been able to talk any of his brothers into helping him down and had ended up falling and breaking his leg.

"C-can you help me get down?" Aaron pleaded.

His heart hammering in his chest, Paul drew in a deep breath and hung the lantern on a nearby nail. "I'm coming, Aaron. Just, please, hang on."

Chapter 22

Paul's hands turned sweaty, and his legs trembled like a newborn foal's as he drew in a deep breath, grabbed hold of the ladder, and slowly ascended it. *Don't think about where you are. Don't look down. Take one rung at a time. Lord, please ease my fears and help me do this.*

"I–I'm really scared," Aaron cried from above. "My hands hurt from holdin' on so tight. I feel like I'm gonna fall."

A chill rippled through Paul. What if the child let go? If Aaron fell from that height, it could kill him. "Be still, Aaron. I'm almost there." Paul didn't want to admit it, but he figured he was probably more afraid than the boy. Philippians 4:13 floated through Paul's mind: *"I can do all things through Christ which strengtheneth me."*

Paul sent up a silent prayer. *With Your help, Lord, I can get Aaron back down this ladder and safely into his mother's arms.*

When Paul reached the rung directly below Aaron, he wrapped his arms around the boy and held him tightly for a few seconds. Aaron stiffened at first but finally relaxed. Paul did the same.

The child sniffed. "H–how are you gonna get me down?"

"We'll go the same way we came up—one rung at a time." Paul kept one arm around Aaron's waist and grabbed hold of a rung.

"D–don't let me go." Aaron's voice shook with emotion, and Paul's fears for himself abated. Aaron was his first priority. All that mattered was getting Barbara's son safely to the ground.

"I'm going to hold you around the middle with one arm, and we'll inch our way down the ladder together. Are you ready?"

"I–I think so."

"Step with your left foot until you feel it touch the rung below. And whatever you do, don't look down."

Paul was relieved when Aaron did as he was told.

Slowly, rung by rung, the two descended the ladder. All the while, Paul kept one arm around Aaron's waist and whispered comforting words in his ear. "We're going to make it, son. Almost there. Just a few more rungs to go."

When Paul's feet touched the ground, he lifted Aaron with both hands, turning the child to face him.

Aaron threw his arms around Paul's neck and clung to him tearfully. "I ain't never goin' up there again—that's for certain sure."

Paul patted Aaron's back as the boy's tears dampened his shirt. "It's okay now. You're going to be all right."

"I shouldn't have run off like I did. Shouldn't have climbed the silo ladder, either." Aaron hiccuped. "I'm sorry for spoutin' off back at the house."

"All's forgiven. It's behind us now."

When Aaron's tears subsided, Paul set him on the ground. "You know what?"

"What?"

"I've been afraid of heights ever since I was a boy. Climbing up that ladder had me scared half to death."

Aaron's dark eyes grew large. "Really?"

"Jah. I prayed and asked God to help us through it, though."

"You're not just sayin' that to make me feel better?"

"Nope. It's the truth, plain and simple."

"Then why'd you do it?"

"Because I care about you, son." The words came surprisingly easy, and Paul paused as he thought about what to say next. This was the chance he'd been waiting for with Aaron, and he didn't want to mess it up by saying the wrong thing. "I know I can never take your daed's place, and I'm not trying to," he assured the boy. "All I want is for us to be friends."

Aaron's lower lip quivered. "It was brave of you to climb up and rescue me. I'll never forget it, neither. Danki, Paul."

"You're welcome." Paul gave Aaron's shoulder a squeeze. "I think we'd better head back to the house, don't you?"

"I guess. But I'll probably be in big trouble for bein' gone so long and all."

"Your mamm has been worried about you."

"You think she'll be real mad?"

Paul shrugged. "That's hard to say. When I was a boy and did something my mamm disapproved of, I always knew she loved me, even if I ended up getting a *bletsching*."

Aaron's eyes were wide. "You think Mama's gonna use the paddle on my backside?"

"I doubt it. Seems to me she'll just be glad to see you're okay."

"Guess I'd better take my chances, huh?"

Paul ruffled the boy's sweat-soaked hair. No telling how long he'd been up on that ladder, too scared to move a muscle. "It's going to be fine—you'll see."

"Jah, okay. Let's go."

Paul breathed a sigh of relief, shut the door leading to the silo, and sent up another prayer. *Thank You, God, for giving me the courage to climb that ladder and for mending fences between Aaron and me. Maybe now he'll allow me to be his friend.*

Barbara finally put the boys to bed, and hoping to calm her nerves, she decided to fix herself a cup of chamomile tea. She had just put the kettle on to heat when the back door swung open. Her heart leaped as Aaron stepped into the room, followed by Paul.

"Thank the Lord, you found him!" she cried.

Aaron rushed to his mother's side and wrapped his arms around her waist. "I'm sorry for sayin' such ugly things before and running out of the house that way. It was wrong, and I know it."

"Your apology is accepted." Barbara leaned down and kissed her son's damp cheek. His eyes were red and puffy, moist with lingering tears. She looked up at Paul. "Where'd you find him?"

Before he could respond, Aaron blurted out, "Way up on the silo ladder. Scared silly, I was, too."

"What?" She gasped. "Oh, Aaron, you know you're not supposed to play in there. It's dangerous. What if you'd fallen? What if—"

"He's okay, Barbara," Paul interrupted. "No harm came to the boy."

Aaron nodded. "Paul climbed up, even though he was scared, and he saved me, Mama. Him and me are gonna be friends from now on." He grinned at Paul. "Ain't that right?"

Paul nodded. "It sure is."

Barbara blinked back sudden tears. This change in Aaron's attitude was an answer to prayer. "I'm so glad, son—about you being safe and Paul becoming your friend." Her gaze went to Paul. "Danki."

"You're welcome."

Barbara glanced at Aaron again. "Your hands are dirty. You'd better wash up at the sink."

He did as he was told, and Barbara turned back to Paul. "Would you like to sit a spell and have a cup of tea?"

Paul shook his head. "I appreciate the offer, but I'd better get home. I'm sure some chores still need to be done." He chuckled. "Besides, knowing Mom, she's probably fretting by now. When I left the house earlier, I only told her I was bringing that busted bridle over, so she's most likely wondering what's taken me so long."

"I hope she didn't hold supper on your account."

"Naw, Mom knows if I'm not home when it's time to eat, I must have found someplace else to take my meal. That's how it's been ever since I was a boy."

Barbara smiled as she walked Paul to the door. "Thanks again for rescuing Aaron. I guess we'll see you at church on Sunday."

"You can count on it." He turned and waved at Aaron, who was drying his hands on a towel. "Good-bye, son."

"Bye, Paul."

On the drive home, Paul replayed the events of the evening in his mind. Even though he hadn't been able to tell Barbara what was on his heart, two good things had happened. He had conquered his fear of heights, and he'd finally made friends with Barbara's oldest son.

"Now, that's a step in the right direction," Paul murmured into the darkness. Maybe tonight wasn't the time to tell Barbara how he'd come to feel about her, anyhow. It might be best to wait until he and Aaron had developed a stronger relationship before he told Barbara that he'd fallen in love with her.

Paul clicked his tongue and jiggled the reins to prompt his horse into moving a bit faster. Maybe sticking around Webster County until the harvest was done wouldn't be such a bad thing after all.

When he arrived home, he was still smiling over his encounter with Aaron. If things went well, he might have a chance with Barbara. If she didn't marry the bishop, that is.

"Where have you been so long?" Paul's mother asked when he walked in the door. "Your daed and I were getting worried."

"I went over to Barbara's to get the bridle fixed and ended

up staying for supper," he replied.

"I told your mamm that's probably what happened," Pop said with a wink in Paul's direction.

"I would have been home sooner, but Aaron got stuck on the top rung of the silo ladder, and I had to rescue the boy."

Mom's mouth dropped open. "But you're afraid of heights."

Paul nodded. "I know, but I couldn't let the little fellow fall just because I was scared to go up the ladder. But after tonight, I think I could climb up there again and not be afraid."

"I'm glad to hear you've conquered your fear," Mom said.

"Jah, me, too," Paul responded. "It was only because I prayed and God helped me through it, though."

"It's good that we can call on Him through prayer whenever we need to."

Paul nodded.

"How are things at the harness shop?" Pop asked, taking their conversation in another direction. "Is Barbara getting along okay?"

"She's managing, I guess. But Samuel's arthritis had been acting up again, and Barbara told me she's getting further behind."

"Harvesting will be done soon," Pop said. "I was wondering if you might consider speaking to Barbara about the possibility of buying into her shop. Sure would make your mamm and me glad if you stayed here instead of going back to Pennsylvania."

"I'll give the matter some consideration." Paul wanted to stay in Webster County and work at Zook's Harness Shop. Whether he did that as Barbara's business partner and friend or as her husband remained to be seen.

Chapter 23

On Sunday, the preaching service was held at Samuel Raber's house. When Bishop John pulled his horse and buggy up to the barn, he was pleased to see Moses Hilty climbing down from his own rig. "Wie geht's?" he asked. "How's your back feeling today?"

"It's doing some better," Moses said, "but I still have to be careful with it."

"That's probably a good idea. Don't want to risk reinjuring it."

"Nope, that's for certain sure." John waited until Moses's wife had headed to the house; then he moved closer to Moses and said, "Have you decided whether to hire someone to take your place in the fields, or does Paul plan to stick around and keep farming for you?"

Moses shook his head. "He won't be staying once the harvest is done, and I already spoke with Enos Miller about working for me. He's looking for a job right now, so it should work well for both of us."

"That's good to hear. Jah, real good." John squeezed Moses's shoulder. "Guess I'd better go inside and get ready for church. Take care of that back, now, you hear?"

Moses nodded. "I'm doin' my best."

As John headed for the Rabers' house, he was filled with a sense of hope. Paul would be moving back to Pennsylvania, Barbara was content to run her harness shop on her own, and Moses would soon have a new helper. Now he just needed to get up the nerve to ask Margaret to marry him. If she said yes, everything would be perfect.

Paul shifted on the hard bench where he sat on the men's side of the room. He was having a hard time keeping his mind on the church service. All he could think about was Barbara. He hadn't been able to speak with her since the night Aaron had climbed up the silo ladder, but he hoped he might get the chance later today. He wasn't sure what he was going to say now that he'd had more time to think about things. Maybe it would be best if he kept his feelings for her to himself and waited to see how things went between Barbara and the bishop. In the meantime, he needed to work on strengthening his relationship with Aaron.

Paul glanced across the room and spotted Barbara sitting beside her mother and cradling little Davey. His heart clenched when she leaned down and kissed the baby's downy head. Paternal feelings he'd never felt before had surfaced unexpectedly since he had spent time with Barbara and her children. If only those boys were his. If only he and Barbara. . .

Paul jerked his attention to the front of the room when Bishop John began reading from Ecclesiastes 4:9–10. " 'Two are better than one; because they have a good reward for their labour. For if they fall, the one will lift up his fellow: but woe to him that is alone when he falleth; for he hath not another to help him up.' "

Is the bishop preaching to himself again? Does he think he needs Barbara as his wife because two are better than one? Paul gritted his teeth. *If only I had the nerve to ask her not to marry John but to marry me instead. But even if I were to do something so bold, she would probably say no. She's given me no indication that she cares for me other than as a friend.*

Paul felt relief when church was finally over and he could be outside in the fresh air. He ate his meal quietly, sitting at one of the tables under a large maple tree in the Rabers' backyard. As he ate, he tried to decide exactly what he should say whenever he spoke with Barbara again.

After everyone had finished eating, Paul decided to seek Barbara out. He wandered around the yard but didn't see any sign of her. He figured she was probably still inside, either visiting with the women or taking care of the baby.

From Paul's vantage near the barn, he noticed Aaron across the yard, watching a group of older children play a game of baseball. It wouldn't be long before the weather turned too cold for baseball.

He pushed his thoughts aside as he approached Barbara's

oldest son. "Hey, Aaron, how are you doing?" he asked, clasping the boy's shoulder.

"I'm doin' okay, but I sure wish the older kids would let me play with 'em."

"Won't be any time at all until you'll be included with the older ones," Paul said, hoping to make Aaron feel better about things. "Why, I think you've grown a couple inches since I first came home."

Aaron smiled, and his face turned a little pink. "You really think so?"

"Sure do." Paul hesitated a moment; then he decided to plunge ahead. "Say, I've been thinking—"

Aaron looked up at him expectantly. "Jah?"

"I'm planning to go fishing next Saturday afternoon, and I was wondering if your mamm might give her permission for you to join me. That is, if you'd like to go."

"Only you and me? Not Mama and my brothers?"

Paul shook his head. "Just the two of us."

Aaron's lips turned upward, and his dark eyes glistened with anticipation. "I'd like that. Jah, I really would."

"Great. I'll speak to your mamm as soon as I find her."

The boy pointed to the house. "I think she went inside to feed the boppli."

"Okay, then. Guess I'll just wait until she comes outside again."

Barbara sat in the rocker and leaned her head back as she fed her hungry baby. She was glad church had been held at her folks' place today. When Davey got fussy, all she had to do was walk a few steps to nurse him in the privacy of her own bedroom.

Feeling kind of drowsy, she let her eyes drift shut, enjoying this special time of being alone with her infant son. *Oh, David, how I wish you could be here to see your namesake—to hold him—talk to him—watch him grow into a man.*

She thought about her other three sons. Zachary had been so young when David died that he would never remember his father. Joseph might not, either. Aaron was the only one who would, and he was the one who had been promised the harness shop someday.

If I sell the shop, it will never be Aaron's. Yet, if I keep it, I'll have to keep relying on Dad's help until Aaron's old enough to take his place. She groaned. *Dad's arthritis isn't getting any better, and it's not really fair to expect him to keep working for me when his hands are stiff and everything he does causes him pain.*

Barbara drew in a deep breath and tried to relax. She knew she needed to quit worrying, stop being so indecisive, and place the matter in God's hands. He knew what was best for her and the children. For now, the best thing she could do was pray and wait on Him to give her clear direction.

As Barbara was putting Davey into his crib, a soft knock sounded on the door.

"Come in," she called.

The door creaked open, and Faith stepped into the room. "Is he asleep?" she whispered.

"Jah."

"I wanted to talk with you, but I guess we'd better do it

downstairs so we don't wake the little guy."

Barbara moved over to the bed, took a seat on one end, and patted the spot beside her. "It's okay. Davey's like his daed—he could sleep through a thunderstorm."

Faith chuckled and sat down.

"What did you want to talk about?"

"Noah said he was by your shop the other day and that your daed had mentioned how far behind you're getting."

"It's true. We've got more work than the two of us can manage."

Faith's blue eyes revealed her concern. "Your daed's arthritis really slows him down, doesn't it?"

Barbara nodded. "I wish I didn't have to rely on his help. But no matter how hard I try, I simply can't do all the work on my own."

"Is Paul planning to come back to the harness shop to help you after the harvest is over?"

"As far as I know, he'll be returning to Pennsylvania." Barbara swallowed around the lump in her throat. She hated the idea of Paul leaving but didn't know what she could do to stop him from going.

"I thought the bishop had asked you to marry him. Whatever happened with that?"

Barbara shrugged. "He changed his mind." She couldn't very well tell her friend that the bishop had taken an interest in Margaret. Not when he'd told her he hadn't asked Margaret to marry him yet. Besides, it was his place to do the telling, not hers.

"You're in love with him, aren't you?"

"The bishop?"

"No, silly. Paul."

"What?" Faith's direct question jarred Barbara clear down to her toes.

"Don't try to deny it. I've seen the look of love written all over your face every time Paul's name is mentioned."

Barbara dropped her gaze to the floor. "I can't allow myself to have feelings for him."

"Why not?"

"I don't want to forget David or let go of what we once had."

Faith slipped her arm around Barbara's shoulders. "Romans 7:2 tells us, 'For the woman which hath an husband is bound by the law to her husband so long as he liveth; but if the husband be dead, she is loosed from the law of her husband.' "

Barbara sniffed as tears formed in her eyes. "I know that verse. But part of me will always love David."

"And well you should. He was a wunderbaar husband and a good daed. However, I'm sure David wouldn't want you to spend the rest of your life pining for him. He'd want you to find love and happiness again." Faith picked up the handkerchief lying on the bedside table and handed it to Barbara. "Dry your eyes and tell me how you feel about Paul Hilty."

Barbara blotted her eyes with the hanky. Then she lifted her head and looked directly at Faith. "You're bound and determined to make me say it, aren't you?"

Faith chuckled. "As you may recall, you were pretty determined that I see my need for Noah after I returned to Webster County a few years ago."

Barbara forced a smile. "I knew your place was here with your family and friends, not on the road trying to make a name for yourself. I also knew Noah could make you happy."

"You were right about that." Faith patted Barbara's hand. "I believe Paul can make you happy, as well."

"But I don't know how he feels about me. One minute I think we're getting close, and the next minute he pulls away. It's almost as if he's afraid of something."

"Maybe he is. Have you asked him?"

Tears hung on Barbara's lashes. "I can't. It wouldn't be right. It would be too bold."

"Humph! You know how I feel about that notion."

Barbara smiled despite her tears. "I think your time of living among the English made you see things in a different light than most people in our community do."

Faith nodded. "I guess you're right about that, but at least I'm not a rebellious daughter anymore, and I know how good I've got it right here with my family and friends." She grimaced. "Back in the days when I wasn't following the Lord, I was silly enough to believe the fifth commandment was to humor my father and mother rather than honor them. Only then, my folks never thought anything I said or did was funny."

"That's all changed, though."

"Right. Often I'll tell a joke, and my daed will laugh so hard he'll have tears running down his cheeks."

"Anything in particular you've told him lately?" Barbara asked, eager for a joke to lighten the mood.

"Oh, sure. I told him the story about the Amish man who went to visit his friend right after a bad storm."

"What happened?" Barbara asked.

"The man said, 'Did you lose much in that tornado?' His

friend nodded and replied, 'Jah. I lost the henhouse and all my chickens. But that was fine with me, 'cause I ended up with four new cows and somebody's horse and buggy!' "

Barbara laughed. "You sure haven't lost your sense of humor."

Faith smiled, but then she sobered. "There's one thing I did not learn while I was living in the English world. It's something I grew up knowing but didn't come to recognize until I moved back to Webster County."

"What was that?"

"The importance of committing every situation to God. I think it's time for the two of us to pray that the Lord will direct you and Paul." Faith squeezed Barbara's fingers. "Keep an open mind and trust Jesus. If you're supposed to be with Paul, it will all work out."

Barbara drew in a deep breath and sighed. "I surely hope so."

Barbara opened the front screen door and discovered Paul and Aaron seated on the porch step. She smiled at the way they had their heads together, talking as though they were the best of friends.

Both of them looked up when Barbara stepped out the door.

"Hey, Mama," Aaron said with a lopsided grin.

"Hey, Aaron. Where are your little brothers?"

"They went for a walk with Grandpa." He grinned up at Paul. "We've just been sitting here talkin' about the fishin' trip he wants to take me on this Saturday."

Paul looked kind of sheepish, and his ears turned pink. "I was planning to ask you first, of course," he said, nodding at Barbara.

Barbara noticed Aaron's hopeful expression. "Would it just be him and you?" she asked, looking back at Paul.

He nodded. "I thought it would give us a chance to get better acquainted."

Barbara stared at the wooden planks beneath her feet as she contemplated the idea. *If he wants to spend more time with Aaron, does that mean Paul doesn't plan to leave Webster County right away? Maybe he's given up on the idea of returning to Pennsylvania.*

"Can I go fishin' with Paul, Mama. . .please?"

She smiled. "Jah, I think it's a good idea."

"Danki, Mama."

"You're welcome," she said, patting her son's arm.

Paul stood. "Well, I'd best be going."

Aaron jumped up, too. "Where to?"

"I've developed a headache and am feeling kind of tired, so I think I'd better go home and take a nap." Paul's long, lanky legs took him quickly down the steps. When he got to the bottom, he looked back over his shoulder. "I'll be by for Aaron on Saturday around one, if that's okay with you."

"One sounds fine."

"And if you have the time, I'd like to discuss something with you then," he added.

"I'll make the time," she replied in a shaky voice. Was Paul going to tell her that he'd decided to return to Pennsylvania? Or could he have something else on his mind?

Chapter 24

John's hands trembled as he tied his horse to the hitching rail near Margaret Hilty's barn. Last night, he'd told his girls of his intention to marry Margaret and was pleased that they'd actually approved. Mary had spoken up right away and said she hoped Margaret would say yes because she was surely a good cook. And when John had explained that he'd fallen in love with Margaret, Betty had said she was glad he'd decided to marry for love and not merely for convenience. John had assured his daughters that he would always love their mother, and they'd said they knew that. Nadine had even told him that she thought he deserved to be happy again.

When John had gotten up this morning, he'd decided this was the day he would ask Margaret to marry him. He prayed she would be receptive to the idea and wouldn't take offense because she hadn't been widowed a year yet.

John found Margaret bent over one of her flower beds, pulling weeds. "Wie geht's?" he asked.

"I'm doing fairly well, thanks to the love and support of all my family and friends." She straightened and offered him a sincere smile. "I saw your buggy come in and wondered if you'd come by to see me or my son-in-law, Jake.

"Came to see you." John shifted from one foot to the other while he raked his fingers through the back of his hair. "I've been wanting to talk to you about something important."

"Oh? What's that? Is Barbara needing more help in her yard?"

"She probably does, but that's not the reason I came by today. Could we find a place to sit while we talk?" he asked, as his stomach did a little flip-flop when she smiled at him again.

"Jah, sure. I'm in need of a break anyhow, so let's have a seat over there." Margaret took off her work gloves and pointed to a spot on her back porch where several wicker chairs sat.

"Sounds good to me." John followed Margaret across the yard, and after she was seated, he lowered himself into the chair next to hers.

"Would you like something to drink?" she asked. "A cup of coffee or something cold?"

"Maybe a cup of coffee, but not until I've said what's on my mind."

Margaret's pale eyebrows puckered. "You look so serious, John. Is there something wrong?"

He shook his head. "Not wrong, really. But there is. . .uh. . . something I need to ask you."

"What is it?"

John swiped his tongue over his lower lip, wishing now he had taken her up on the offer of something to drink. But he needed to get this said before he lost his nerve. "I. . .uh. . .well, during the time we've spent visiting these past few months, I've come to realize that we have much in common."

She nodded slowly.

He leaned slightly forward and stared at the porch floor, unable to make eye contact with her. "I've become quite fond of you, Margaret, and I've enjoyed the time we've spent together."

"I've enjoyed being with you, as well."

He lifted his gaze and turned to face her. "Enough to become my wife?"

Margaret's mouth dropped open, and her eyes widened in obvious surprise. "You—you want to marry me?"

He nodded. "I know it hasn't been a year yet since Dan died, but I'm willing to wait until the proper time if you feel it's too soon."

Margaret's cheeks turned pink, and she placed both hands against them. "Ach, my! This is such a surprise. I never expected—"

He held up one hand. "I'm sorry if I've been too bold—too presumptuous. Maybe I'm out of line in thinking—"

She shook her head. "It's not that. It's just that I'm a few years older than you, and I—well, I thought you were interested in Barbara Zook."

"You did?"

"Jah. In fact, someone mentioned not long ago that you had asked Barbara to marry you. So I just assumed—"

He lifted his hand again. "I can't deny it. I did ask Barbara to marry me, but not because I'm in love with her."

"Why, then?"

"I thought she needed someone to protect her."

Margaret tipped her head as she pursed her lips. "Protect her from what?"

John swallowed hard. He couldn't come right out and tell Margaret that he thought her brother-in-law was out to get Barbara's harness shop. On the other hand, he couldn't think of any sensible reply.

"What do you think Barbara needs protecting from?" Margaret persisted.

"I. . .uh. . .well, she's been so tired since her boppli was born, and it's getting harder for her to run the harness shop. I felt it was my duty as her bishop, and as David's friend, to see that she and her boys were cared for and that no one came along and took advantage of her." He reached up to swipe at the sweat rolling down his forehead. He decided it wouldn't be right to tell Margaret that he had originally been looking for a younger wife who could give him more children. "I've come to realize that it wouldn't be right for me to marry Barbara when it's you I love."

Margaret stared at her hands, clasped tightly in her lap. After several seconds, she turned to face him and smiled. "When the proper time has elapsed for me to set aside my mourning clothes, I would be honored to marry you, John Frey."

"I would be equally honored." He reached over and took hold of her hand. "Now, if that offer of something to drink is still open, I think I'll take a glass of cold water."

On Saturday afternoon, Barbara was about to begin working on a new harness for Noah Hertzler when she spotted John Frey's rig coming up the driveway. Since her father was in the back room taking stock of their supplies, she knew she would have to be the one to wait on the bishop.

A few minutes later, John entered the harness shop wearing a grin as wide as the Missouri River. "Just came by to share my good news," he said, removing his hat.

"What news is that?"

John looked around, as though worried that someone might hear them. "Are we alone?"

"Dad's here, but he's in the back room right now."

"I have some news I wanted to share with you, but for now, I'd rather not tell anyone else. I would ask that you not mention it to anyone, either."

"Whatever you say won't leave this room," Barbara promised.

"I've just come from seeing Margaret Hilty, and she's agreed to become my wife."

Barbara smiled. "That's good news. The last time we talked, you said you wanted to marry her."

"Jah, I was just waiting for the right time to ask." He twisted the brim of his straw hat in his hands. "We won't marry until Margaret's set her mourning clothes aside, of course." He took a step closer to Barbara. "Are you going to be okay here on your own? If I thought for one minute that you—"

She shook her head. "There's no need for you to worry about

me, Bishop John. I'm praying about what God would have me do with the harness shop, and I'm confident that He'll show me the way."

He patted her arm in a fatherly fashion. "Jah, I'm sure He will."

Paul was glad the hay had finally been harvested and that his dad had no problem with Paul taking off to go fishing with Aaron.

"It sure is a nice day for fishing," Pop said as Paul hitched the horse to his buggy. "Bet they'll be bitin' real good, too. Won't be long before the weather will be turning cold."

"How about you and me going fishing sometime next week?" Paul asked.

"Sounds good. I'll be looking forward to it." Pop gave him a nod. "I hope you and Aaron enjoy your day."

Paul grinned and hopped into the open buggy. "I'm sure we will."

Fifteen minutes later, he pulled into the Zooks' yard, eager to take Aaron fishing and anxious to see the boy's mother. Much to Paul's chagrin, he noticed Bishop Frey standing outside the harness shop talking to Barbara. As far as Paul was concerned, the older man stood much too close to the woman Paul wanted to make his own.

He clamped his teeth together and jumped down from the buggy.

Trying not to appear as though he were eavesdropping, Paul stroked his horse behind the ear and strained to hear what the two of them were saying.

"I'm glad you agree," John said, giving Barbara a wide smile. "I think we'll be very happy together."

Barbara nodded in return. "I think so, too."

A knot formed in Paul's stomach, and he nearly doubled over from the pain. Apparently, Barbara had decided to accept the bishop's marriage proposal. Paul felt like climbing back into his buggy and heading straight for home, but just then, Aaron rushed across the yard waving his fishing pole and grinning from ear to ear. Even though Paul wasn't in the mood to go fishing now, he had promised the boy, so he would see it through. When he brought Aaron home, however, he planned to tell Barbara he was leaving Webster County for good. He'd come back home planning to stay only a few weeks but had ended up staying several months. There was no point in him staying any longer.

With a sigh of resignation, Paul helped Aaron into the buggy, gave a halfhearted wave to Barbara, and pulled out of the yard.

"Sure have been lookin' forward to this day," Aaron said, nudging Paul's arm.

Paul nodded. "Me, too."

As they rode in companionable silence, Paul relished the sounds of birds singing from the trees lining the road and the steady *clip-clop* of the horse's hooves against the pavement. It was quiet and peaceful on this stretch of road. For that matter, all of Webster County was quiet compared to the area he'd left back in Pennsylvania. Paul would miss all of this, and he sure wished he could stay. But it would be hard to stick around and watch Barbara become the bishop's wife. Of course, if she married John, she would probably decide to sell the harness shop. Paul could offer to buy the place, and that would mean he could stay here and live near his folks. But owning the harness shop didn't hold nearly the appeal anymore. Not without Barbara at his side. No, the best thing he could do was return to Pennsylvania and try to forget he'd ever allowed himself to foolishly fall in love with Barbara.

Aaron poked Paul's arm again, pulling him out of his musings. "Sure can't wait to catch me some big old fish today."

Paul smiled. "I hope they're biting real good."

A short time later, they pulled up by the pond. Paul hopped down and secured his horse to a tree while Aaron ran off toward the water.

They spent the next few hours sitting on a large rock, visiting and fishing. Paul was pleased that they'd each hooked a couple of big catfish. It would give Aaron something to take home to show his mother, and Paul would have some fish to contribute to his meal at home tonight.

"Guess it's time for us to head for home," Paul finally said, reeling in his line.

"Do we have to go so soon? It seems like we just got here."

"It's getting close to supper," Paul said, ruffling the boy's hair. "And I don't want your mamm to worry about you."

"Aw, she won't worry 'cause she knows I'm with you."

"Even so, I think it's time for us to go."

"You gotta catch me first!" Aaron hopped up and started running along the banks of the pond.

Paul set his pole aside and quickly followed. He'd almost caught up to Aaron, when the boy's foot slipped on a rock, and he fell toward the pond. Paul reached out his long arm and grabbed Aaron just in time. "Got you!"

Aaron looked up at Paul, his dark eyes wide and his mouth hanging slightly open. "You did it again, Paul. That's the second time you've saved my life."

"I don't really think your life was in danger this time, Aaron. I just saved you from a chilly dunking, that's all," Paul said, his voice thick with emotion.

"I hope you stay in Webster County forever." Aaron clung to Paul's arm. " 'Cause I sure do need you."

Paul swallowed around the lump lodged in his throat. He knew he would be leaving soon, but he sure didn't want to go.

Paul and Aaron didn't return home until nearly five o'clock, so Barbara figured they'd had a good time. She couldn't wait to hear about their fishing trip and find out what Paul wanted to discuss with her. He hadn't said anything before they left, but she'd been busy talking with John Frey. Paul must have decided the matter could wait until he'd brought Aaron home this evening.

When Paul halted the horse, Barbara stepped up to the buggy. "Did you two have a good time?"

Aaron jumped down holding a plastic sack with a couple of fish tails sticking out. "We each caught two nice catfish, and I almost fell in the pond."

Barbara's gaze went immediately to Paul. "What happened?"

He shrugged. "Aaron was running along the edge of the pond, and he slipped. He nearly fell in, but I caught him before he hit the water."

Aaron's dark eyes shone like two shiny pennies. "That's the second time Paul's saved me now."

A lump formed in Barbara's throat. It was wonderful to see Aaron enjoying Paul's company and appreciating him so much. "I'm glad you're okay and didn't get wet." She smiled at Paul. "Danki, Paul."

He nodded.

"Are you two hungry?" she asked.

Aaron's head bobbed up and down. "Jah, sure. I could eat a mule."

Barbara chuckled. "I'm afraid your grandpa might have something to say if you go after one of his mules." She looked at Paul. "Would you like to stay for supper? I've made a big pot of beans and some corn bread."

A shadow crossed Paul's face, and he avoided her gaze. "I appreciate the offer, but I'd best be getting home."

"Aw, can't you stay awhile?" Aaron asked with a pout. "I know my little brothers would like to see you."

"Sorry." Paul leaned over and handed the boy his fishing pole. "I promised my mamm I'd be home early tonight, so I'd better be on my way." He climbed into his buggy and quickly gathered up the reins.

"What about the talk we were supposed to have?" Barbara asked. "I thought you had something you wanted to discuss with me."

"It was nothing important. I just wanted to let you know that I'll be leaving for Pennsylvania early next week." Paul stared at her with a strange expression. "I hope you have a good life, Barbara." Before she could respond, he drove swiftly out of the yard.

"Sure wish he could've stayed to eat with us," Aaron said dejectedly.

Barbara nodded slowly. She wished Paul would have stayed, too. "Maybe some other time, son."

"But you heard him, Mama. Paul said he'll be leaving soon." Aaron's lower lip trembled, and his eyes filled with tears. "And just when we were becoming good friends."

Barbara gave Aaron a hug as she fought to control her own emotions. "I'm awful sorry. I guess some things just aren't meant to be."

***

"Are you coming to bed?" Noah asked as Faith stood in front of their bedroom window, staring at the night sky.

She turned to face the bed, where he sat holding his Bible. "I'm not sure I can sleep."

A look of concern flashed across his face. "What's wrong? Are you worried about one of the kinner?"

Faith shook her head and sat down beside him. "I spoke with Margaret Hilty today, and she gave me some surprising news."

"What?"

"Margaret told me that John Frey asked her to marry him."

Noah's eyebrows shot up. "That's sure a surprise. What'd she tell him?"

"She said yes. But they won't be getting married for a few more months. Not until she has set her mourning clothes aside."

"I guess that makes sense."

"I knew the bishop had been making calls on Margaret, but

until today, I had no idea they had developed such a personal relationship or that he'd proposed marriage." Faith's forehead wrinkled. "At one point, the bishop was after Barbara to marry him. But the last time I spoke with Barbara, she told me John had changed his mind about marrying her, and she was glad because she's not in love with him." She grunted. "My good friend never said a word about John proposing marriage to Margaret, though. It makes me wonder what happened to change his mind."

Noah reached for Faith's hand. "After spending so much time with Margaret, John probably realized he'd fallen in love with her."

Faith nodded as she pursed her lips. "I wonder. . . ."

"What's going on in your head?"

"Since Barbara won't be marrying John, I wonder if Paul will ask her to marry him."

Noah squeezed Faith's fingers. "Now, fraa, don't you be trying to play little matchmaker. If it's meant for Paul and Barbara to be together, then you'd best let the Lord work things out between them."

She nodded and kissed him on the cheek. "I promise not to meddle, but I can sure pray."

Barbara sat straight up in bed. She was drenched with perspiration from having tossed and turned most of the night. She'd seen David in one of her dreams, kissing her good-bye before he headed to town to pick up her anniversary present. John Frey had been in another dream, calmly telling her of his plans for the future. The last dream had Paul Hilty in it, driving away from her house and out of her life forever.

Barbara slipped out of bed and padded across the room to the dresser. She massaged her temples a few seconds, then leaned over the basin of water on top of the dresser. As the cool water hit Barbara's face, she allowed her anxieties to fully surface.

"I've got to sell the harness shop," she moaned. "There's no way I can keep running it on my own." She had prayed long and hard about this matter and, under the circumstances, felt it was the only thing she could do.

Barbara dried her face on the nearby towel and grimaced. *If Paul leaves Webster County, who will I find to sell the place to? Nobody else in our community does harness work. And without a harness shop, people will have to go to another town to get their work done.*

She sighed as she glanced at her infant son sleeping peacefully in his crib. *At least someone in the room isn't feeling the burdens of life.* She moved over to the window and lifted the dark shade. A light rain fell, dropping more leaves from the trees in her yard and matching the tears Barbara felt on her cheeks.

She drew in a deep breath. *Paul has to buy the shop. I should have spoken up yesterday when he was here and asked if he'd be interested.*

She reflected on Paul's announcement that he'd be leaving in a few days. *I should have been more prepared for that news, but it caught me off guard. Paul has seemed so settled here of late.* Ever since he had helped Aaron down from the silo, he had acted like he cared about the boy and wanted to be his friend. *That will never happen if he leaves.*

Barbara paced the room in quick, nervous steps. There was

only one thing she could do, and that was to ask Paul outright not to go. Maybe when he heard her offer to sell him the harness shop, he would decide to stay.

"But I'd better move fast," she murmured.

Chapter 25

"Where you going, son?" Paul's mother asked.

"Thought I'd take a ride. Since I'll be leaving in a few days, I'd like to see the countryside one last time."

Mom frowned. "I still can't get over the announcement you made last night. I don't see why you have to go and leave us again. Don't you know how much your daed and I will miss you?"

Paul nodded. "I know, and I'll miss you, too. But with Barbara getting. . ." His voice trailed off.

"With Barbara getting what?"

"Oh, never mind." He grasped the doorknob.

"Will you be back in time for the noon meal?"

"I don't know."

"We're having Margaret over, along with your brothers and

their families." She paused. "And there'll be a couple other guests, as well."

Paul did want to see his sister-in-law again, if just to see how she'd been getting along and to tell her good-bye. "I'll try to be back by noon."

"That's good," she responded. "This might be the last time our family can all be together for some time."

"Okay, Mom."

As Paul trudged across the yard toward his buggy, he felt the weight of the world on his shoulders. All his plans and dreams had gone out the window in one brief moment when he'd overheard Barbara and the bishop speaking about their upcoming marriage.

He stepped into his buggy and grabbed the reins. Maybe some time alone with the wind blowing in his face and the smell of crisp autumn leaves tickling his nose might calm his anxieties. He could also do some serious praying.

"Giddyap there, boy," he called to the horse. "You and me have got some riding to do."

As Paul headed down the road, anxious thoughts tumbled around in his mind. He loved Barbara, but she was going to marry Bishop John. He'd come to care for her boys, but they could never be his. He enjoyed being in Webster County, but he didn't belong anymore. He loved working in the harness shop but would probably never own one of his own.

Sometime later, the smell of sweaty horseflesh drifted up to Paul's nose, and he grimaced when he realized that he'd been making his poor gelding trot for the last several miles. He had thought this buggy ride would make him feel better, but by the time he returned home, he was even more agitated than when he'd headed out. He didn't want to leave his friends and family again, but he didn't want to stay and see Barbara marry the bishop, either.

In a brief moment of desperation, Paul had considered driving straight over to Barbara's and begging her to marry him instead of John Frey. But he'd quickly decided that it was a dumb idea. *She's already chosen him. I'd only make myself look like a fool if I barged in and declared my love.* The best thing he could do was to get back to Pennsylvania as quickly as he could and hope he'd be able to forget about Barbara and her boys.

Paul took his time unhitching the horse and putting him in the barn. He dreaded the meal with all his family present. Goodbyes would be hard, especially with Mom and Pop so set against him leaving.

When Paul headed around the back of the house, he was surprised to see Bishop Frey sitting in a chair on the porch. Beside him sat Dan's widow, Margaret.

What's he doing here? Paul fumed.

Gritting his teeth, Paul stepped onto the porch.

"Wie geht's?" the bishop asked.

Paul forced a smile. "I'm fine, and you?"

"Good. Real good.

Paul looked over at Margaret. "Are you doing okay?"

"I'm fine and dandy." She grinned up at Paul, and he noticed for the first time since Dan's death that Margaret looked quite relaxed. Maybe she'd been counseling with the bishop and Paul had interrupted. Best he should make a fast exit.

He grabbed the handle on the screen door and was about

to open it when the bishop said, "Your mamm tells me you're planning to go back to Pennsylvania sometime this week."

Paul gave a curt nod. "I'll probably see about getting a bus ticket tomorrow morning."

"That's too bad," the older man said. "We were hoping you'd be here for the wedding."

Paul's body became rigid. What was the bishop trying to do—rub salt in his wounds? "I didn't think there was any need for me to see you and Barbara get married," he said stiffly.

Margaret gave a little gasp, and John's bushy eyebrows drew together.

"I'm not marrying Barbara Zook," John said with a shake of his head.

Confusion settled around Paul like a thick fog rolling in. "But I thought—"

"It's me John is planning to marry," Margaret said, her face turning crimson.

Paul felt as if the air had been squeezed right out of his lungs. He grabbed the porch railing for support. "When? How?" he stammered.

"We've been seeing each other for a few months now," the bishop replied. "And last week, Margaret agreed to become my wife. After the proper time for her mourning to be finished, of course."

"But—but I saw you at Barbara's harness shop yesterday. I overheard you saying—"

"I was telling her about Margaret accepting my proposal."

Paul continued to lean heavily against the rail. If John was going to marry Margaret and not Barbara, that meant Paul still had a chance. At least, he hoped he did.

Drawing in a deep breath, Paul said, "I'm happy for the both of you." He started for the steps. "Would you tell Mom I have an errand to run and won't be able to join the family for lunch after all?"

"She'll surely be disappointed," his sister-in-law said.

He turned to look at Margaret, whose pale blue eyes held a note of concern. "I'll try to be back in time for dessert." Paul hopped off the porch and raced for the barn.

As Paul's buggy sped out of the yard, John looked over at Margaret and frowned. "Now, I wonder what's gotten into him? As soon as we told him of our plans, he hightailed it right on out of here."

She shrugged. "I don't know, but he did seem to be in a hurry to go somewhere."

"Do you think he might be upset because I'm going to marry you?"

"I can't imagine why he would be," she replied.

"Well, it *was* Paul's brother you were married to. Maybe he thinks it's too soon for you to find another husband. Or maybe he doesn't think I'm good enough for his sister-in-law."

"He said he was happy for us, remember?"

John nodded slowly. "Even so, he's never been all that friendly toward me, and it could be that he doesn't want you to marry a bishop."

Margaret reached for his hand and gave his fingers a gentle

squeeze. "I don't care what anyone thinks. You're exactly what I need."

John smiled, relishing in the warmth of her hand and delighting in the look of love he saw on her sweet face. "You're just what I need, too."

⁂

Barbara felt relieved when her mother agreed to watch the boys. Mom was always so good about it, but Barbara didn't want to take advantage of her mother's willingness to help. Mom assured her she enjoyed spending time with the children. Today, when Barbara said she wanted to take a buggy ride and be by herself awhile, Mom had readily agreed.

As Barbara guided her horse down the lane, she was glad she hadn't told her mother the real reason for this buggy ride. She didn't want to tell either of her folks that she was planning to sell the harness shop until she had a buyer. Dad had said many times that he didn't mind helping out, even though he wasn't able to do a lot. He knew how important the shop was to her and said he'd do whatever he could to see that it kept running. And Mom, even though she often reprimanded Barbara for working too hard, had often said that she knew Barbara enjoyed her job and needed to keep working in order to support her family. Even so, she was sure they would support her decision to sell the place.

Barbara glanced at the darkening sky. "Looks like it could rain some more," she muttered. She was glad she'd thought to bring an umbrella along. An open buggy offered little protection from the unpredictable fall weather.

She'd only made it halfway to the Hiltys' home when the wind picked up and droplets of water splashed against her face. As she reached for her umbrella under the seat, Barbara spotted another buggy coming from the opposite direction.

Barbara snapped the umbrella open as the buggy approached. She recognized the driver immediately. It was Paul, and from the way his horse trotted down the road, she figured he must be in a hurry to get somewhere.

She slowed the buggy and waved at him. Paul slowed his rig, too, and motioned for her to pull over to the side of the road.

They stopped under a nearby tree. Paul tied his horse to a sturdy branch, then came around to the passenger side of Barbara's buggy and climbed in.

Barbara scooted over so they could share the umbrella. "The rain sure hit quickly, didn't it?" she asked, feeling suddenly nervous and unsure of herself.

Paul nodded. "I just spoke to Bishop Frey over at my folks' place. He informed me that he plans to marry my sister-in-law Margaret."

"That's what he told me yesterday afternoon, about the time you were picking Aaron up for the fishing trip." She smiled. "I'm glad for them. I think they'll be good for each other."

"Jah." Paul cleared his throat. "I. . .uh. . .wanted to speak with you yesterday, but after hearing what the bishop said, I figured it was pointless."

"What does the bishop marrying Margaret have to do with your talking to me?"

"I thought it was you he planned to marry. And since I only

heard part of your conversation, I got the impression you had agreed to become his wife."

Barbara shook her head. "He told me several weeks ago that he wanted to marry Margaret and that he didn't love me." She smiled. "I felt relief hearing that, because even though I have great respect for our bishop, I'm not in love with him. I loved David very much, and the truth is, unless love was involved, I could never marry another man."

Paul sat, looking perplexed. "I totally agree with that, Barbara."

"So what did you want to say to me yesterday?"

"I had a business proposition to discuss. But now that I've had time to think it over, I've decided it's not such a good idea."

She tipped her head. "Funny thing. I had a business proposition for you, too."

His eyebrows lifted. "Really? What was it?"

"After much prayer and thought, I've come to the conclusion that I can no longer run the harness shop on my own."

Paul leaned closer. So close that Barbara could feel his warm breath against her face. "Maybe you won't have to," he murmured.

"That's the deduction I came to, as well." Barbara bit her bottom lip, hoping she wouldn't give in to the tears pushing against her eyelids. "I have decided to sell the business, and I was wondering if you might be interested in buying it."

Paul shook his head. "I could never do that. I had thought I could at one time, but not now."

"Why not? Is it because you prefer living in Pennsylvania?"

Paul lifted Barbara's chin with his finger and stared into her eyes. "I'd rather stay here with you and your boys."

She swallowed hard. What was he getting at? Could he possibly mean. . . "If you want to stay in Webster County, then why not buy my business?"

He inched his head closer. "If I stay and work at the harness shop, it would have to be on one condition."

"What's that?"

"That it be as your husband." There was a pause as he took her hand. "I'm in love with you, Barbara."

The shock of Paul's words sent a shiver up Barbara's spine, and she let the umbrella drop to the floor behind them. "Are— are you asking me to marry you?"

"Jah, if you'll have me."

Barbara thought about the verses from Ecclesiastes that talked about two being better than one. She thought about the feelings Paul evoked in her whenever he was around and about how much her boys liked being with him.

She swallowed again. "I can hardly believe the way God has answered my prayers."

He raised one eyebrow. "A prayer to keep your shop open, or a prayer to find love again?"

She touched the side of his face. "Both. But mostly to find love again. I do love you, Paul Hilty, but I've been afraid to admit it."

"Why?"

"Because I was scared to open my heart to love again. And I didn't know if you felt the same way toward me."

"Does this put your fears at rest?" Paul's lips sought hers in a kiss so gentle and sweet she felt as if she could drown in it.

"Oh, jah," she murmured as she stared at his handsome

features. "I don't want to be on my own anymore. I need someone to share my life with—the joys and the sorrows, the present and the future. I want that someone to be you, Paul."

"Does that mean you'll marry me?"

She nodded slowly. "I want you to be my life partner as well as my business partner. . .for as long as we both shall live."

Epilogue

Eighteen months later

$\mathcal{I}$ can hardly believe our first wedding anniversary is next week," Paul said as he cut a hunk of leather and handed it to Barbara.

She smiled and reached up to stroke his beard. "Would you mind very much if I give you my gift now?"

"A whole week early?"

"I can't wait a moment longer."

"Sure, go ahead." Paul chuckled and set the leather aside. "I always did have a hard time waiting for things."

She grasped his hands and placed them against her stomach, her heart hammering like a stampede of horses. "My gift to you is a son or daughter of your own."

His eyes grew large. "A boppli?"

She nodded. "Are you happy about that?"

Paul wrapped his arms around Barbara and pulled her close. "Oh, jah. I'm very happy."

"Does that mean I'm gonna be a big bruder again?"

Barbara and Paul turned at the same time. Aaron stood off to one side, his arms folded and a strange look on his face. Barbara hadn't realized he'd come into the harness shop. "That's exactly what it means," she said, praying he wouldn't react negatively.

Paul moved toward the boy. "I hope you know that the boppli coming won't change anything between you and me or affect the way I feel about Joseph, Zachary, or Davey."

Aaron grinned up at him. "I know. You've been my new daed for almost a year already, and I won't let nothin' change that—not ever."

Paul gave Aaron a hug, and Barbara joined him. "Now we need to tell our other three sons," she said, blinking against tears of joy.

Paul nodded and gave her a kiss.

"Aw, do you have to do all that mushy stuff?" Aaron asked, shaking his head.

"You'll be doing the same thing someday when God brings the right woman into your life." Paul chuckled and boxed the boy playfully on the shoulder. "And if you're really lucky, she'll be able to make Webster County Fried Chicken as good as your mamm's."

Aaron grabbed a chunk of leather and headed for the back room. "I ain't never gettin' married," he called over his shoulder.

Barbara smiled at Paul.

He winked, then kissed her again. "When the time comes, I hope our boy finds someone as wunderbaar as his mamm."

She smiled and nodded. "No one should spend their whole life on their own. I'm glad I finally realized that I couldn't do everything on my own. And that I trusted God enough and made the decision to spend the rest of my days with you, for two really are better than one."

Barbara's Webster County Fried Chicken

1 cut-up frying chicken
1 cup sifted flour
2 teaspoons salt
½ teaspoon pepper
Shortening

Combine flour, salt, and pepper. Sprinkle some additional salt over the chicken. Roll the pieces of chicken in the flour mixture. Melt a few tablespoons of shortening in a heavy frying pan. Add the chicken and brown on both sides. Then cover the pan, turn the heat to low, and continue to cook until the chicken can easily be pierced with a fork.

ABOUT THE AUTHOR

WANDA E. BRUNSTETTER enjoys writing about the Amish because they live a peaceful, simple life. Wanda's interest in the Amish and other Plain communities began when she married her husband, Richard, who grew up in a Mennonite church in Pennsylvania. Wanda has made numerous trips to Lancaster County and has several friends and family members living near that area. She and her husband have also traveled to other parts of the country, meeting various Amish families and getting to know them personally. She hopes her readers will learn to love the wonderful Amish people as much as she does.

Wanda and her husband have been married for forty-four years. They have two grown children and six grandchildren. In her spare time, Wanda enjoys reading, ventriloquism, gardening, stamping, and having fun with her family.

In addition to Wanda's novels, she has written several novellas, stories, articles, poems, and puppet scripts.